DEATH
ON THE WATER

PATH

OF THE WATER

Praise for CJ Birch

False Horizons

"[A] solid scifi heavy book that relies more on the world building and scifi elements than its romance. It's a nice change of pace."—*Colleen Corgel, Librarian, Queens Public Library*

Unknown Horizons

"The concept of the whole memory loss thing was very intriguing and it got quite exciting when we find out why it happens! The story became very fast-paced and I was immersed in it!"—*Too Much of a Book Nerd*

"The characters and story were engaging and well-written. I couldn't put the book down."—*The Lesbrary*

The Edge of Yesterday

"I'm glad I took a chance on this book, because it is fantastic… If you do like science fiction, like me, I think you'll find both the technological and philosophical issues around time travel adequately explained, and better, to make sense. Five out of five stars. Highly recommended."—*Seasons in the Soil*

By the Author

Between Takes

The Edge of Yesterday

Just One Taste

An Intimate Deception

Death on the Water

New Horizons Series:

Unknown Horizons

Savage Horizons

False Horizons

Visit us at www.boldstrokesbooks.com

DEATH
ON THE WATER

by
CJ Birch

2023

DEATH ON THE WATER
© 2023 BY CJ BIRCH. ALL RIGHTS RESERVED.

ISBN 13: 978-1-63679-497-6

THIS TRADE PAPERBACK ORIGINAL IS PUBLISHED BY
BOLD STROKES BOOKS, INC.
P.O. BOX 249
VALLEY FALLS, NY 12185

FIRST EDITION: NOVEMBER 2023

CREDITS
EDITORS: JERRY WHEELER AND STACIA SEAMAN
PRODUCTION DESIGN: STACIA SEAMAN
COVER DESIGN BY W.E.PERCIVAL

Acknowledgments

A great big thanks to Bold Strokes for all their amazing support, especially Jerry and Stacia, my editors, for making the process so smooth and almost painless. I appreciate all the work you do.

One of the first things I was taught about writing (besides the difference between a noun and a verb) was to write what you know. Surprisingly, it's only taken me eight books to follow that advice. I spent a small chunk of my early and mid-twenties working on cruise ships, and in those short years I amassed a ton of memories, some of which I've shared in this book.

Besides the murders and subsequent investigation, most of the stories I've shared are based on true events. People do die on cruise ships, and there probably have been several murders on board. The pay is horrid, the hours worse, and there really were twins whose allure did get a shipmate fired. And he truly did believe they were worth it.

I'd like to thank my wife for always supporting me in my endeavor to mash words together to form sentences. As she points out, they don't always make sense, but are at least entertaining (especially the unintentionally funny typos).

And last, but by no means least, I'd like to thank my readers for joining me once again on this journey into my crowded brain. I hope you enjoyed the ride.

For all the tireless workers on cruise ships.

CHAPTER ONE

It all started in a long, narrow alley.

The moment before, my focus was on the lanterns strung above, through the arches, between the buildings—it reminded me of Christmas—when my focus should've been on the mass of people streaming through the alleyway. That number of bodies could kill, and would, given the chance.

I'd let the flow take me, forfeiting control of navigation so I could observe the Sanja festival with its parades, ceremonies, and dancing. Even now, as the swarm closed in like birds undulating on the wind, I could hear the ever-present drums. The beat seized my heart, overwhelming my senses, which still hadn't alerted me to my current danger.

A hand grabbed me from behind, violently swinging me out of the way and knocking my head into the brick wall to my left. My cheek scraped the hard sandy surface. I tried to feel the damage with my hand but found my arms pinned to my side by the press of people. In a matter of seconds, I felt the panic around me as we, as one mass, moved farther into the narrow alley, like a river after winter thaw.

I began to slowly spin, although that makes it sound like I had a choice in the matter. The spinning happened as my backpack caught on someone moving faster, and once I'd twisted, I saw in horror the crowd behind me pushing us through the constricted gap.

Fear and panic welled inside me like I'd never felt before. I'd faced down teenage punk gangs in Croydon with chips on their shoulders and a man with a knife in New York. I'd been shot at, followed home from interviews, threatened, and on one memorable occasion had a bomb threat called in at my office. And yet nothing compared to this.

The absence of control and the knowledge that I couldn't do anything about the thousands of people pushing and pulling me in all directions contributed to this sense of impending death. I may have found myself in deadly situations before, but for the first time in my life, I knew I would die. I could feel my blood leaving my extremities. They'd already become cold, like I'd cut them off and given them to the crowd.

And then I stumbled.

My body arched back, and instead of the crowd, I saw the glowing lanterns overhead. My head hit the cobblestones with a crack, someone stepped on my hand, and my vision went black.

I awoke with a start, focusing on my strange surroundings. For a moment, I thought I'd woken back in the hospital in Tokyo, but the subtle crash of waves and sunlight streaming through my balcony reminded me of my current predicament, my editor and publisher conspiring to send me on vacation as a way to get over what had happened.

I sat up fully when I heard a scream coming from the hallway. I peeked my head out the door to find a woman screaming from the door next to mine, "He's *dead*."

One Day Earlier
Claire—Sunday afternoon: Fort Lauderdale

"This way, miss." A deeply tanned man in a polo shirt pointed me toward a queue on the far side of the building. He reached for my elbow, as if to grab it and pull me along, belying the "miss" he'd thrown at me. My phone rang before I had time to swat his hand away. The next person that touched me got a poke in the eye or a heel to their foot.

I never signed up for this.

"Hello?" I spoke into the phone as if I had no idea who had called, but I knew it was my agent. For the fifth time that day.

He knew this. He knew that I always answer as if it were a landline in the 1980s. "Did you make it on board yet?"

"I haven't the faintest idea what you're talking about. I'm at home sitting on my back deck with a vodka tonic enjoying a good book."

"You better not be. I paid good money for that ticket."

"The publisher paid, not you." I joined the queue under the red VIP sign. "They've invited me to this inaugural ceremony. Do I have to go?"

The invitation arrived by email, not even one of those fancy emails they dress up to look like real mail, inviting me to sit for a ceremony to christen the ship. I would rather be buried up to my neck in manure with fire ants eating my eyeballs than sit for three hours in the humidity listening to some stiff plonk drone on about the wonders of this monstrosity.

"You're on vacation, Claire. You don't have to do anything but enjoy yourself and relax. That last word is an actual order from the publisher. Me personally? I'd love to have front row seats to your eventual nervous breakdown, but for some reason they like it when you're sane and can make them money. The selfish bastards."

I've known Rick my entire career, which started twenty-five long years ago in a dingy old office at the *Evening Standard*. Before he became a literary agent, he worked in the admin offices toiling away on Windows 95. We ditched before it became free and, quite frankly, went downhill.

Rick acts as my anchor to the real world, otherwise I'd get too caught up in my projects and drown. Rick worries about me, which is sweet but sometimes unhelpful when you write stories about people who may want to kill you for it.

I once sold an article to the *New Yorker* about a gentleman who sat on the same corner in London every day selling roses for 50p, which is rather a little less than the going rate of four pounds. Of course, he wasn't selling roses. He sat there, day after day, as lookout for the men who used ladies in the hotel across the street.

You could purchase a perfectly functioning rose from the man. It would smell like a rose, and the thorns would prick you the same. But if the bucket stood empty, it meant the police had come.

I spent two months writing that article, figuring out how their system worked. Needless to say, they weren't fans of the article. Unknown to me when I'd started the project, I'd stumbled onto a sex trafficking ring. The police busted them shortly after the article came out. Rick's not wrong when he says I take chances. I'd no idea what I'd gotten myself into. He likes to remind me I won't always come out on top.

"This is hardly my idea of a relaxing vacation. I've read the brochure. This thing is like a floating water park swarming with children."

"What's wrong with children?"

"They're loud."

"The back pool deck is twenty-one only. I want you to get into your bathing suit, grab a vodka tonic, and take a book back there. Most people would kill for this vacation."

"Perhaps you should've found one and given them the cruise."

"Claire." He said my name like a parent cautioning their five-year-old. "You need to slow down." I know he's seen the pills. He knows what my doctor's told me. My high blood pressure is a direct result of my stressful job. I find it hard to take his advice. I need to relax, to stay calm, and not work for one whole month. My publisher thinks this chaos before me will make everything better.

I hung up with Rick and proceeded forward, relinquished my passport to the cruise ship for the week, and shuffled to the next queue. And there I stood, about to embark on the first vacation I'd had in fifteen years, unaware that three people would be dead by the end of it.

CHAPTER TWO

Moira—Sunday morning: Fort Lauderdale

I slipped a crisp twenty dollar bill from my dark blue uniform shorts and snapped it taut, flapping it in front of Jimmy's face. His eyes hardened, a clear sign that I hadn't offered him enough.

The sun beat down. Even in the shade, it bounced off any shiny surface to find us escaping the heat. Earlier, I'd slathered myself with a thick 60 SPF, a morning ritual before braving the outside. I may have grown up on the Italian Riviera with its beaches and sun worshippers, but if anything, it taught me the need for protection.

Jimmy hadn't taken this precaution. His skin looked like old leather, crinkled and worn. His usual quick smile, now hiding behind a scowl, showed deep laugh lines that spread out from his mouth like ripples in the pool.

I sighed and pulled out another twenty. I came prepared to offer him whatever it took. His eyebrows crawled up his textured forehead, so I knew I was getting closer.

A long horn blared in the distance, and a gruff voice shouted over the PA system, "Code bravo, code bravo, main galley." We both ignored the alert. A fire team drill. One last training exercise before the inaugural voyage of the *Ocean Summit*.

The main pool deck, where we'd taken cover under the awning of the central bar, filled and emptied with crew, an ebb and flow like water lapping and receding at the shore. Blue and white chaises convalesced in a semicircle around the pool while two attendants placed tightly rolled pristine white towels on each. They moved with efficiency, a hint of their experience and expertise. The faster they finished, the sooner they could escape the sun and disembark the ship for leave.

I slid my hand into the opposite pocket and pulled out a ten, now up to fifty. Jimmy pushed a hard bargain.

He held out his hand. "Coward."

I shrugged. I could handle Jimmy calling me a coward if it meant I didn't have to face the crew's wrath.

"They aren't going to like this."

I dropped the money into his palm. "You make it sound like they're planning mutiny here. I'm only asking a favour."

"Favours don't come with tens and twenties, Moira love." His eyes twinkled, and the ripples returned to his face. He'd do this for me. "A bit of advice? They may call you princess, but it's an act. Don't piss them off, or they'll make your life hell. I've seen it before." Jimmy, whose real name died several decades ago, was what I called a lifer. On ships there are those who come and go, a contract here, maybe a few, and realize they don't fit in this world. They have a few great stories, a little bit of travel, but the real world beckons, with real jobs and real money. Then there are people like Jimmy, who started as a busboy at eighteen to escape life in the Philippines and realized there was money to be made if you could get into the right jobs.

"It's not cancelled forever, okay?" I said. "But I can't do anything about the lights not working in the aft pool area."

He folded my crisp bills and slid them into the breast pocket of his Hawaiian shirt. He slapped the bar and hopped off the stool, sauntering away fifty dollars richer.

"So, you'll tell them?" I called after him. "They've only postponed it?" He didn't answer.

Had I known then what I know now, I would've taken Jimmy's advice as solid. But that's not how things happened.

Moira—Sunday morning: Fort Lauderdale

As I meandered through the immaculate chaises on the pool deck, the morning sun followed my path. "We Sell Fun" embellished every possible surface. We don't. Fun is the by-product of selling everything else we push on passengers: excursions, jewelry, copious amounts of booze, pictures—finger quotes, memories—and future cruises.

The last few hours before embarkation, when the ship bobbed empty of passengers, or pax, as the crew called them, made me believe in perfection. The world was without demands, where everything seemed flawless and sublime. No passengers were pushing chairs together, destroying hours of thoughtful work. No kids screaming, running, splashing, breaking the morning calm.

The corridors stood empty, vacuumed, free of debris or parked mobility scooters. The ship belonged to the crew. Only we knew the best place to watch the sunset was on the back deck where several decorative sculptures kept the wind at bay. Or which café had the best coffee. That you should only eat seafood Mondays to Wednesdays before it became questionable. Or when the seas got rough and you needed a place to compose your rolling stomach, you could go to the back booth in the bar outside the casino.

Only a short time existed before passengers became possessive and discovered these things for themselves.

This being the maiden voyage of the *Ocean Summit*, even the crew hadn't discovered the ship's secrets yet. But it wouldn't take us long. The *Summit* had a sister ship, the *Ocean Zephyr*. Both were the same length, height, and width, but with a few differences. The *Zephyr* doesn't have a casino since they cruise in Europe and have few sea days. Most countries have laws that don't allow casinos to be open when we're docked.

We also had an addition that the *Zephyr* didn't: a hot tub spanning the aft of the ship. Thick glass extended along the far wall allowed passengers an unparalleled view from the back of the pool deck. It was only for pax. The crew tested it last week during final prep. Granted, our view of the Fort Lauderdale port refueling station sparkled less than most ports and ocean views, but it was still a thrill.

I ducked into the glass elevator midship and rode it all the way down to deck three, where I had a staff meeting. The elevator cut through the inside of the ship. Several restaurants zipped by, the main promenade with shops, cafés, and reception, then into the bowels of the ship. No outside light penetrated this area. In fact,

I stepped off into flickering lights, yet another thing maintenance hadn't fixed. Our maiden voyage loomed hours away, and yet every deck needed repairs.

I opened a side door with the words Crew Only painted in blue and found myself in a stark and sterile world. No bright busy carpets, smooth finished bulkheads, and calm lighting here. This world screamed hospital, utilitarian, psych ward. The metal bulkheads smelled of fresh paint. Red and blue lines pointed away from the door to various areas, the harsh reality behind the curtain.

I strolled into the cargo room for my staff meeting to find only two people had shown up on time. Even Amy, the cruise director, was late.

Jamie and Austen, my two go-to people, had pulled several boxes out from our skid and sliced them open.

"We haven't found the bingo sheets yet." Austen pointed to a box on their right. "According to the manifest, this skid has loads of them. Not true." He held up a pile of junk. "Playing cards and Scrabble."

If I could create a perfect entertainment staff member, Austen would fit the mould. He could follow orders, land a joke at the right time during bingo, and keep his hands to himself. Clean cut and drama free. The less drama in my life, the better.

My one perk as ACD? I make bingo commission, my consolation prize for dealing with all the drama of my staff.

I plucked the clipboard from his hands and scanned the sheet searching for the playing cards and Scrabble boards. The box label read Green 22. I pointed toward the far end and had Jamie slice open one of the boxes.

It's a misconception that all Canadians sound the same. That stereotypical Canadian accent exists only in a small percentage of the country. But from my experience, the closer to a big city they grew up, the more alike they sound—softer and generic like Heinz ketchup, too bland to cause a stir but familiar and pleasant.

Jamie flung open the box. "Voilà." She replaced English words with French every chance she got. She reminded me of a kindergarten teacher: kind, forgiving, and easy to manipulate. "They must have mixed up the manifest."

My crew phone rang, and I unclipped it from the ridiculous

holder on my belt. I didn't even have a chance to say hello before Amy's voice skipped over the line.

"Were you planning on joining us?"

I searched the hold; the three of us were still the only ones here. "Where are you?"

"In the conference room on deck nine."

"I thought we agreed the cargo hold so we could do inventory."

"I changed my mind."

I sighed and replaced the phone on my belt. "The meeting moved." I checked my watch. "And we're all ten minutes late." *Crap.*

CHAPTER THREE

Claire—Sunday afternoon: Fort Lauderdale and at sea

For once I'd taken Rick's advice. As soon as I boarded, I donned my bathing suit, grabbed a book, and found the twenty-one-plus section of the pool deck. I traded the vodka tonic for their signature drink because why not? I'm on vacation. Plus, tequila gives more bite, and I believed I'd need to be at least partly inebriated in order to survive this week.

I'd seated myself on a chaise at the very back of the ship with a view of the port below. As I settled in, the stewards and luggage handlers looked like ants from this height, scurrying to get all the baggage on before we sailed.

The entire area stretched before me with its wide, shallow pool and wraparound bar, designed to look like a jungle. Beside me a hot tub stretched along the back with a glass back to view the churning of the water as the ship's props propelled us through the ocean.

The brochure, which my publisher had sent a month ago with a bouquet of flowers I let die a slow death on my kitchen island, boasted of grandeur, of gluttony, and it didn't lie. From what I can tell, they constructed the *Summit* to kill people with food. A large two story dining room sits at the back of the ship ten decks below a buffet that runs the entire eleventh. The *Summit* has no less than six specialty restaurants, ten bars, three cafés, an ice cream shop, a pizza parlour, two Starbucks, and a cupcake emporium. Even if you had a mind to, you couldn't possibly eat in all of them. Their mission brags of choice, a haven for the eternally bored. Unless, of course, you're me.

Cruise vacations are for the extrovert or people living with ADHD. The ship reeked of voracity and edaciousness, and reminded me, for some strange reason, of *Hansel and Gretel*. In many ways, the ship felt like it should be edible.

Consumption was the word of the day.

Very few other passengers had picked this pool. Many, I imagined, had chosen the main pool, which I could hear had live music. The speakers in this section of the ship, hidden amongst the shrubbery, played soft classical music. A woman and her teenage daughter wandered in but soon an attendant approached and whispered to the mother. They stepped back out, leaving me with a wrinkled man in sagging skin who'd fallen asleep with a John Grisham novel open on his belly, and a woman in her thirties with beach blond hair who had been recording herself with her phone every five minutes.

One long horn, almost sad in its calling, blasted, and I felt a jerk as the ship began to edge away from the wharf. The gap between the dock and the ship grew wider as we gained speed. I sipped the last of my cocktail, and before I could even place it on the ground, an attendant arrived with a tray.

"Can I get you another one, miss?"

I smiled and shook my head. As my father always used to say, "Never have more than one drink before dinner. But make sure it's large and strong." Ian Fleming, whom my father adored, used to say something similar. I suspected, if my father could've gotten away with it, he would've worn a bow tie and used a cigarette holder to smoke. He would've looked foolish, and James Mills never looked like a fool. I had to give him that.

I checked my watch and noticed the late departure. The itinerary said five o'clock sharp, and my watch read half past. That only gave me half an hour to get ready for dinner. Tonight I decided it would be easiest to dine in the main hall. They'd seated me at six p.m., which is far too early to eat, but my only other option was nine thirty, and that's far too late. I can understand having to accommodate all the passengers, but it meant I'd probably find an alternate tomorrow.

Seven thirty is the perfect time to eat dinner. And tomorrow, I promised myself, I would eat when I wanted. Seeing as it was a sea day, I would have all day to figure that out.

As soon as the automatic glass doors parted, the music from the main pool slapped me in the face, along with the wind. The ship had picked up speed, and the beaches along the shore coasted by.

The sail away party had spilled from the main pool onto the entire top deck. A band played on a stage overlooking a large kidney-shaped pool in the centre of the ship. People danced and clapped along to the music, most still wearing their bathing suits from earlier as if the party sprang up out of nowhere.

I weaved through the throngs of partygoers, trying to make my way to the elevators and down to my cabin. No easy feat.

The song ended, and a tall woman with blond, wind-blown hair stepped onto the stage, her face stuck in a huge grin. "Welcome, my friends, welcome. I'm Amy, your cruise director, from Canada. I'm here to make sure you have fun."

Someone coughed into the sound system and Amy paused, looked to the heavens, confused, then her face broke out into an impish grin as a young brunette stepped onto the stage from the wings. "Fun? We can do a little better than fun."

"Of course. Fun is for amateurs. This is my assistant cruise director, Moira from Italy." She went on to explain all the different more-than-fun things the ship had to offer that week, but I'd stopped listening. I watched Moira from Italy as she jumped from the stage to mix among the spectators. She'd secured the front of her long brown hair with tiny braids and let the rest of it flow in the wind behind. She smiled as much with her eyes as she did with her mouth, delightfully engaging with passengers as she wandered by. Her merriment infected everyone around. They couldn't help but smile when she neared.

She stopped at a man in loud shorts and an Atari T-shirt who had packed up his things to leave. She put her free arm around him, supporting the microphone with the other. She looked down at his socked feet. So did he. "I like your socks." She had a beautiful musical voice, and her Italian accent played with the words.

He appeared confused. "My socks?"

I couldn't see the socks, but Moira described them for the audience. "They're R2-D2, right?"

He nodded.

"Where are you going?" she asked him. "The party's only getting started."

I took my chance and pushed through the crowd before I became a victim of her gaze.

Those words must have been a cue of some sort because the first chords of Madonna's "Holiday" blasted through the speaker.

Later that night, as I settled on my balcony, the calm sound of waves washing below and the soft, warm wind at my feet, I sipped gin and leafed through one of the books I'd brought for the trip. My head lolled. It had been a long day, and my exhaustion had caught up.

My head flung back and hit the metal bar of the chaise. I felt disoriented. I must have fallen asleep. I looked out to see the land long gone, the horizon empty. The full moon shed light on my balcony. I checked my watch: 12:45 a.m. I groaned and peeled myself off the chaise. Next door two men talked in a low murmur. I fell into bed, not giving anything a thought until I awoke the next morning to screams coming from next door. I popped my head out into the corridor and saw one of the cleaners hysterical. She kept screaming, "He's dead!"

CHAPTER FOUR

Moira—Monday morning: at sea

The crowd was mine. I had them on their feet swaying to some god-awful dance anthem from the 90s, clapping their hands, screaming, "I *love* bingo!" like they actually meant it. The first game of the trip cements the week. If you can make it as fun as winning at a casino, they'll come back again and again.

The prize for the first game always includes a suite upgrade. Other ships I've worked on, we got the big megasuite most of the time because few people want to spend twenty-five grand to visit Ocho Rios. This being the inaugural cruise, the best we could do was a grand suite, which sounds luxurious but is really only a balcony room with a few added square feet and concierge service.

Of all the gambling that happens on this ship, bingo is by far the biggest scam because it gives the illusion of being the most inclusive and safe. There's always a winner, sometimes two, but when you're competing against fifty to a hundred other players, your odds aren't great. Blackjack has the best odds, but it requires some skill. If you can hear and dab, you can win at bingo. I try to make it as fun as possible, or at least give them a show for their money.

"All *right*!" I scream into my microphone. "Who's ready to play some *bingo*?"

The room went nuts.

"Okay, you crazy kids, sit down so we can start." I always host the first bingo experience. The rest of the week I can pass off to staff, but this game is important. I'm playing a role. I give them humour, a little bit of cheek, and just a touch of Sophia Loren. This crowd was perfect for me because most of them grew up in the 50s and 60s, just the right age to appreciate a cheeky Italian girl.

"My lovely assistant Jamie will call out the numbers. When you get close, I want you to stand up and make all the other people jealous."

A family I'd met last night during the first seating at dinner waved to me. I remembered them as high energy and good sports, so I could play off them for some laughs.

The final bingo round had five potential winners, all standing with their bingo sheets clutched in their hands, dancing back and forth on their feet as if they had no-see-ums crawling up their legs. Out of the corner of my eye, I saw Austen waving me over, a look of concern on his face. I handed the mic to Jamie and excused myself.

"Someone could be moving to better digs in a few minutes," Jamie cheered as I left the lounge. The slang sounded odd coming from her mouth, but the crowd loved it and whooped as she read another number. I heard someone scream bingo from the stairwell. Yep, everyone loves a free upgrade.

"What's wrong?" I asked.

"Sick bay called the office for you," he said, picking at a dried paint drip on the railing of the stairwell. Austen had that pretty boy gone to pasture look. When I'd first met him two years ago, you might've mistaken him for a boy band member. He'd grown up barrel racing horses in Calgary and had that sculpted Greek statue look, with his full puckered lips, high cheekbones, and brown curly hair. After two years of drinking cheap beer in the crew bar and eating buffet style every night, he'd packed on a few pounds, which had rounded out his face, and now, instead of a Greek statue, he looked more like Cupid after a bender.

This couldn't be good news. As if I didn't have enough work to do, I also performed duties as crew welfare ambassador. It sounded fancy, but like most things with this cruise line, it made something boring and meaningless appear fun and important.

They created the role as a way to boost crew morale. I organized parties, raffles, karaoke in the crew bar, and of course, bingo. I also worked with the bar department to order supplies for the crew store and bar. I took the role, however, because I saw an opportunity to advocate for the crew. Many came from countries with very few rights or freedoms and struggled to see that they could have a voice and air their concerns. It meant occasionally, I helped crew get out of a bad situation.

Austen filled me in on our way to deck four. One of the cleaning crew had discovered a dead body, an apparent suicide, in one of the cabins they cleaned and had become, as Austen put it, "hysterical."

But when I entered the medical centre, I saw very little hysteria. Perlah, the woman who'd found the dead body, sat subdued and quiet on one of the exam beds. I'd met her a few weeks ago when she signed on for her first contract. I like to meet crew who haven't worked on ships before. Being aboard is a unique experience not everyone can prepare for ahead of time. I like to ease them in if I can.

Relief washed over her face when she saw me. I put a calming hand on her back. "I heard what happened. I'm so sorry, Perlah."

"In my orientation, they told me this could happen. I didn't think it would on my first day." Her petite frame and large brown eyes gave me the impression of a child, but she was closer to thirty than twenty.

The doctor had dimmed the room, which stole some of its starkness. The crisp white walls relayed sterility in a way that wasn't so much as comforting as it was bland. Few passengers saw the med centre. Most of the people who came down suffered from heatstroke or seasickness. Occasionally accidents or emergencies happened. For that reason, the cruise line hadn't spent the same kind of money to glam up this part of the ship. It was functional at best.

"I'll talk to your supervisor and make sure you're reassigned to a different area. Take today to rest, okay?"

"I'm all right, really. I don't want to cause problems. But I have a favour to ask you." She looked down at her hands pressed tight together in her lap and then back up at me with sad, scared eyes. "My son's birthday party happened today. I wanted to call after to see how it went and wish him happy birthday. I brought my phone with me, I know it's not allowed. I didn't think anyone would know."

"Are you worried you'll get in trouble?" I shook my head, not understanding what favour she needed from me. Unfortunately, I only had so much influence with the housecleaning supervisor.

"I dropped it in the room. And if they find it, they'll know I broke the rules. I had to call during the day because of the time difference."

"You'd like me to go get your phone?"

She brightened. "Could you?"

Armed with Perlah's keycard, I went to deck ten to find Perlah's phone. By now they would have removed the body to the morgue. Death on a cruise ship happens more often than people think, especially cruises out of Florida. I doubt people intend to die. But it happens. They come on board with family and die in their sleep and get discovered by someone like Perlah.

Accidents happen often as well. People get drunk and do something stupid like crawl from one balcony to another. Or lean too far over and fall overboard. We don't always find the bodies. Murders do happen from time to time, usually spur of the moment due to alcohol. A jealous wife or husband, in a fit of rage, pushes their spouse overboard.

Of course, everyone loves a good mystery, and we have plenty of those. Over the years hundreds of people have gone missing on board ships, less frequently now because cameras watch every surface. And on playback, ship's security discover they've fallen overboard. A lot of those are suicides.

In this particular case, they would keep the body in the morgue until we docked in Fort Lauderdale. Depending on the wishes of the family, the local coroner would perform an autopsy and then ship it to them.

I entered an empty corridor, a bit of a relief that. Crew members like myself can't enter passenger rooms. Only crew whose job requires it, like Perlah, can enter. I slid Perlah's master keycard in and slipped inside.

The room creeped me out. It appeared unused except for an unpacked suitcase on the couch, unworn clothes spilling out of the opening as if they could escape the darkness. The constant sunshine streamed in through the balcony door, which someone had left open, allowing the curtains to billow inward.

As the door shut, I got an uncomfortable sensation someone else was in the room and turned to find a woman standing behind the door as it closed. I screamed, which prompted her to scream, her hand to her chest as if I'd given her the fright of her life.

"I didn't mean to startle you." Her accent was British, posh. She wore long, silk pyjama bottoms, a camisole, and a worn, multicoloured robe. Her bare feet were stark against the dark green carpet.

"What are you doing in here?" I asked, suspecting a passenger who got off on morbid things.

She lowered her hand, which held a wallet.

"Are you stealing?"

She looked down at the brown leather wallet in her hand and over to the safe that stood open in the closet next to her. "No. I swear. I'm not doing anything nefarious, I promise." She opened the wallet and showed me a driver's license. "I only wanted to find out his name." The name read Colin Avery. His picture, as with most DL photos, looked like the before image for an ad curing chronic depression.

"So the safe was open?"

She sucked in a breath, looking at the ceiling. "These safes all have a reset code. I'm familiar enough with this make." She placed the wallet back in the safe and closed it.

Confused by all this, I stepped farther into the room, away from the woman. Her perfume filled the air, something floral, pretty. It didn't match the surroundings.

Very little evidence existed that anyone, let alone Colin Avery, had used this room. A few pill bottles lined the back of the bedside table next to the room-to-room phone. A blank pad of paper sat on the rumpled but made bed. It still had yesterday's lame towel animal, a sea turtle, sitting between the pillows.

And then something occurred to me. "How did you get in?"

She pointed outside toward the ocean. "I climbed over the balcony."

My heart dropped to my toes. "Are you crazy? You could've gone overboard. Didn't you read your safety guide?" I looked down at her slinky, oversized pyjama pants and realized how easily she could've slipped. And for what? "If you're not stealing, why are you here?"

She folded her arms and gave me a hard stare. Apparently, few people had the audacity to admonish her. "And what exactly is the assistant cruise director doing in the cabin of a murdered man?"

"Murdered? He committed suicide."

"What are they basing that on?"

I shrugged. I'd gotten my information from Austen, who had heard it from the doctor. I doubted Austen would confuse that point. "They obviously found evidence to suggest he killed himself. What makes you so sure it's murder?"

"Last night I heard arguing. One of the men was very upset that the other gentleman was in his room. He kept saying he shouldn't be there. It just seems odd he would be mad the person was there and then kill himself."

"Or what if it was the other way around? The man who killed himself was the one who shouldn't have been on the cruise. He felt guilty and killed himself."

The woman gave me a look to suggest I'd skipped a couple of important logic blocks. "I also found this." She handed me a blank piece of paper from one of the branded notepads that come standard in each cabin. It had the imprint of something written on it. "Someone wrote something on the pad and took it with them. I can make out the first few words, but they don't make any sense to me. Fox, justice, walk. Maybe it's a code."

"Maybe he's playing Wordle."

She placed the paper back in her robe, intending to keep it. Could it be evidence? If someone murdered this man, did I have an obligation to report it? Report her for pocketing evidence? "Come on." I started to lead her out of the cabin, then remembered the purpose of my visit. I searched the floor looking for Perlah's phone. Nothing. I bent down and peered under the bed. It must have rolled when she dropped it because I found it a foot under there.

"Whose phone is that?" the woman asked.

"You ask a lot of questions for someone who should be on vacation." I paused, then added, "It belonged to the cleaning woman." I shouldn't have to explain myself, but it felt important to prove I had a reason to be there that didn't include snooping around dead people's rooms.

"Of course. I didn't mean to imply anything by asking. Just curious. I'm Claire, by the way. Claire Mills." She held out her white and freckled hand.

"Like the writer?"

"The very same."

"You're Claire Mills? The woman who exposed the sex trafficking ring in London?"

She nodded slowly. Things started to fall into place. Maybe she couldn't help herself. Even on vacation, she needed to investigate.

Claire Mills had worked for some of the most influential newspapers and magazines in the UK. Her detractors described her as a bulldog who never let anything go, and her admirers called her a brilliant observer of human nature. She intimidated the hell out of me.

"Why do you think someone murdered him?"

She shrugged and dropped her hands into her robe pockets. "A hunch."

"You must get those a lot. How often do they pay off?"

"More often than not."

I escorted her out into the corridor, careful to make sure it was still empty. "I'm not sure what you're planning to do with that information, but—"

"I'm going to see what else I can find. If someone did murder him, there'll be plenty of evidence." Out in the corridor, she pointed to a dark dome protecting one of the many cameras on board. "I'm sure if you had security check, they could find out who was in his cabin last night."

"Hmm." I nodded, in a noncommittal way, unsure if I should tell her they didn't work. Hardly any of the cameras on board did. The *Ocean Summit* left dry dock a year and a half behind schedule, and instead of giving crew an extra few months to fix any bugs, the company plowed forward with the inaugural cruise. It meant half the systems needed attention. When connecting the cameras to the system, security prioritized the embark deck and, of course, the casino.

Instead of telling Claire any of this, I said, "It's a cruise vacation. Why not enjoy yourself and relax instead?" I had a feeling this didn't happen often. She had a reputation as a bulldog for a reason. "I'll tell you what, why don't you come up to the pool deck around eleven?" I checked my watch; it was ten to. I would have to leave Perlah's phone in the entertainment staff office for her to get. "I'm hosting a cannonball contest at the pool, and I think you'd make a great judge. As payment, you get the signature cocktail of the day while you watch, and I'll make sure you're out of the splash zone."

She wavered, peering back at her cabin door as if it held sanctuary.

"The whole thing will take you less than an hour, and then you're free to find somewhere for lunch."

"What would I have to do? To be a judge, I mean."

"All you do is hold up a premade sign with a number on it." I could tell it wouldn't take much to win her over now. "And before you ask, the signature cocktail today is a kiss on the lips, which is coconut rum, peach schnapps, and frozen mango. The perfect morning cocktail."

Claire laughed. "The only morning cocktail, according to my father, is a kir royale."

I shrugged and slipped my hands in my pocket. "Doesn't sound as fun as a kiss on the lips. Plus, what could be better than front row seats to people making asses of themselves?"

She leaned against the railing that ran the length of the corridor and folded her arms, studying me. "Do you like your job?" It felt thrilling to be under her stare. I wondered what her sharp observational skills told her about me.

"Why?" A strange answer for me. Usually I'd lie and say, "How can I not? I get to travel for a living." A standard answer for any crew member. If you tell a passenger you hate your job, it ruins the illusion for them. They want to assume the crew live happy and carefree lives. I didn't say that this time because I felt certain she'd spot a lie.

"You're excellent at enticing people. I doubt they pay you enough." Truer words.

"I like a good challenge." Very true. Part of what bored me about this job was that I'd been doing it so long. Ten years on ships, but before that I'd worked in a hotel from the age of twelve. I couldn't escape the tourism industry no matter how much I tried.

"As fun as this sounds, it's not up my alley, but thank you. You're very good at your job. Now, if the signature cocktail had been tequila based, I may have said yes."

"I don't believe that for a second. If I'd told you the signature cocktail was a forbidden kiss, you would've chickened out all the same."

She raised a delicate eyebrow above a golden brown eye, and it occurred to me this was more flirting than my job required. She had lovely eyes. It struck me how much her appearance seemed to change from a few minutes ago when I thought she'd pilfered her neighbour's wallet.

"What's in a forbidden kiss?"

"Tequila, vodka, apple juice, and a splash of grenadine."

She smiled, which brought out tiny dimples on her cheeks. This had an effect I wasn't expecting, and I found myself hoping she'd say yes so I could watch her smile for the next forty-five minutes. "You're right. I still would've said no." She pushed herself off the wall and turned to her cabin and realized she'd locked herself out. I could easily have let her in with Perlah's card but instead I sauntered off.

"Shame about that. Next time maybe you should bring your keycard when you climb over other people's balconies and break into their rooms."

Chapter Five

Claire—Monday afternoon: at sea

I lounged on my balcony in solitude, a book open on my lap, yet I hadn't absorbed anything in the last half hour. Every few minutes, I could hear a loud splash and then the cheers of the crowd above me on the pool deck. Moira's voice filtered down over the loudspeaker. Not for the first time did I worry I'd made the wrong choice. Should I have said yes?

It's not in my nature to participate. I observe. I study. I watch. And I love what I do. There have been far too many people in my life recently telling me I should slow down. For what? I suffer from high blood pressure, and my doctor has sent me into a tailspin of worry that my stress at work has caused these health issues.

This forced vacation couldn't have come at a worse time. My latest book was in its last round of edits, and I couldn't have been more disappointed with how it had turned out. It would need rewrites, and having my life hijacked to lounge on a cruise for a week didn't help.

Rick had colluded with Diane, my editor, and confiscated my laptop. They'd reiterated my doctor's instructions: No work. At least for a week.

This must be what withdrawal felt like. Maybe Frank was right. For years he complained that I spent too much time with my head on work and not enough on him. "Oh well, you can't live life on maybes," I said to myself. I snapped my book shut and left it on the balcony's tiny table, a napkin sticking out of the top as a reminder I would return later.

I dressed in a loose skirt and wraparound top. As far as casual clothes went, I didn't own much. I'd purchased these for a trip with Frank to Spain a few years back. I shut the top drawer and looked up at the mirror, remembering that I'd cancelled that trip last minute because a source had gotten back to me, willing to do an interview, and I couldn't pass up the chance.

What I saw reflected in my image I couldn't say. Guilt? Contrition? My phone buzzed and I lifted it up. The display read four missed calls and three text messages, all from the same person. I left it on the top of the dresser. It could wait. If I wanted to master this thing called vacation, I needed to let go of more than my work.

Along with book edits, my divorce could wait.

Moira—Monday afternoon: at sea

I picked up my cardigan offstage behind a speaker where I'd left it before the contest and stopped when I saw Jimmy. My eyes narrowed. "Why do you always do this to me?"

He grinned, not even a little sheepish at playing songs he knew I hated. "Amy requested the song specifically. The cruise director trumps assistant cruise director."

"Ah, but my friendship should trump all."

"She fills out my evaluation."

"No. I fill it out, the cruise director signs off on it. You think she's going to take the time to read what I say?" They never had before, but he tilted his head to the side, evaluating.

Amy had signed on last week, and none of us had worked with her before. She'd transferred from another company. So far she'd proved to be somewhat controlling and anal. I didn't blame Jimmy for questioning whether she'd read my evals. It seemed likely.

Jimmy looked at his watch and waved. "Gotta go. Lunch and then back up here for the afternoon beach party."

"I know where your loyalties lie now."

"Yeah, with a steady paycheque," he called. "But I think maybe that's the least of your problems."

I had no idea what he meant by that, choosing to ignore it, which would come back later to bite me in the ass. I shrugged on my sweater and entered the crew area from a door made to look like it blended in with the mural of beach balls and sun umbrellas. The AC hit like an Antarctic storm. The amount of AC used on ships always baffled me. Why make it so cold? The point of vacationing in the Caribbean was to experience warm weather.

Inside the walls, hidden from passengers, the ship came alive. Like an ant colony, you only ever saw the opening in a crack on the pavement and one or two ants scurrying around coming with food or going to look for more. As soon as I entered the crew area, the corridors sprang to life with crew members hurrying from one place to another running the mechanisms of a relaxing vacation all the while behind the scenes, hidden as if even seeing the act of work would ruin all the relaxation going on.

The office was empty when I entered. On the *Summit* we had office space behind the reception area in the main atrium. You'd think after ten ships they could manage their space better. But every new ship it was the same thing; the crew areas got smaller while the passenger areas got bigger. Amy had her own desk, a wraparound which took up most of the space. Behind and to her right stood another tiny station for the cruise staff admin, and then a communal computer for the rest of the staff to share.

I took a seat in Amy's chair. Any computer would accept your login, and I figured, why not? I hated the communal computer, the keys always got stuck.

Amy and I still hadn't figured each other out. In the past week, I'd learned she took her job very seriously to the point where each day of the week had a specific outfit meant to coordinate with that day's theme. I knew this because she'd already filmed her morning shows for the week ahead even though we'd only set sail yesterday.

Andrew, the last cruise director I'd worked with, hadn't filmed one at all, because he hated talking to a camera lens. But Benny and I always used to do it together each morning first thing. It was cheesy as hell but passengers loved us for it. It made them feel like they knew us.

If assistant cruise directors live and breathe by bingo, it's pax comment cards for cruise directors. Good comments mean you can make more money, great comment cards mean you get the best ships in the fleet.

It should've been Benny and me together on the *Summit*. However, he'd retired a few months ago and, for some reason, head office recruited outside the company. An inaugural cruise wasn't the time to throw two unknowns together.

I suspected Amy's desk mirrored her personality. She'd positioned what few items adorned the shiny surface in a zigzag pattern. She had one of those clay whistles from Cabo San Lucas that the local children sold, running up and down the pier blowing them at tourists as they skirted by. A fake cactus with two googly eyes stared at me, and a blank picture frame decorated with sand and sea shells stood between the two. All of it a little too cutesy, like Amy. Yet that soft outer shell hid something much harder and dangerous.

As soon as I woke the computer, it showed Amy hadn't logged out of her account before leaving. I quickly signed out and into mine. I hadn't had a chance to input that morning's bingo numbers. Not stellar numbers yet. I'd need to promote more during the show openings and closings to get more people to come out for our bingo sessions.

I jumped in my chair, startled, when the door swung open and Amy entered with Brad and Noah. Those two, in the past week before sailing, had begun following Amy around like a bunch of lackeys. I hadn't worked with Brad before, but Noah was your all around kiss-ass. Every group has one, and Noah was ours.

I logged out of my account and stood as soon as she entered. I could see the words forming on those pink pale lips to get out of her seat, and whether she would be polite or rude, I didn't feel like hearing it. Her chair had cushions and swivelled. I could sort of understand why she didn't want other people sitting in it. The rest of us had to make do with hard plastic chairs that were neither cushioned nor did they swivel.

We skirted each other, sidestepping around the desk in the cramped space. She plopped down and arranged the few trinkets she had as if it were a throne and I'd sullied her things with my presence. She pulled a mug out of her top drawer and reached toward Noah.

"Could you be awesome and fetch me some coffee? I know they keep a pot in the galley next to the bridge."

Noah's smile faltered. "That's for bridge crew."

Amy scrunched up her face like that one girl everyone knows who thinks if she pretends she's sweet about it, she'll get things she doesn't deserve. "I know, but it's so good. The stuff in the mess tastes like burnt tar."

I took a seat at the admin Andreea's computer and shuffled the mouse to wake it up, waiting to see if Noah would risk the wrath of the officers. He accepted the mug, but the smug cheer had disappeared. He slithered off as if she'd asked him to bag a dead rat.

Brad kept his back to us, head down, filling a bag with packs of playing cards. I scanned the schedule on the corkboard behind Andreea's computer. Brad had less than five minutes to get up to the library to start the euchre tournament.

I logged in and opened up the bingo spreadsheet as Brad gave a weak salute in the doorway and left.

As soon as he'd gone, Amy stood and removed her cheap pink blazer, draping it over the back of her chair. Beneath the blazer, she wore a loose, sleeveless camisole that cut wrong and made her biceps look like freckled sausages. The skirt, also pink, cut her legs off mid-calf, making her appear short. She held her blond hair back with two wooden clasps and let the rest fall limp to her shoulders. Instead of screaming professionalism, her outfit reeked of trying too hard.

If you'd asked me if I thought Amy was pretty, I'd say yes because gossip travels fast on a ship, and I don't like pissing off my boss. But in truth, I could never see past her sour expression.

Amy opened her second drawer and pulled out a portable fan. The whizzing filled the tiny space like an invading mosquito. Her lank hair flapped dully as she waved the fan back and forth.

"How can you stand this heat?" By not wearing pantyhose in thirty-four-degree weather. I looked down at my summer uniform of shorts and a light blue polo shirt. She too could wear this uniform. But the more I got to know Amy, the more I realized she liked to separate herself from us lowly cruise staff, which irked me all the more. If Benny had taught me anything, it was that you should never take yourself too seriously.

"Did you hear about the suicide?" Amy asked. Word travels fast around a ship.

I nodded. "A man named Colin Avery." When I didn't hear a response, I turned to find Amy staring at me. "Did you know him?"

"No." She shook her head, lank hair slapping her cheeks. "Sounds young." With barely a pause, she switched topics. "I'm glad I have you here." She blew out the left side of her hair with the hand-held fan. "I caught your closing of the welcome act last night." Then the right side of her hair lifted up. "We need to talk about that." I sat mesmerized by the rhythm.

I picked up a pen and clicked the top as if I were about to take notes.

"You need to stop using the openings and closings of the shows to promote your bingo games."

I clicked the pen shut and set it aside. I crossed my arms. What balls.

"Bingo is boring. It's for old people. This isn't Holland America. We're trying to cater to the young and hip."

I stood and spoke for the first time since she'd entered. "I hate to tell you this, but the young and hip can't afford these cruises. You know who can? People who like bingo." That's what I wanted to say, what I should've said. Instead it came out, "That's our only revenue source for this department."

"I don't care. It stops now. Period. It's on the list of activities guests receive in their stateroom newsletter every morning. If they like bingo as much as everyone thinks, they'll come to you." She clicked the fan off and dumped it in her drawer.

My mind boiled. I could scream, my insides shook with so much fury. First she'd questioned me on scheduling, then on activities, now she'd begun meddling with my livelihood. I strode to the door, ready to leave before I exploded.

"Oh, and from now on, use the staff computer." She pointed over her shoulder. I turned away and smirked. If she wanted to do petty, I could do petty.

CHAPTER SIX

Claire—Monday afternoon: at sea

"No one brews tea right on this ship."

The tepid tea I'd scrounged on deck eleven cooled beside me as those words came from a familiar voice behind me. I flicked my gaze back to confirm—yes, my almost ex-husband had crashed my one vacation in fifteen years. Could I try and ignore him? I had for the last seventeen years, why stop now?

He slipped into a chair opposite me at the café I'd chosen for lunch.

"Spectacular view," he said, unfolding a napkin and placing it on his lap. I'd chosen this spot for that exact reason. From here I could see the lower decks as they fanned out below, and beyond that, the real spectacle, a wide expanse of roiling, frothing cobalt blue ocean.

I stared pointedly at him, hoping he'd get the hint that I wanted to eat alone. I'd gone on this vacation to get away from my problems, not have them follow me on board.

We didn't work out because of this display of inconsiderateness. He could bemoan my work hours all he wanted, but in truth, he never respected my needs.

He pushed back a flop of red hair to reveal a sweaty forehead. Of course he'd chosen to wear what I considered his uniform, trousers and a polo shirt, in this weather. Dark rings of sweat settled at his armpits, while his pasty skin pinked and freckled under the unrelenting sun of the Caribbean. He looked like a guppy in pants.

"How'd you know where to find me?"

"Rick."

"That bloody traitor."

He held up a hand before I could get started on a good rant. "Don't be mad, he didn't know I planned to come."

"Why are you here?"

He signalled one of the servers standing around and ordered a scotch.

"A bit early for that, isn't it?"

"I've called and texted you a dozen times in the last few weeks, and you've ignored them all."

"Frank, this is a divorce. We speak through lawyers now."

"So that's it, then? Twenty years down the drain." The server set a neat scotch on the table in front of him. He lifted and swirled it, then drained it and signalled for another.

Disgusted, I put my napkin on the table and stood. "I have very little interest in watching you drown yourself in scotch. I have a good book"—and a murder to solve—"back in my cabin."

He pulled a mopey face like I was the unreasonable one. He reached for my wrist, but I pulled away.

"Claire, please? I wouldn't have gone to this extreme if I didn't have something important to discuss." He pointed to the empty glass on the table. "I'll sip the next one like a good boy. Just please, sit down." He scanned the other tables, afraid we might make a scene. Always more worried about impressions, Frank had a knack for appearing spineless.

I sat back down. "So. What was so important you flew to an entirely new continent and boarded a bloody ship?"

"Can we eat first? I need something in my belly." He pulled the menu from its anchor on the table and opened it to the first page.

I settled back, seething. Frank would take his time, as he always did when he held the upper hand. I decided to play his game and see where it got me.

Lunch arrived. I'd ordered a salad, the quickest thing I could eat in case I got fed up and wished to leave before he got to the point.

Frank chewed with his mouth open. It was the reason I'd stopped loving him. Okay, not true. On our honeymoon, we ate in a restaurant in this little seaside village in the south of France. He used a knife and fork for everything, even prawns, taking small tiny bites, scooping the food with his knife onto his fork and placing it in his mouth. So refined. Which would all go to hell when he began chewing with these great big chops like he was killing the food before swallowing. I found it endearing.

And then one night last October, it stopped being endearing.

I pushed my salad, long finished, to the side and waited for Frank to finish his beef sandwich, which of course, he ate with a knife and fork. Once he'd placed them neatly together in the middle of the plate, I said, "What is it, Frank?"

He patted his stomach. "Not on a full stomach. Give me a moment. It's important and could change the nature of our lives. It requires…" He used his hands to grab at the air as if he could pull the word he was looking for from it. "Brevity."

I stood, dropping my napkin onto the table, shaking my head at my foolish belief he could change. Without saying another word, I walked away.

"Claire, wait." He pushed his chair back to follow. He stopped short when the server handed him the cheque for his drinks.

I swept into the first corridor I could find and took the stairs down two decks to my cabin. Once inside, I leaned back against the door afraid, but not sure why. Frank was harmless. I wasn't worried about him. Our marriage had dissolved because of little decisions. Choices that seemed inconsequential at the time but built up until they equaled bad decisions. We hadn't even fought that much. Instead of going out with a bang, our marriage had fizzled.

I pushed myself off my door and wandered back to my balcony, my book no longer sitting on the tiny table where I'd left it. Instead, I found it blown by the wind in a mess of pages near the edge about to topple over. When I picked it up, I noticed a tiny pill lodged in a groove near the edge. It was small and round, and I recognized it immediately as Rozerem, the same brand of sleeping pill Colin had had on his nightstand.

I placed the pill in the palm of my hand and studied it. How had one of Colin's sleeping pills ended up on my balcony?

CHAPTER SEVEN

Moira—Monday afternoon: at sea

The last thing I saw before I was completely submerged underwater, the salty fluid filling my mouth and nostrils, was Amy, her arms folded and a deep scowl on her face. I flailed briefly, pinwheeling my arms to stop my downward momentum until a pair of strong hands caught me and pulled me back to the surface.

Austen perched at the edge of the pool, arm outstretched to yank me out. An entire pool of water sluiced off my body as I stood sputtering for breath. Austen took the now dead mic from my hand and passed me a folded towel from a nearby chaise. "I didn't see what happened. Did someone push you?" he asked, concern all over his face.

"I'm fine." Amy had disappeared.

The volleyball players in the crew versus passenger game I'd been reffing were still bobbing in the pool like apples in a bucket. I opened the towel and dried the ends of my hair. It seemed the calm from minutes ago was back.

I had come out to the pool like usual and dipped my foot in, wishing I could play instead of referee. With the sun high and the breeze taking the edge off, you couldn't ask for better weather on a sea day. Billowing white clouds meandered across the sky, as if they too were on vacation. Watching the sea calmed me. Whenever I felt life rushing by out of my control, I could gaze up at the sky or the stars or out to sea and ground myself.

Back home, at the hotel my family worked at, I used to go up on the rooftop terrace and stand against one of the pillars facing the ocean, out of sight of the guests, and stare out at the blue expanse. It seemed endless. The more I gazed out at the rushing waves, pushing against the sand, and then back out again, bringing every possibility imaginable, the more I wanted to explore the world across that ocean.

I closed my eyes, and the hot sun bathed me in its warmth. I needed this. The uncertainty Amy brought nagged at my precious equilibrium. I allowed two deep breaths and then opened my eyes. Game time.

The *Ocean Summit* had four pools, each with its own special feature. Long and narrow, this pool was for sports. I'd served on the sister ship, which had an identical set-up. In the mornings, passengers could swim laps. And at the beginning of every cruise week, passengers diligently woke up eager to maintain their exercise regimes. But by midweek, the pool sat empty, the lane indicators dipping and swaying with the motion of the ship.

The packed pool deck had quieted as I raised the mic. "Who's ready for some serious crew versus passenger pool volleyball?"

Two men in baggy swim shorts had pumped their hands in the air and shot forward.

I'd laughed. Every cruise I met guys like these. Tanned, fit, and eager to show off to the ladies. "We've got some passengers eager to lose, I see." They'd flexed their muscles while puffing out their chests. "This isn't the hairy chest competition, no need to audition." The gathered crowd laughed. The men laughed with them. I waited until I had a full team of passengers, mostly big men, but some women and one lanky teenager who kept pulling his swim trunks up, before introducing the crew team.

The *A-Team* theme song blared out of the speakers as an impressive stream of men and women strode onto the deck. They looked like they could win gold medals in the Olympics, and some probably could, but mainly I'd pulled them from various departments because they looked impressive. Winning isn't always about ability, sometimes it's about intimidation. And nine times out of ten, it worked.

Both teams jumped in the pool, deciding their starting positions.

We always give first serve to the passengers as a sign of goodwill. It relieves some of the initial sting of seeing our team. I'd picked up the volleyball and glossed over the rules, then tossed it to the passenger team. Ten minutes later, I noticed Amy and her scowl observing from the deck above, and the next thing I knew, I was underwater. I don't remember how I got into the water.

Through the gathered crowd, I saw Claire Mills watching me—the passenger from that morning who claimed there'd been a murder on board. I didn't believe that for a second. I imagined curiosity served her well in her career, but it had no place here on this ship.

Austen motioned for me to change. "I'll finish off the volleyball game."

Claire intercepted me before I could make it into the crew corridor. "Are you okay?"

"I'm fine." I ran my fingers through my hair, knowing a losing battle when I saw one. I untucked my shirt from my shorts and twisted the end; another pool full of water gushed out. It splashed over my bare feet and onto Claire's leather sandals. I looked up to see Claire watching, and it electrified me. I performed for a living, yet this felt different, more intimate than being in front of a crowd. Something in the way she watched held me there, the wet heavy fabric clinging to my skin. I shivered in the heat.

Behind us, the volleyball game resumed. Claire coughed and the moment passed.

Before I could step around her, she said, "I found this on my balcony." She dropped a tiny white pill into my reluctant palm. I turned the pill over with my finger but was unable to find anything significant.

"Why is this important?"

"Colin had two empty prescription bottles on his nightstand. I recognized the prescription, they're sleeping pills. This pill is from one of those bottles." I still didn't follow her logic. How could she be sure? "If Colin committed suicide by taking sleeping pills, then why was one on my balcony?"

"It could've been from a previous occupant in your room."

"It's a pill, Moira. How long is it going to last outside on a ship balcony? Besides, isn't this the inaugural cruise?"

"Fair point."

"Let's say someone *did* kill Colin, and they wanted to make it look like a suicide. How would they stage that? The cleaning crew would discover him the next morning dead without any visible wounds on his body and an empty bottle of pills next to him. It makes sense to jump to that conclusion. So the killer poisons him and then dumps a bottle of pills overboard."

I nodded along with her. "And naturally there's a good chance some of them would blow back on board."

"Exactly, they warned us about that in our safety drill. It's why we shouldn't throw lit cigarette butts overboard, because anyone who has an open balcony door could have that blow back into their room and start a fire."

"But we still don't know for sure how they think he died."

"That's why we need to see the body and take a look at their report."

"What? You want to see his dead body?"

"To prove someone murdered him."

"Why do you care so much? Let the authorities handle it."

"I think a better question is why don't *you* care? It's obvious they're mishandling it, which means someone on board is about to get away with murder. How can you stomach that?"

I stared at her, wondering what it must feel like to have that much fire in you. Here was a woman who'd put herself in danger, stood up against the mafia and police and prosecutors who wanted her sources. And she never once backed down. How did someone get that much courage?

I certainly didn't have it. My list of priorities that afternoon included getting into dry clothes and finding a way to enact revenge on my boss for being an anal bitch. I should care about this, but I also didn't have the same privilege Claire Mills had. If they found her in the morgue, they would either ask her to leave the ship or, and this was more likely given who she was, give her a soft reprimand not to do it again. I, however, would get fired. Dropped off at the next port with all my belongings and told to piss off and get myself home.

"Why me?" The salt water from the pool had begun to dry on my skin. It felt sticky and itchy. I wanted to get out of these clothes as soon as possible.

Claire shrugged. "You happened to be in the wrong place at the right time."

I sighed. "I can't help you."

"Can you point me to someone who might?"

"No one's going to help you, Claire. We all need our jobs."

"What about justice?"

"Justice doesn't pay the bills." I walked away unable to look her in the eyes. Claire Mills would risk her job for justice—she probably had several times. I couldn't face that kind of disappointment.

I shlepped down to my cabin on deck three. As assistant cruise director, I got my own cabin, and on this ship it even had a porthole. Most of the crew slept below the waterline, some six to a room. To have my own room felt decadent, a privilege I tried never to forget or misuse.

I opened a door off the main corridor into a side hallway where they housed a few department heads, guest entertainers, and some of the lower officers. You could call this the mid-management section of the ship. I stopped halfway down in front of my door and slipped my keycard into the slot. When I opened the door, a wave of water leaked out, spreading down the hallway slopping back and forth with the motion of the ship.

I rushed inside to find one of the taps gushing water in my sink. I turned the knob, but instead of turning the water off, it kept spinning. I grabbed the comforter off my bed and shoved it into the sink to try to sop up some of the water and pulled out my ship phone to dial maintenance.

The real reason fire was so dangerous on ships wasn't the fire itself. It was the water necessary to put it out. Too much untamed water on board could capsize a ship. Even one this size.

It didn't take long for three of the maintenance crew to show up in their blue coveralls and tool belts. I pointed to the washroom and they stormed past me.

I stomped down the corridor, still wet, with a change of clothes. I hoped Kaitlin was in her cabin.

When I knocked, I heard a muffled "Hmph."

"Thank God. Let me in."

"Who's me?" a groggy voice asked.

I kicked the door with my foot a second before it opened to probably the closest thing I had to a best friend. She beckoned me into her tiny room with its scattered clothes and faint smell of liquorice.

She scanned my wet hair and clothes. "Did Amy throw your arse off the ship?"

"Not yet." I peeled my polo off and chucked it into the bathroom sink. I hadn't thought to get a bra.

Kaitlin slept most afternoons because she managed the nightclub bar. Her cabin held a double bed, a slim locker, and a squat dresser with two suitcases stacked on top. The both of us took up the remainder of the space in the room.

"Not that I don't love the impromptu striptease," she said, lifting one perfectly sculpted eyebrow. Kaitlin, originally from South Africa, grew up in Wales where her father worked for a company that manufactured copper pipes. Like Kaitlin, her accent had travelled the world and hadn't settled down in one place yet. Nor were her looks an indication of her heritage. Many mistook her for German. She did, after all, bear a remarkable resemblance to Marlene Dietrich and had the same no-nonsense air about her. It's fair to say I found her gorgeous.

We'd both met on our first contract, she a lowly bar server and me, a cruise staff shlep. Her father had died a few months earlier, and instead of following her mother's wishes and getting married and pushing out babies, she'd rebelled. We never talked about it, but I assumed her rebellion came with the loss of her inheritance.

I'd led a similar rebellion in not following my dad's wishes. He'd wanted me to take over his position as manager at the hotel I'd worked at since I was twelve. But I knew the second I stepped into that role, I wouldn't step out again until retirement. Granted, working on a cruise line didn't scream tattoos, sex, and rock and roll like some of my classmates' revolts.

Surprisingly, Kaitlin and I had only worked on one other ship together over the years. This reunion made me ecstatic to have her close again.

"My sink tap won't shut off. It flooded my cabin with an inch of water. Mind if I take a shower and change?"

"They should never have allowed this ship to leave wet dock." Kaitlin turned on the kettle and pulled a ramen soup package from her cupboard.

"If we make it back to Fort Lauderdale I'll buy you a drink."

"I'll be surprised if we make it to Belize."

"That might prove true," I said. "I've gotten some complaints from the crew that some of the safety alarms aren't working in the engine room, so they've posted crew to monitor in shifts."

Kaitlin plopped down on her bed and crossed her legs as if she'd discovered her favourite show on TV. "So this whole ship might go kaplow?" She cackled, enjoying this too much.

I filled her in about Amy sabotaging my bingo earnings, and the dead body they'd found on deck ten.

"See? This is why I don't need drama in my life. I live vicariously through you."

I smacked her in the arm. "I don't court it, drama finds me."

She leaned back, still in her sweats from her afternoon nap. Later, she would dress up in her tight skirt suit uniform that, thanks to a few alterations, made her legs look dynamite, and she would saunter up to the nightclub, which usually didn't close before four a.m. She cultivated a certain look because men tipped better, she said. We each owed part of our livelihood to the intricacies of human nature. Kaitlin for tips, and I for bingo commission. We likely bonded over this unfortunate circumstance.

Kaitlin pulled a pillow over, hugging it to her while I dropped my shorts and lugged them into the sink to join my polo. "You don't think someone murdered him."

"I don't care if someone did or not. I don't want to get involved."

"Ah." The way she said it, like she'd summed up and understood and had solved my entire dilemma, made me want to scream. "You've been saying for years how you want to get out and do something else, anything else as long as it doesn't involve tourists. Yet here you are, keeping your head down complaining that solving murders isn't in your job description."

"Well, it's not."

Kaitlin sat up and threw her pillow at me. "You're not thinking of the bigger picture. This is your opportunity to impress Claire Mills. She probably has a lot of connections. If you help her out with this, chances are she'll help you out. But if you sit on your arse and do nothing, then you get nothing in return. Be a go-getter."

I stepped into the bathroom, a short distance from where I'd stood a second ago. "I hate your pep talks." I closed the door.

"It'll be fun," she said from the other side. Leave it to Kaitlin to find solving murders fun. She could find the fun at a funeral if you gave her half a chance.

CHAPTER EIGHT

Claire—Monday evening: at sea

"You want to go see a dead body?" Moira's voice filtered through my cabin phone. "Meet me in front of reception." Her sultriness belied the content of the conversation. In my mirror, the bright red of my dress glared back at me. The attire for the night was formal even though they no longer turned you away at the door if you chose to wear jeans or, God forbid, shorts. But I had to ask, was it too much for a morgue? Not that the dead would care what I wore, but it felt wrong to dress up for the occasion. Viewing a dead body seemed more of a dress down sort of affair.

My shoes had an accusatory look about them as well, as if the anticipatory click-clack on the hard floor would be too much for anyone to bear. I debated changing. Why did I want to go out to dinner anyway? I had more of a chance of bumping into Frank out there. I stared hard at myself in the mirror. I'd had this same pep talk at least three different times this afternoon and not once had I won, which seemed strange since I was arguing with myself.

It went like this: Not one but two of my close friends forced me on this vacation because I had a tendency to overwork myself. As they'd pointed out. I had several health conditions as a result. I always counter that I should've been born in Japan. The Japanese even have a word for this: karoshi. It literally translates as overwork death. They see the beauty in loving work so much that you give your whole body to it.

When I think of this word, I picture a man, usually a man but sometimes a woman, sitting alone on a stool at an outdoor yatai forcing noodles into their mouth with chopsticks. The sun has long disappeared into a forgotten day and the streets have birthed a chaotic night life.

Their eyes blankly stare out at the tourists and youth who pack the streets as they nourish their bodies before going home and collapsing on their beds. The next morning, before the sun has risen, they will wake and do it all over again.

I lose my own argument because of this image. It sits forlorn in my mind, a sad oil painting of a pointless life. As romantic as it seems at first, to actually have a word for overworking yourself to death doesn't live up to the puffery. Because in reality, I know deep in my soul the man or woman who sits ramming noodles into their mouth doesn't love their job.

My life doesn't resemble theirs even a little. I love what I do, and it infuriates me that I should have to justify that. Still, I wasn't questioning whether I should go down to the morgue to investigate a possible murder, something I shouldn't even get involved with. No. I was debating whether I should change back into capris pants or wear my flowy red dress and go out to dinner after. I was debating what a dead body would prefer to see me in.

I plopped down on my bed before my head exploded. What existed inside me that created this need to know? I needed to know if Colin Avery killed himself. I needed to know if there was someone on this ship who wanted him dead and killed him, making it look like a suicide. I needed to catch this person. I needed to know they would not get away with it. The need was neurotic, all consuming, and dangerous. My work in itself is not dangerous, no. It's the need to know that will get me killed.

I stood at the centre of the reception area, also the heart of the ship, waiting for Moira to show up. The main atrium felt big and impressive. The open space towered several floors above me, giving the impression of antebellum grandness. An odd mix of passengers streamed by, some in swim shorts and smelling of sunscreen, others, like me, in dresses and suits, perfume and cologne trailing behind. Every minute or so I spotted a man who looked like Frank, and I turned in the other direction. Perhaps I should have countered with a less public meeting place.

"I noticed you doing that on the pool deck. Who are you avoiding?"

I turned at the sound of Moira's voice and took a step back, surprised at how different she looked out of uniform. She wore a tight black dress which cut mid-thigh, showcasing her long athletic legs. She'd tamed her long dark hair into a voluminous braided updo, but a few strands had escaped, framing her face. And her three-inch heels equaled out our height difference. Only the name tag at her breast signalled her as crew. She reminded me of an advert I'd seen of a woman stepping out of a speedboat onto a pier, with beautiful European architecture as the background. Dark hair, dark lips, and dark eyes without a care in the world. Moira had the confidence of a woman who looked more beautiful than anyone else in the room, so nothing else mattered.

"I ran into someone I know on the cruise, and now I'm avoiding them." I spotted him heading our way the second I said it. "Bugger." I turned to face away, knowing he'd seen me.

"What?" Moira stepped closer facing the same direction and whispered. "Did you spot them? Is it someone we should hide from?"

I sighed. "An annoyance, really."

"Claire. Where have you been hiding?"

We both turned and found Frank standing in a variation of his uniform—darker trousers, nothing light for the evening would do, a polo, and a dinner jacket. He'd combed his recently washed red hair, and it had since dried and flopped onto his forehead like a red patch of twine.

"Are you heading in to dinner?" he asked. "Maybe we could persuade someone to change seats and sit together?" The hope in his voice made me cringe.

"We have a prior engagement." I grabbed Moira's wrist. "Sorry." For some unknown reason, I didn't want to hurt Frank. I wanted him out of my life, but I wanted him as happy about our divorce as I was.

Strange how you spend years with someone without noticing

how much you dislike them and then suddenly, or at least it seems sudden, you want nothing more to do with them. You want them gone, a lost memory that only appears late at night after you've woken from a distant car alarm, soon forgotten as your head hits the pillow and you drift off to better dreams.

Frank didn't belong in my life anymore, and the sooner he realized that, the happier we'd both be. Me, because I wouldn't have this crushing guilt hanging over me, and him? Well, I didn't really care why he should be happy. He was the one who cheated. Then I cheated, but only because he did. With the same person.

I tugged on Moira's wrist to get her to move, but she appeared momentarily stunned by Frank. I wanted to get out of there before Frank said anything else.

"We still need to talk. We have things to talk about. I never got a chance to say what I needed to say this afternoon."

"Because you stalled through the whole lunch, Frank. It's over." I pulled Moira away, resisting the urge to look back and witness a crushed man. I didn't have it in me to care anymore.

After steering us through a few corridors, Moira brought me to a service lift. As we waited, she asked, "Frank's your husband?"

"Ex-husband. As soon as the paperwork comes through."

"Ah." She nodded knowingly.

"What does that mean?"

"It explains the tension between you two. I see it a lot. People come on cruises thinking a vacation can save their marriage. But what it does is prove how little you have in common. And only one person will get that. The other will think everything went well, they enjoyed themselves. The unevenness, it shows."

"How old are you?"

Moira smirked at me, lifting an eyebrow to chastise me for asking her age. "Old enough."

"I didn't mean to… You act older than you look."

The lift chimed, and the doors opened into a tiny box big enough for one person, two if you squeezed.

"Sorry about this. These are the crew elevators. I usually take the stairs everywhere. They tend to treat this like a clown car."

I didn't understand what she meant until we stopped one deck below and three crew members tried to push on. Moira waved them off, telling them to take the next one.

One of the men nodded and said, "Sure thing, princess."

"Princess?"

She sighed and leaned her hip against the wall of the lift. "I'm crew welfare ambassador. I don't know why, but some of them call me princess. I haven't figured out if they mean it as an insult or a show of respect. I basically organize parties and order supplies for the crew bar. Nothing fancy."

"Nothing that would warrant the title princess?"

Her radiant smile brightened the space. "I think you might have solved my conundrum there." She laughed.

"You can pretend."

The lift stopped and opened on to an austere deck. Nothing of the warmth of the passenger area remained. The colourful plush carpets on the floors, the fine art on the walls, the whimsical statues and topiaries every few yards were all gone, replaced with white everything.

"Which suits me fine. Pretending is what we do best here." She pointed to the right and I followed her, aware for the first time in a while that at the end of this maze we'd find a dead body.

Our heels clicked along the hard floor and echoed off the empty walls. The capris would have suited this excursion better, I thought at that moment.

"Where is everyone?" I asked.

"This area doesn't get used much during sailing. We use it for tenders. So when you get off the ship in Belize, you'll have to come down here to board the tender boat to take you ashore." She steered us to the left into a waiting area that seemed an in-between world of passenger versus crew. It didn't have the sterility of the crew area, nor the warmth of the passenger area, but instead the appearance of mediocre décor. As if it had tried, failed, then tried a little less hard to meet some standard of presentation. There was a carpet, for instance, but thin and beige. The plastic chairs had armrests but no cushions, and the walls had informational posters instead of fine art.

"Welcome to the medical centre." Moira guided us behind the small reception area into the back where few passengers saw. Two closed doors stood on either side of the hallway and a large watertight door anchored the end of the corridor. Moira led us through this and knocked on a door just inside.

A tall, very blond man in a white lab coat opened the door and smiled at Moira. "I heard you got this assignment," he said with a strong South African accent and pulled her into a hug. After a moment, he noticed me standing off to the side. "A medical problem?"

Moira turned to me. "This is Claire Mills, and she has the cabin next to the deceased man." He nodded as if my being here for that reason made sense. "Claire, this is Dr. Jan Steenbok." He grasped my hand and pumped three times very quick. When he smiled, his cheekbones took over his face, making angles and creating shadows from the unfortunate lighting. His deep blue eyes, the only colour on his face, stood out like two beacons, duelling lighthouses on a bluff searching for lost souls.

"It's nice to meet you, call me Jan." He looked back at Moira. "What can I help you with?"

Moira beamed at him. "We want to view the dead body."

"A dead body?" He leaned into Moira and whispered in a voice so loud they could hear it all the way back at the lift, "A little macabre for a date, don't you think, Moira?" A chime from the front tinkled back to us. "If you'll excuse me for a moment, I have customers."

The silence spread out before us, like pâté on a cracker, uneven and delicious. If Rick knew I had convinced this poor woman to bring me down here to investigate a dead body, he'd tell me I needed therapy. I could imagine his argument now: "If you can't even take a few days off to enjoy yourself, what does that say about your mental state?" Right as always. Nothing calms me more than a good old-fashioned mystery. And I may read them as much as I like, but a book has nothing on the real thing. So, in a way, my vacation was shaping up nicely, thank you very much, Rick. Of course, I would never tell him about any of this. A lark, to pass the time.

"I like your dress," I said, to break the silence.

She leaned forward, peering down. "Thank you. I borrowed it from a friend. My room is…undergoing maintenance."

The slight pause gave her away. Something private I didn't feel the need to pry into at the moment.

"So Frank. Did you know he would be on board or—"

"Total surprise, or shock. Yes, I like shock better. I had no idea. He still thinks he has a chance, which he doesn't. Are you married?"

Moira shook her head. "I can't say that I want to be. I don't know many married people."

"It's a bit of an odd duck, marriage. And you never know whether it's going to be a good one until you're in it. Marriage is a bit like having a place to store everything. I liked to keep the milk in the door on the fridge, and Frank always put it back on the top shelf. You know where the milk goes, or that particular dish in the cupboard? When they don't match up, you have trouble. Frank spent seventeen years thinking the colander went beneath the microwave when it hung on a hook on the island." I shrugged.

Dr. Steenbok strode back through the door. "Nothing to worry about. A couple of ladies with seasickness. I gave them some pills and sent them on their way. Now, what's this about a dead body?"

"Claire thinks the suicide verdict—"

"Someone murdered him and we'd like to—"

"*You'd* like."

"Yes, I'd like to examine the body for any foul play that—"

"I missed on my examination?" Dr. Steenbok said.

I tilted my head from side to side. "Well, did you do toxicology?"

Steenbok shook his head, a laugh almost bubbling to the surface. "I don't have the equipment or proper storage facilities to do any of that, nor the authority, I might add. If they want to do that when we arrive back in Fort Lauderdale, they can."

"But after a nine-day cruise, won't most of that be useless?"

"Sure will."

"So if I wanted to kill someone, wouldn't a cruise ship make a great place to do it?" I spread my arms out to indicate the surroundings. "The authorities on this ship did very little investigation before claiming Colin died by suicide. And now his body will sit decaying beyond the time for a proper autopsy and toxicology testing, which means the authorities in Florida will likely rule it a suicide, and the killer gets away with it."

"I don't generally think of these things, but yes, likely it will happen that way."

"We just—"

"You." Moira corrected me again.

"*I* just want to take a look, see if anything out of the ordinary pops up. How did they think he killed himself?"

"Sleeping pills. They found an empty bottle on his bedside table."

"A suicide note?"

He shook his head. "And what happens if you examine him and do discover something? What then?"

"Nothing. I satisfy my curiosity."

Dr. Steenbok looked dubious, and I didn't blame him. He turned his stare to Moira and softened. He must have owed her a favour because he agreed. I tried not to squeal with excitement. People who know me wouldn't call me a squealer by any means, but excitement bubbled up inside me, like I'd won something.

He led us to the morgue, a tiny room with three metal doors on the wall. It looked like every morgue I'd seen on TV and one memorable time in my early twenties while working on a story about missing homeless people.

Dr. Steenbok yanked up the handle and flipped the door open. Two feet with colourful socks poked out the end. He undid a latch under the bed and pulled it forward to reveal a very dead Colin Avery.

Moira held back, waiting for Dr. Steenbok to exit the room, or maybe she'd decided she didn't want to see a dead body. He hadn't begun to smell yet, and I wondered how long it took. I pulled back the sheet. He was still clothed, wearing an Atari T-shirt and cargo shorts.

Moira went to the foot of the table and examined his socks. They had R2-D2 from *Star Wars* on them. She stepped to the side and peered into his face. "I remember him from the sail away party. I liked his socks." She closed her eyes. "He didn't say much. He was soft spoken. Amy had to hold the mic close to his mouth."

We spent a total of fifteen minutes up close and personal with what used to be Colin Avery and found nothing. I'm not exactly sure what I thought I'd find. A pinprick from a syringe? Some bruising that hadn't shown up in the initial examination? What a stupid thing to think we could do a better job than Dr. Steenbok, the only person in this place who held a medical degree. I started to doubt myself and realized I might have brought Moira in on this for no reason. She was risking her career so I could play detective.

Dr. Steenbok leaned against the door frame. "The one wrench in your theory is that Colin was alone on his vacation. How do you get someone on board to kill them without them knowing it?"

I'd spend the rest of the evening pondering that.

CHAPTER NINE

Moira—Tuesday morning: Cozumel, Mexico

I stood at the bow of the ship as we crawled into Cozumel. At this speed, I would arrive faster if I jumped overboard and swam, but the ship's draw—how deep it sank into the water—wouldn't allow for fast navigation through the corals. I watched as the pilot boat sped away, still in the shadow cast by the *Summit*. The pilot navigator, who would be familiar with the local water depths, shoals, and sandbars, would help the captain navigate to the pier where the ship would dock in less than an hour.

Earlier, the sun, which now peeked over the trees on the mainland, had sent rays dancing through the palms, casting light on the small island buildings. I imagined the shops preparing for the onslaught of tourists pouring out of cruise ships like ants descending on a piece of fruit left to rot on the road. They could have the main shops with their cheap trinkets and tourist traps, I only wanted to escape the ship, find a decent restaurant, and eat something that hadn't gone through several rounds of food prep before the staff mess.

As the pier came into focus, so did the Señor Frog's, Starbucks, and Hooters. Not much had changed in ten years, or even twenty. Thirty years ago, however, this island boasted a quaint local village where tourists could enjoy virgin beaches and local cuisine. The cruise ship industry, far more efficiently than the colonialists and pirates of the sixteenth century, had defeated the Caribbean and warped it in their own image.

I'd like to imagine one day, once the environmentalists have their way, the islands of the Caribbean Sea will revert to their former selves. Like a university student slinking back to their residence after a night of binge drinking and emerging for class dressed in the semi-conservative outfits they wear to impress current professors and future employers.

At the sound of voices, I saw Amy push through the gate and enter the bow area, followed by a short man with a beer paunch and flamboyant toupee. I came here specifically to hide from people because only crew could enter, and at this time of the morning, they were either working or sleeping. From my position off to the side, I stood hidden by a support beam for one of the lifeboats.

Years ago, ships allowed passengers near the bow, but after *Titanic* came out, too many people wanted to recreate that iconic scene. The practice faded over the years, but this area still remained off limits.

"I wanted to surprise you. I couldn't tell you before I got here because that would have ruined it." He stepped forward and tried to grab her hand, but she pulled away, facing the approaching island. "I had it all planned out. I got reservations at Da Nella's and everything."

She turned, her eyes slits and her mouth a thin line. "You told me your mom died. But that wasn't true."

He held up his hands and stepped up onto a large coil of rope to even out the height difference. "I lied, but for a good reason. I know it doesn't get me off the hook."

"It doesn't. You…" She gestured at his body and hair. "Don't look anything like your pictures."

"Oh come on, who does these days?"

"Um, Amy?" The voice came from behind. Simon, the broadcast technician, stood at the rail with a video camera and a mic pack. "Do you want me to come back later?"

Flustered, Amy shook her head, smoothing down her hair. "No, I want to get this done while we're coming into port." She turned to the man standing on the rope. "I have to work now."

"We'll talk later," he said as he stepped off the rope and headed toward Simon. "Maybe at dinner?" he said hopefully, but Amy didn't respond.

Simon, wearing the all-black uniform of the tech department, hoisted a camera on his shoulders and pointed to the very front of the ship. Amy, who wore her Cozumel outfit, stepped over the large ropes holding the anchor tight against the ship, her heels slipping on the slick deck. She looked out of place, crawling around equipment in a light blue skirt suit.

"Make sure you get the pier in the background," she said.

Simon gazed around at the bow. "You'll need to stand on something. The railing is too high."

"In these heels? I'd break my neck." She scooped them off by the ankles and tossed them to one side. "They won't see them anyway." She clambered onto a python-sized coil of rope and gripped another steel lifeboat beam to steady herself.

Lucky for her the ship was only doing three or four knots.

"Aren't we waiting for Moira?" Simon asked.

Instead of a response, Amy tilted her head to the side as if to say, "What a silly suggestion."

"That's a shame, you guys have really great banter."

Amy shook her arms like an athlete getting ready for the 1500-metre dash, then plastered on her fake smile that puffed out her cheeks but didn't touch her eyes. "Let's get this done. I want to get off the ship as soon as we dock."

"Okay. We're rolling."

Her voice melted into a warm cadence as she recited her monologue, clearly rehearsed a million times. "Welcome to Cozumel, home to the second largest barrier reef in the world. If you're here to do some diving today, you've picked the right place."

I listened for a few more seconds before slinking away out of sight. It didn't matter to me if Amy wanted to do these spots with me or not. It meant extra work, and I already had too much work to begin with. Let Amy have the spotlight. I slid past a group of passengers watching land come into view from the port side of the ship and walked into the main atrium. It would take two or three hours for the majority of the passengers to disembark, then the crew members could go ashore.

I took the stairs two at a time in search of coffee. The place swarmed with people waiting to get off the ship. I needed a quiet place to think, something I thought I'd found on the bow. If someone had murdered Colin Avery, and it looked like a possibility at least, then they were still on board. Claire had said the next thing to look at would be the motive. I had my doubts. How could we figure that out? There could be a million reasons to kill someone, although Claire mentioned there tended to be only four real reasons—the four Ls: love, lust, loathing, and loot. I couldn't wrap my head around any of those since I didn't know the first thing about Colin.

Instead, I had other things to worry about, like how to get revenge on Amy. That seemed easier and more straightforward than delving into the mind of a murderer searching for a motive.

I spotted Dominic coming out of a hidden door in the side of a corridor. Just the person I needed. I called to him and he turned, laden with a tray full of silver domed plates.

"Can you let me in?" I pointed to the door he'd stepped out of.

He tsked at me. "One of these days I will start saying no."

"But not today, right?"

He grinned, pulled a keycard out of his pocket, and slapped it across a section in the wall. The door clicked, and I pushed it open.

"I owe you a beer later."

"If I recall correctly, you owe me several. But I will call it even if you can get me extra time on a computer station tonight."

"Done." I stepped into the hidden room, which revealed a small galley complete with a full pot of coffee. I, of course, wanted to find out about Colin. Claire had lit a curiosity in me, but first I had more important things on my mind. I needed to find the purser and take care of Amy's shore leave.

Claire—Tuesday morning: Cozumel, Mexico

The sun cast a sharp ray across the bed, beaming into my eyes as the ship turned sharply. I slipped out of bed and opened the balcony to find the ship turning in place alongside the pier. We'd made it to Cozumel, but a large building stood in my way, so this could be any number of ports. The navy blue water, churned by the ship's propellers, bounced between the ship and the pier, forming tiny waves.

Four men stood on the dock, ready to secure the mooring lines which shot out toward them, landing in the water a few feet from the dock. They pulled them up and dropped the big loops over small yellow pillars, at first slack and then taut as the ship reeled the lines in, pulling them closer to the pier.

I watched as several crew slid disks, like saucers cut to the middle, up each of the mooring lines. Curious as to what they did, I filed it away as yet another thing to ask Moira.

As much as the murder case intrigued me, I had to admit, so did Moira. What possessed someone to work on ships? I didn't know much about her personally, something I hoped to change, but I couldn't shake the feeling that it meant giving up so much. Why hide herself away on ships when she could accomplish so much more anywhere else? She had talent and charisma, she obviously had a brain in her head, and of course, she was gorgeous, sadly one of the most important keys to opening doors these days.

Back in my room, I filled the kettle from the sink in the bathroom, tilting it almost on its side to fit, then pushed the button to start the water boiling. I'd brought my own tea bags from home, knowing they'd muck it on the ship.

I flipped on the television as background noise and began the arduous task of choosing which swimsuit and coverup to wear. I'd packed several, knowing I didn't plan to wear much else. I had no plans of getting off the ship. If anything, I looked forward to a day without other guests. I had my book—a deep dive into the real cost of colonialism—and a plan to stake out a spot by the pool and not move until my stomach growled for lunch.

A roar from the crowd turned my attention to the television, which played an edited version of the sail away party. "Celebrate" by Kool & the Gang came on as a montage of people dancing flicked past on the screen. I grabbed the remote, ready to switch it to something, anything else, when I saw Colin flash up on screen. Moira and Amy had cornered him as he tried to squeeze through the crowd. Alive, he appeared young and timid, his voice so soft. Amy jammed the mic in his face.

"What's your name?"

He whispered something.

"So the rest of us can hear." Amy moved the mic so close he was practically eating the thing.

"Colin Avery."

Amy paused at that, thrown for a moment, but continued on. "Colin. And where were you heading?"

"My cabin."

Amy'd spread her hand out toward the crowd. "The party is right here, Colin." He'd given her a shy smile, probably something practiced over the years when encountering overbearing people. Easier to smile and nod than tell them to sod off. "Where are you from, Colin?"

"Michigan."

"Big place. Whereabouts in Michigan?"

"Bay City."

"And what brings you on the *Summit*? Celebrating anything special? A birthday, anniversary?"

He'd shook his head. "I won a contest."

The scene changed to people dancing.

I switched the channel, tired of listening to that dreadful song and Amy's overly friendly voice. She didn't do subtlety. So Colin had won a contest. That made things interesting. I finished getting dressed with a new plan in place. The pool deck and my book would have to wait. I wanted to see if I could find anything out about this contest and specifically Colin Avery. Maybe the contest people had a bio or some blurb to tell me more about him. The more I could find out about Colin, the closer I would get to finding who killed him.

By the time my kettle boiled, I'd already left the cabin in search of the computer lab on deck six.

Moira—Tuesday morning: Cozumel, Mexico

My room still didn't feel like mine. They'd gotten the tap to stop gushing, but everything still smelled damp, and my carpet left little squishy footprint trails. Last night I'd crashed in Kaitlin's room until she got off work at three a.m. and kicked me out of her bed. I spent the rest of my night on my rock-hard loveseat. I'd called down three times to get a new comforter but still hadn't heard anything.

If I still didn't have one by tonight, I would go down to laundry and steal one. Why did this have to happen this week? I already had too many problems. And as soon as that thought reached consciousness, my on-board cell rang.

"This is Moira."

"Hi, Moira. This is Fatima from reception. I have a woman here who has asked for you."

"Does this concern yesterday evening's bingo? I know we had some mix-ups but—"

"No. She said her name is Claire, and she has some information about…" Fatima paused, listening to someone on her end. "Colin. She says it's urgent."

I promised Fatima I'd get there in a few minutes, finished dressing, sighed as I surveyed my room one last time knowing I wouldn't see it for a while, and closed the door. As a precaution, I took a clean uniform to store in the cruise staff office for when I got back on board.

Claire stood to the side looking chic in tight capri pants and a white wraparound sleeveless top. Her pixie cut made her appear younger, as did her almond eyes surveying every detail in the atrium. I got the impression nothing slipped by her. I imagined she'd need that kind of skill as an investigative journalist, as well as curiosity, which she had in spades. Two things I knew about Claire right away: one, she was the kind of person you wanted to have in a bad situation, and two, I didn't want to get on her bad side. Ever.

She spotted me, and her face bloomed into a smile. "Oh good. I need access to a computer." She waved her hand at me. "And before you even say it, I've already checked the passenger computer lounge on deck six. It's full of old ladies emailing their grandkids. Is there a shop in Cozumel that sells laptops?"

"You want to buy a laptop? While on vacation in Cozumel?" She gave me the look my sister used to give me as kids when I asked questions I knew the answer to. In other words, stupid questions. Of course she wanted to buy a laptop while on vacation. I could ask why she hadn't brought her own, but I already suspected I knew the answer. "Someone forced you to take this vacation, didn't they?"

She gave me a sly smile. "They confiscated my laptop too. But luckily I have a credit card with me, and I've met the perfect guide."

"To enable your workaholism."

She looped her arm through mine and steered me toward the

elevator. I guess viewing a dead body bonded us in some way. She still hadn't convinced me someone had murdered Colin in the first place. "I've never understood why people always use such a negative term for dedication," she said.

"Is it dedication or obsession?"

"There you go again. Can't it be a healthy obsession?"

"I believe that would be an oxymoron."

Claire laughed.

The bulk of passengers had already disembarked for the day, leaving the few strays waiting for excursions or choosing not to go ashore milling about. When we reached the elevators, I guided Claire to the stairs as I couldn't use the passenger elevators but felt embarrassed to say so for some reason. Perhaps because, for once, Claire didn't treat me like a crew member, which happened often. Passengers saw the name badge and automatically assumed they could treat me differently.

On deck four, we came upon a mass of crew lining up to get off the ship. We had to wait until the majority of passengers got off before we could disembark. Up ahead, I saw Amy talking with a crew member, waving her arms and jabbing her finger at something on a computer screen.

As we moved closer, I could hear part of the conversation and smiled to myself.

"I can't possibly have more than two hundred dollars on my bar bill."

"It says right here you owe three hundred and fifteen dollars, and you will have to pay that before you get off the ship." The man stood three inches shorter than Amy and had a quiet, calm voice and a close-cropped haircut. His accent told me he came from somewhere in Eastern Europe.

"I understand the rules," Amy said. "What I'm saying is that there has been a mistake."

The man held his hand out for her card, sighing, his expression bored. He swiped it, waited, and then pointed to the screen. "No mistake. If you want to get off the ship, you will have to find the purser and pay what you owe."

I could see the debate in her eyes. Should she try to throw some weight around or suck it up and go explain the mistake to the purser? I knew the right answer. The look on this man's face told me he didn't care if she was Elizabeth II, she had to follow the rules like everyone else.

Other crew members had stopped to stare.

Amy huffed as she pushed her way through the crowd.

"What was that all about?" asked Claire.

I shrugged.

We made it off the ship without any problems and stepped off the gangplank onto the concrete pier in San Miguel de Cozumel. Claire stood at the edge looking into the cyan water.

"They say you can still find pirate treasure in the reefs," I said. "This whole island used to be a pirate haven."

Claire turned back to me. "Have you ever gone looking?"

"I don't dive." Not that I wouldn't. I'd never found the time to get certified.

"Shame. Might be fun to go looking for pirate treasure."

We meandered through the crowd, past the Señor Frog's with the drink girls outside enticing patrons to come get drunk. The farther away from the main drag we got, the fewer tourists we saw.

As we turned onto a busy street, several vendors bombarded us with souvenirs, cheap things that every city in Mexico carried. Sometimes you could ignore them and they would melt back into the crowd, but other times you had to get aggressive. One old man in particular wouldn't leave us alone. He held out a few fans with the word Cozumel splashed across the front, and I knew if we'd travelled to Cancún they'd have the same crappy fans, only with Cancún printed on them. As a last ditch hope of enticing us, his eyes lit up and his grin turned mischievous as he held out a lighter and flicked it on. When he turned it sideways, he said, "It lights by the pee pee." He grinned and held it out to us as if he'd found the secret to us giving him money.

Claire stopped, took the lighter, and turned it over in her hand. "Why do they make these? They're crude." She tried to hand it back, but he refused to take it, instead insisting we pay him a hundred pesos.

"I'm not giving you a hundred pesos," I said, which was around five American dollars.

"A hundred pesos?" Claire exclaimed. "That's outrageous."

"Seventy-five," he countered.

I shook my head, took the lighter, and tried to hand it back. He held his hands up as if we'd offended him in some way.

"Oh, for crying out loud." Claire pulled a wad of money out of her pocket and waved a twenty peso bill at him.

His mouth scrunched up and his brows furrowed.

I took the bill from her and pushed it into his hand. "Take it or leave it. And get out of our face." I waved him away. He scurried down the road and around the corner.

"How much did we pay for this ridiculous thing?" she asked, pushing down the tiny penis as a flame popped up.

"About a dollar."

"So the joke's on him."

I took the lighter and put it in her knapsack. "The joke's on the person who now owns a dirty lighter."

We continued on our way, finally stopping in front of a dilapidated storefront with broken fake palm leaves and a faded sign that read "Surf the World Wide Web."

The door squeaked as Claire pushed it open to reveal six giant computer monitors, yellowed from years of sun and nicotine, on two tables of three each. She turned back to me and said, "I wanted to buy a laptop."

"I think that would defeat the purpose of your vacation. This way you save money and still get the knowledge you seek." We stepped inside. Two ancient fans gyrated above. "What did you want to look up?" I asked.

"I'm looking for who killed Colin Avery."

Chapter Ten

Claire—Tuesday evening: at sea

My stomach growled in protest as I stood waiting for Moira. I stepped out onto the deck to watch the sun sink below the horizon of the waves. The coast of Cozumel lay behind, a small speck of darkness.

At first I worried I was going to spend much of the week over my toilet, but luckily my stomach had proved itself hardier than I'd given it credit for. A few people passed behind me still dressed in beachwear, with pink arms and noses. As a Brit, I'd endured many heat waves over the last few years, and if that had taught me anything, it's that British people melt when the temperature gets above twenty-five. I couldn't fathom spending my vacation on a beach in the sweltering heat.

The internet café, straight out of the late nineties, hadn't proved fruitful. We'd found nothing online about the contest Colin might have won. In fact, we hadn't found much of anything on Colin. He had no social media accounts that we could see. Moira pointed out he might have used a nickname. A lot of people used different names these days, especially since most employers investigated these things during the hiring process. My generation certainly benefited from not having every minute of our lives plastered over the internet. I don't think many of us would be employed now if that were the case.

I'd enjoyed the afternoon more than I'd expected to. After we didn't turn up anything at the café, Moira had taken me out to lunch. The place looked as run down and out of touch with reality as the café, but what it lacked in appearance, it more than made up for with food. I'm embarrassed to say I'd never eaten real Mexican food before. Back home we have the usual Tex-Mex. Most people love a good fajita, but nothing I'd ever eaten matched what I ate today.

They made a special mole sauce which could be the most complex thing I've ever tasted. I grew up with boiled chicken and mashed potatoes and naturally fell in love with curry the first time I had it because British food is where flavour goes to die.

The woman serving us also ran the kitchen and owned the restaurant, and when I asked how she made her mole, I lost count after the tenth ingredient. After that, I ordered several more dishes because I wanted to try everything. Moira stopped me from ordering for a third time, promising me she'd take me to a great restaurant in the next port.

As we walked back to the ship, my stomach full and happy, I realized why Rick had pushed me to come. I could travel all over the world, immerse myself in a particular culture for a story, and still wouldn't have experienced it in the slightest for myself.

I live and work for my readers.

I was so caught up in the revelation, my eyes welled with sudden emotion, and I had to turn away from Moira, afraid she might see and think me mad. Why had it taken her and, of all things, trying real Mexican food for the first time to make me realize this? I felt silly and didn't say much on the way back. Walking past tourists with their heads in their phones and scooters with entire families hanging on, I felt the clinginess of the tropical air and knew this vacation would stay with me for years.

I needed to relish it. To make every moment count. Why had I spent the first two days trying to find a murderer when even the authorities on board thought Colin had committed suicide? I needed to drop it and have fun, relax, and every other thing Rick had told me to do for years.

So why was I waiting for Moira so we could go look at unused footage from the sail away party?

When I got back on ship, I fully intended to embrace this new me. The one who looked forward to the next port where I would find an out-of-the-way restaurant and try the local food. Hell, I even signed up for an excursion to a Mayan ruin.

Then Moira called my cabin and said it might be a good idea to see if Simon, the person who had shot the sail away party, had gotten anything else of Colin. I know I'm a workaholic. I also know I'm weak when it comes to setting new boundaries and goals that don't involve work. So I promised myself I would do this one thing, but then I would stop and enjoy the rest of my vacation.

I felt a tap on my shoulder and turned to see Moira in nice pants and silk blouse with her name tag above her left breast. The heat didn't ever seem to bother her. I'd always kept my hair fairly short because it didn't take much maintenance. In this weather, it made me doubly happy because it would be a frizzed mess by now. Moira's hair, on the other hand, looked radiant. Her dark, almost black tresses fell around her shoulders and seemed to bounce as she walked, so shiny the moonlight glinted off them.

"I'm taking you to an area that's off limits to passengers, so I nabbed this for you." Moira handed me a name tag with my name and country of origin on it. I snapped the magnetic back off and clipped it to my shirt. I had decided I couldn't handle dinner in the large dining room and had opted for casual, jeans and a sleeveless top, which would be acceptable in one of the buffet restaurants. "If anyone asks, you're a guest entertainer."

Moira led me through a labyrinth of hidden corridors to see Simon, the person responsible for filming the sail away party. I felt an instant chill as we stepped into his office. A maze of servers and digital displays crowded the tiny room, with four monitors wrapped around his swivel chair like we'd stepped into the control room for the universe. Dozens of screens lined one wall, each playing something different. One had a view of the front of the ship, another played a cheesy Meg Ryan and Tom Hanks movie, and a third played the cannonball contest Moira had asked me to judge yesterday.

Simon spun around. "Hey, Moira. Why exactly did you want to see the sail away footage again?" He tracked me as I stepped into his office, struggling to find a spot where I couldn't break anything.

His tight curly hair hugged his head like a swimming cap and almost looked like a wig, but his arms were also covered in dark curly hair, with a definite patch in the vee of his polo.

"I wanted to check the performance. We got a note, and it's bugging me."

He twirled back around and took a swig of a giant travel mug, clicking away with his mouse. "Okay, let's see. I have a nice wide shot of the crowd from the static camera mounted above the stage." He hit Enter on the keyboard, and one of his screens began playing a distorted wide angle video of the entire pool deck.

Moira leaned in closer to the monitor. "Do you have anything up close?"

"Sure I do. I've got what I took on my camera as I weaved through the crowd." As he spoke, he worked the keyboard and mouse, pulling up another video, this one more erratic than the other. It dipped to the ground, swinging as he moved through the crowd, then back up again, zooming in and focusing in on a couple dancing by the pool. "I keep it recording so I don't miss anything. No one's supposed to see the unedited stuff."

Moira clapped him on the back. "No problem. I really appreciate this."

We spent the next ten minutes watching Simon work his way through the crowd. He tilted his head back toward me, whispering to Moira, "Who's that?"

Moira turned back to look at me, a mischievous smirk on her lips. "Oh, that's Claire. She's one of the guest lecturers on board. She teaches people how to play bridge in the library every afternoon."

I almost laughed. I knew less about bridge than I did about flying an airplane.

"She asked to come along," said Moira. "She doesn't usually get to see much of the ship. And this is a pretty cool ship, wouldn't you say?"

"If they can get everything working right."

After another ten minutes, the interview Amy did with Colin came on the screen. I moved closer. Simon hadn't edited it at all, and when Amy had finished, Simon dropped the camera to his side, still recording. Simon paused the video.

"Can you keep playing it?" I said and stepped closer.

Simon turned to Moira and, after getting her nod, hit a key on the keyboard and the footage began to play again.

"Strange, isn't it?" I said to Moira, and we all watched as Amy and Colin's legs stood in place, neither one moving away after Amy's interview.

"Can you go to the wide angle?" asked Moira.

"Sure. This thing's pretty cool, huh? They installed them all over the ship. They record directly into a hard drive up here. In fact, I don't even have to remember to record. I can program all the shows in for the week, and it will do it automatically."

Moira patted his shoulder, obviously not caring in the slightest.

Simon pulled up the wide angle, jumping to the same point. Amy and Colin carried on a lengthy conversation before Amy stormed away in a huff. Then Simon refocused his camera on Moira, who had begun interviewing an old woman in a caftan and large sun hat.

"There's no way to get audio on that?"

Simon shook his head. "I'm guessing you aren't here looking at your performance. What exactly are you looking for?"

"You heard about the guy that committed suicide?"

Simon nodded. "I heard he hung himself in his shower."

"Why would you think that?" I asked, disgusted that people would add their own gruesome details.

Moira pointed to the frozen frame of Colin on the screen. "Well, that's the guy, and this was his last night alive."

"You think he didn't kill himself."

Moira looked over at me, perhaps gauging my reaction to telling him, but I didn't know this man from Adam. I shrugged.

"We think someone staged it to look like a suicide." Moira leaned against his desk and crossed her arms.

Simon didn't appear fazed by this revelation. "Have any leads yet?"

"Everyone's a detective these days."

He held up his hands in surrender. "Just making conversation."

"We know he won his trip in a contest and now it seems like he maybe knew Amy, or I don't know."

"Pissed her off, that's for sure," said Simon. "I've only worked with her for over a week now, but she is one anal bi—"

"Well, thanks for your help, Simon." Moira clapped him hard on the back.

"Hey, Moira, aren't you supposed to be taking off the magician tonight?"

"Yeah." She checked her watch as Simon pointed to a screen showing a wide view of the stage where a magician stood atop a glass table. "Balls!" she screamed and rushed for the door.

By the time Simon finished saying the magician was on his last trick, the door had already slammed shut.

"So you don't like Amy?" Moira hadn't mentioned it, but I could tell she didn't think much of her. And apparently, no one seemed to.

"You're not really a bridge instructor, are you?"

"That obvious?"

"No, I could totally see you as a bridge instructor. I just wondered why you're interested in a murder, that's all."

I turned to leave, my ego bruised, and find something to eat. Maybe a glass of wine, or several.

I'd discovered if you wanted low quality food, eat at the buffets. I'd already decided I didn't feel up to dining in the big hall, which didn't leave me a lot of options. It occurred to me that they had several good restaurants on board, but the chances of getting a table at this hour seemed slim. Plus I would have to change.

As I pulled the door open, Simon asked, "Have you eaten yet?" He stood up, clicked a few buttons on his keyboard to put his computer to sleep, and pushed the chair in tight. "Because it's roast night in the staff mess, and I know someone who can answer a lot more of your questions about Amy."

I pointed to the door. "After you."

Moira—Tuesday evening: at sea

I jumped down the crew stairs, two sometimes three at a time, gripping the railing when needed to stop me from breaking my neck. I slammed through the door into the hallway next to the theatre, taking down a server in a red suit. His drink tray flew out of his hand

and crashed to the ground. I didn't see the chaos I'd left behind, only the faint tinkle of broken glass.

I'd pay for that later.

I checked my watch in a blur. Balls. He had two minutes left, tops. I could picture the dead silence when the Magnificent James finished his last bow and no one came onstage to thank him and promote the next event of the evening.

I ripped open the entrance to backstage and lunged up the stairs, halting next to the curtain tech just off the wings, gulping in air like a fish flopping on the side of the pool looking for water.

I paused when I realized it wasn't the Magnificent James performing. I turned to the curtain tech, Brad, and asked between mouthfuls of air. "Who is that?" I pointed to the man standing onstage wearing a suit he might've stolen from a nineteenth century circus announcer. Or perhaps he *was* a nineteenth century circus performer.

His purple and red striped suit sparkled in the stage lights, and when he tipped his top hat, revealing bouncy curly blond hair, it too shone as if dipped in glitter. But what stood out the most was the almost white goatee he had gelled to a fine point that stood at attention a few inches from his chin.

"Magnificent James missed the ship. Guess he's not so magnificent." Brad chuckled as he pressed a button to lower a scrim at the back of the stage. "This is Bandini the Great."

"Never heard of him."

"And you'd heard of the Magnificent James before?"

"Good point. Any good?"

Brad turned to me as if I'd told him Siegfried and Roy had good taste. "He's a magician who performs on ships."

I turned to focus on Bandini, who stepped to the side. Amy now stood front and centre, but she took time to give me a brief death stare before switching her attention back to Bandini.

"And now, Amy, what do you have to say to our audience?" He spoke in an overdramatized Italian accent.

She opened her mouth and began saying nonsense words. "Fox, quick, ocean, justify."

"Whoa, whoa, whoa." Bandini put his hand over her mouth.

"How did you know my Bitcoin passphrase?" He exaggerated his expression of astonishment, then took his hand away as Amy continued to spout nonsense. His hand went back over her mouth. "I really must insist. I have a lot of money stashed away. Let's finish this." He waved a multicoloured scarf in front of her face and then motioned for her to talk again.

This time when she spoke, the words formed sentences. She thanked him for his show and encouraged people to come back tomorrow to watch one of the all-time great comedians no one had ever heard of.

When the curtain sank to the stage and she came offstage, she strode over to me, death rays streaming from her eyes. "You're late."

"I got here in time to take him offstage." I looked over at Brad to confirm I had been standing in the wings the whole time.

"Bandini's last act needs a crew member. I asked you to be here twenty minutes before his performance ended. You're lucky I happened to be watching from the wings."

She hadn't told me that, and I suspected it was on purpose.

"If this happens again, you'll be on report."

So that was the deal. *Okay, Amy. Game on.*

Chapter Eleven

Claire—Tuesday evening: at sea

Apparently a fake name badge got you far, or deep, into the underbelly of the ship.

No one questioned whether I belonged, especially with Simon at my side, as we weaved our way through corridors, down metal stairs, and through several watertight doorways that looked heavy enough to crush bones.

When I didn't think we could go any lower, Simon opened a door and we stepped into a busy cavernous thoroughfare I learned everyone called the I-95 based on the visa most crew needed to work on ships. It reminded me of New York, everyone in a hurry to get somewhere.

"This way." Simon steered me to the right, guiding me through the crowd and up another flight of stairs. How did they remember where to go? If Simon left me stranded, I'd have no idea how to get back to my cabin. Past the narrow stairs, we entered a busy cafeteria full of crew members in various uniforms.

Two-person tables lined one wall and six circular tables dotted the room in a random pattern. A buffet of food took up space on the opposite wall of the tables. A weak salad bar, two large stations with white rice, a few more vegetables in several different states of wilting, and at the end a tall man in a white apron and scowl carving a large roast.

Simon grabbed a tray and plate and handed it to me. "So, how well do you know Moira?"

"Meaning?"

"Have you been friends long? We worked together on a ship a few years ago, my first contract, but I got transferred after a few weeks to do vacation relief."

So that's why he invited me to dinner. He had a thing for Moira and hadn't yet figured out she dated women exclusively. Although I suppose I couldn't say for sure if she only dated women. However, I got the distinct impression Simon had zero chance with her. I felt it not my place to tell him. Instead I lied, something I'd become good at over the years. I always amazed myself at how fast I could pull information from years of hearing about other people's lives. Like going to a grocery store and deciding which vegetable to pair with which protein.

"I met Moira about three years ago. I can't say I know her any better than the rest of you."

He placed a hand over mine to stop me from grabbing the tongs for a stew-like dish. "I wouldn't, I'm pretty sure they recycle the food here."

I replaced the tongs, not worried for a second that the food had been another dish previously. Perhaps he'd gotten caught up in the rhetoric of hating your employer. I saw it all the time, people willing to believe the worst about a company simply because they felt short-changed by them for one reason or another. I thought it very unlikely a cruise line this large would risk fines to save money on food costs, something they'd have factored into doing business in the first place.

"Do you know if she's seeing anyone?"

I shrugged. At this point, I didn't feel hungry anymore. I wanted information if I could get it, so I followed behind Simon, taking what he took and ending the line with a large slice of roast on my plate.

He pointed toward a door at the back of the mess once we had full plates and a cup of stale coffee in mugs. It opened up onto a small deck at the back of the ship. Unfortunately, it had no ocean views, only a large wall with the words "Please to Put Loungers Back to Finish" painted next to a pile of plastic chaises.

Looking up, I could see passenger balconies hanging over the side, and at the very top, the café Frank and I had eaten lunch at just the other day.

We sat at a picnic table in the corner and Simon introduced me as the bridge instructor, a friend of Moira's, to several other crew. I still couldn't tell if Simon knew I was a passenger or not.

One woman, Kaitlin, stared longer than the others. She reminded me of a Russian model I'd interviewed once, all blond and ice, but when she spoke, she had a clearly west Londoner accent. Chiswick or Hampton maybe?

I also met Alan, a Romanian who worked in what he called the surveillance department. He watched cameras all day. If, for instance, someone fell and tried to make an insurance claim or lost something and claimed someone stole it, he would search through hours of footage to help disprove them.

"Sometimes they don't lie, but mostly they do," he said. "When I worked on the *Ocean Zephyr*, I once had to look through five days of footage in the main restaurant area because a woman slipped on a wet floor and claimed no sign was up. Turns out she fell right on the sign. It practically went up her ass. And then there was the time a woman lost her engagement ring. Said someone stole it. Turns out she took it off in the fitness centre to run on a treadmill. Set it down and then left it there when she'd finished. An old man picked it up and pocketed it. We followed him back to his room on cameras and got the ring back. All happy endings." He had short cropped black hair which he gelled down even farther, making his head look painted. He wore a simple black suit and tie.

"Sounds boring," I said.

"Very, but I make okay money. Better than back home. Plus, someday I hope to be one of the art dealers. They work very little and make the big bucks. Thirty thousand a month. Can you imagine? All for holding a couple of auctions during the week. They don't even do the heavy lifting of the art. They hire the chorus dancers to do that. All cash, all under the table." We lost him after that. He finished his dinner and headed back to work.

We didn't spend a lot of time talking about Amy, but I did find out from Simon she'd asked him to take a few professional pictures of her. "Not like that," he said. "Like in her 50s poodle skirt and her

70s catsuit. And then a few of her looking off into the sunset. She didn't say what they were for."

"Probably online dating." Kaitlin twisted open a bottle of water. "Knowing her, she thinks the kitschy photos make her look fun instead of the sad, pathetic woman she is."

CHAPTER TWELVE

Moira—Wednesday morning: at sea

I pressed the button and watched the cream stream into my cup, honestly my favourite time of day, the first hint of espresso filling my nostrils with that almost bitter scent.

The ship swayed starboard, and I braced myself against the edge of the stainless steel counter. Most passengers didn't feel the swell of the waves, especially in the Caribbean Sea, which didn't tend to get rough except in areas where it met up with the Atlantic. However, the higher up on the ship, the more noticeable the sway, and I was as high up as you could get.

The door to the tiny galley kitchen opened, and I froze. This was the captain's galley. Only a few select crew members had access. If I got caught, I might get written up, which wouldn't look great on my records but wouldn't ultimately get me fired. It would also put an end to my favourite thing every morning.

I relaxed when Sammy walked in. He smiled and waved a hand at the tray he carried. "Would you like a croissant and some smoked salmon?" Sammy worked this galley exclusively. It didn't sound terribly exciting, keeping this minuscule galley stocked for the captain, but it came with a certain amount of privilege and prestige. Sammy could get you anything you wanted. Because of his job, he had access to everything and everyone on the ship. If the captain wanted some mint chocolate ice cream at four in the morning, Sammy could get it for him. If he wanted some pistachios at ten a.m., then he'd make that happen too. Since he could get things for you, people treated him well—they made sure he always had phone cards to call home, they bought him beers at the crew bar, and they let him skip the line to get off ship or use the computers in the crew lounge.

We all did nice things for Sammy so that when we needed a favour he would happily return it. Sammy let me use the captain's galley to get coffee in the morning, and in return I threw him a calling card every week and made sure he was first up for crew karaoke. We both held power positions on the ship, and we'd become fast friends.

"No thanks," I said. "Too rich for me. I'll stick with coffee."

"Fake energy, you'll be empty in an hour."

"Which is perfect timing for my second coffee of the day. Listen, have you heard anything about the man they found dead in his cabin?"

Sammy placed the tray in the fridge and nodded. "They were talking about it yesterday. The staff captain came in to tell the captain they'd informed his family and arranged to have the body shipped back to Michigan. That's where he lived with his mom."

"Anything else?"

Sammy sucked in his lips, thinking. "No, just that the staff captain had informed head office and that they would make a statement to the media about it. The usual stuff about tragic circumstances, blah, blah, blah." He cocked his head. "Why are you so interested?"

"Perlah, one of the new staff, found him. I thought I could find something useful to tell her to make her feel better."

He nodded and smiled. I knew from that smile he didn't believe me for a second. One of the most important commodities on ships was information. And we both collected it like sunken treasure.

Having grabbed coffee and very little information, I headed to the main concourse to talk with the future cruise staff to see if they knew anything about which contest Colin might have won.

I've always thought of cruise ships as microcosms of the real world. After all, they engineer them to make you feel like you've stepped into a tiny world, and every employee has an obligation to make you believe that.

We have restaurants, cafés, a tiny shopping mall, casinos, a theatre, nightclubs, an art gallery, library, event space for weddings and birthdays, and a tiny office with two people whose sole purpose on board is to make you buy into it all over again.

They offer you deals that seem like bargains—on-board credits—if you book before you leave. Some of them can rope you in without all the sleaze, but most of them remind me of used car salespeople who care more about their commission than steering you in the right direction.

Phil and Carla, the duo on this ship, summoned up thoughts of Boris and Natasha, the villains from *The Adventures of Rocky and Bullwinkle*, and not entirely because they have Russian accents. They always looked like they were scheming, which I knew was all in my imagination. Probably. They also embodied that dark, brooding I'm-planning-your-murder kind of vibe. I successfully avoided them most days.

Today, however, I found myself outside their office on the main concourse a little after nine in the morning. Each had their own desk in the small alcove, designed to look like a well-to-do law office, with plants and rosewood desks.

"Carla, hi," I said, taking a seat across from her. I tried to deal with her exclusively. She felt safer for some reason, a little warmer, which didn't say much about Phil. Today she wore a business skirt suit with a large red scarf that dwarfed her small head even more. She'd pulled her black hair into a severe bun at the back of her head, which gave her a schoolmarm look.

She nodded to me but didn't say anything.

"I wanted to ask if you guys ran a contest for this cruise? Or know of any contests? One of the passengers mentioned he'd won a cruise during the sail away party."

Carla turned to Phil, who had put down the tablet he'd been reading. He shook his head. She turned back to me. "The cruise line didn't run any contests. It's the inaugural cruise, we practically had to beat people away with sticks." The way she said it, with her thick accent, made it sound like she would've enjoyed that.

"Is there any way to find out about who ran a contest?"

A small indulgent smile formed on her dark purple lips. "Hundreds of contests exist for this. They have whole websites for this."

I nodded. Of course. I hadn't expected much, but as I rose from my seat, Phil said, "If you really want to know, why not ask the person who won the contest?"

Thanks, Phil. Bold idea. I gave them a weak smile and left, knowing I'd hit another dead end.

At that point, I didn't have any more ideas. I decided to switch focus and work on one of the many problems at hand, because quite frankly, if someone killed Colin Avery, and that was a big if, it was the least of my problems.

I made it down to deck two, stopping first at deck six to use one of the room service galleys to get more coffee, nowhere near as decadent as my first, but my body needs caffeine to function like a ship needs water to float. I entered the ship laundry with two steaming cups of coffee in hand. When asking favours, it always helps to bring gifts.

Claire—Wednesday morning: at sea

I lounged, my feet up, on my balcony as I read the *New York Times.* A service on board allowed you to order newspapers to your room. I usually read at least four every morning with my tea. Not on a computer or phone—I liked the feel of real newspaper between my fingers, even if it did make a mess.

The wind made it difficult. Every turned page meant a few more slapped in my face, but you couldn't beat the view or the fresh air. At home in Highgate, a quaint little village in North London, an ancient balcony overlooks my small garden out back, and I like to bring my tea up when the weather allows and devour the news every morning. I used to live in Mayfair, but I prefer the green space we have in Highgate. Even with all the parks, Mayfair has too much concrete, and I didn't have a terrace or a garden.

This morning when I woke up, for a second, I thought it was my own bed back home until the ship swayed, something I'm not entirely used to yet.

Vacations throw you off your routine in such a strange way. Normally by ten I'd already have left the house. It felt odd to have nothing to do. I hadn't even checked the day's schedule because I had no plans to join in.

I had just gotten to the Lifestyle section when my cell phone rang. It didn't have any of the fancy features the new phones had, which made it a bit of an antique. It's ridiculous to even think that something that fits in my pocket and allows me to talk to people halfway around the world is obsolete.

"Hello, Rick." I didn't even need the Caller ID. I knew who would be calling, almost like a sixth sense.

"Finally upgraded your phone, did you?"

"If this is about work, I'll have you know I'm under strict instructions not to do any while I'm away on vacation."

"Funny that. I grabbed a coffee with Susan this morning, and we got around to talking about new projects and then she asked me about your new project, the one dealing with some guy named Colin something or other. And I said to her, 'That's silly, Claire doesn't have a new project.'"

I sighed and closed the paper. "It's not what you think, Rick. I'm not planning any story."

"Then why're you calling Susan to do research for you?"

Because you stole my laptop and I didn't get a chance to replace it yet. I couldn't say that to Rick. I knew he meant well. "Perhaps I have other interests besides work. I'm thinking about investing in a couple tech companies and I wanted to check this guy out."

"Says the woman who thinks her Nokia from the '90s is high-tech enough for her. Pull the other one, love."

I refused to say the words out loud. That I had stumbled upon a death and all by myself declared it murder and started investigating like I worked for the CID. "I don't do well at cold turkey, Rick. You know that."

I could hear his laughter on the other end. Traffic noise filled the air. I imagined Rick on his way to some meeting, busy as always, and I envied him that.

"Did Susan find anything for me?" I bit my lip, breath held. Maybe I'd gone too far asking.

"She said she emailed you what she'd found, but seeing as how you don't have your laptop and your phone only does phone calls, it can wait until you get back." He paused for several seconds before sticking the knife in my heart and twisting. "I'm worried about you. Medical professionals have told you, if you keep going the way you are, the stress will kill you. Not might, will. I don't say this often to people I work with, but I like you too much to watch that happen. Claire, promise me you are taking this seriously."

I heard a loud bang from next door—the cabin that now stood empty since the occupant had relocated to the morgue.

I stood up and went to the edge of the frosted glass screen that separated my balcony from Colin's.

"Claire? Did you hear me?"

"Yes. I promise I am taking this vacation seriously. I love you but I have to go. I'm late for bingo." I hung up before he could call me on my bull and peered around the glass to see if I could spot anything. The shape of a person's shadow crossed by the window, hidden by the closed curtains.

It couldn't be anyone cleaning the room. I imagined they'd wait until embark and do a thorough clean when they turned over the rooms. It had to be the person who Colin argued with on the night of his death. In other words, the killer had returned to find something. But I knew I wouldn't see anything from this angle.

And looking a long way down at the waves rushing past, I might add, I didn't want to climb over onto the next balcony. He'd spot me in an instant. I decided to wait until he came out into the hallway. Then I could perhaps follow him and find out who he was.

I stood for what felt like a million years waiting to hear the door shut. When I did finally hear it, I rushed to my door and yanked it open, cautiously peering out into the hallway to find nothing. It was empty and quiet.

I ran back to the balcony and leaned over as far as I could to see if I'd mistaken the sound of a door, but no, the room too sat silent. Was I not fast enough? A possibility. A successful break-and-enter required speed. The person must have rushed around the bend before I got to the door.

Perhaps I could talk to Moira about the cameras. She seemed to have a way to get access to areas you wouldn't think an assistant cruise director would have access to. Plus, it would give me an excuse to contact her.

She excited me in a way that even Frank hadn't. Our relationship had evolved from convenience. In my own way, I loved him. A different man, someone more forthright, and it might have lasted, but Moira had a charisma, an essence that drew people to her. She excelled at her job because of it.

Logically I knew nothing would come of it, but what else was I supposed to do on vacation? I'd read by the pool, and frankly if that was all I did, I would be bored to death. Yes, the pool was lovely; yes, I enjoyed reading, but too much and I'd go mad.

I picked up my activity schedule to see if I could search out Moira and ask about the cameras. Someone had gone in to Colin's room, and it wasn't the cleaning staff.

CHAPTER THIRTEEN

Moira—Wednesday afternoon: at sea

I spotted Claire in the back of the room almost as soon as she entered, milling about trying to get my attention. At first I thought she might be here for bingo, then quickly realized she would never waste money like that. I've noticed she doesn't spend without a good reason. Bingo is never a good reason.

When we came back from lunch in Cozumel, I asked if she wanted to buy any souvenirs and she looked at a display table edged against an old building and said, "I don't buy nonsense." I guess she's right. I bet most souvenirs, the mass-produced ones, end up in people's trash more often than their display shelves. I stopped bringing home souvenirs from my travels years ago. But then again, I stopped going home years ago.

I handed the reins over to Austen and watched in dismay as the last few stragglers come in. Half full, the lounge should be standing room only by this time in the week. I can usually wrangle more than this by the second sea day. I, of course, blamed Amy, and while I weaved my way through the paltry crowd, I thought of more ways I could pay her back.

Claire made her way toward me in khaki pants, a tank top, and a button-up rolled to her elbows. For someone who doesn't vacation much, she managed to look relaxed and so put together every time I saw her. It must be a journalist thing. Her makeup said "I know I'm gorgeous without it," but there's nothing wrong with a little enhancement.

She smiled warmly and said, "Do you think Alan could get us in to see the cameras? Someone was in Colin's room this afternoon but they ran out too soon, I couldn't see who. But it got me thinking about the night of the murder too." She dropped her voice as she looked around, and for the first time in a very long time, I was tempted to get to know a passenger more than I should. That low sultry voice with those large luminous eyes, talking about of all things, murder, and I was suddenly a pool of mush. It saddened me to crush her dreams.

"The cameras in the halls don't work yet. One of the many wonderful things about doing the inaugural cruise. Nothing really works yet. Besides, Alan would never let us in his area. He'd get fired in a heartbeat, and you'd get kicked off the ship."

"I suppose Simon shouldn't have taken me into the mess."

I'd heard about that little adventure and had smacked him upside the head.

"If you'd gotten caught they would have booted you at the next port. Plus, the staff captain would've fired Simon, so next time someone on the crew tries to lure you into a crew area, just say no."

She smirked at me. "Didn't you lure me into a crew area?"

"That was different. The morgue is practically in the passenger area."

"And Simon's office?"

She had me there. I'd forgotten I took her up there, which is why Simon probably took her down into the mess in the first place. "Let's make a new rule. No going into crew areas."

"How are we going to find out who was in Colin's room? It must have been who killed him."

"Do you know why they were in his room?"

Claire shook her head. "The only way in for me was over the balcony, and I believe you told me never to do that again."

"It's nice to see someone listens to me." I still had Perlah's keycard, which meant I had access to Colin's room in a way that didn't require risking our lives. "Meet me at your room in twenty minutes. I have to take care of something first." She nodded and turned to leave. Halfway to the door, she glanced back, that same smirk on her face from earlier.

Once back at Colin's room, I slipped Perlah's key in and

pushed the door open. Everything appeared the same as before. Claire strode in with purpose, going to the balcony door and turning back to face me. She raked over every surface as if she'd memorized it from before and wanted to compare it. I knew she probably had memorized the contents of the room.

"What's this?" Claire pointed to a door on the wall.

"It's a door to the adjoining room." I walked over and tried the door. Locked. "Sometimes the cruise line will sell adjoining rooms as suites. Like if someone brought their kids but still wanted privacy, they may get two rooms that connect. The staff doesn't unlock them otherwise."

"If Colin won a contest, don't they usually come with two tickets? Maybe he was travelling with someone?"

"Two tickets for the same stateroom. If he did come with someone, they would've been in this room as well."

Claire shoved her hands in her pockets and looked about the room. She had an almost gleeful expression on her face.

"You seem very happy about someone breaking into Colin's room."

Claire sighed and took a seat on the bed. "Truthfully? I'm relieved. For the past few days I've worried perhaps I led you astray, and Colin did, in fact, commit suicide. What do we actually have to go on except for a pill I found on my balcony?"

"We have that note you found. What were the words again?"

"How do we even know if they have anything to do with his death? The words didn't even make sense. It was just nonsense like fox and justice and quick."

"You're right. We have nothing." I flopped down on the bed beside her, dejected. "They make it look so easy on all the detective shows."

Claire placed a comforting hand on my leg. "The trick I've found, and it's a hack for life really, is to never give up. Keep going and eventually you'll get there. Which means we need to keep looking, and eventually we'll find something." Claire kept her hand on my leg, and I felt the pressure of it. She glanced down, realized it was still there, and removed it.

"We also know someone was in his room late the night he died," I said to sail us out of any awkwardness in the situation.

Claire nodded, then cocked her head to the side. "Where'd his laptop go? He had a laptop sitting on that side table, and now it's gone." We both stood and began searching the room but came up empty after a few minutes.

As we left Colin's room, I felt a little demoralized we hadn't found any more clues, but Claire reminded me that if Colin had committed suicide, no one would care about his laptop. We might not have found anything concrete, but we were more certain than ever that someone murdered him.

"Maybe they killed him for what's on his laptop?" I asked.

"Then why didn't they take it that first night? It hadn't moved. We need to focus on the cameras."

"They don't have cameras in the hallways."

"What about the elevator area?"

We walked down the hallway, stopping at the next group of elevators. Claire looked up at the camera dome attached to the ceiling. "I can ask Alan if they work, but he's not going to let us in that area. Even I don't have access to it. But I can see if he'll take a look." I stopped before descending the stairs and turned back to Claire. "What should I say we're looking for?"

"We want to know who used these elevators around the time of the murder. And see who came back this way shortly after. This is the only access to the floor. Even if they used the stairs," she said, pointing to the line of sight of the cameras, "they'd see whoever came up or down." A lot of ifs existed in this plan, but at least we had one.

CHAPTER FOURTEEN

Claire—Wednesday evening: at sea

I waited for what felt like hours before finding a spot at a computer. I shouldn't have let Moira talk me out of buying a new laptop the other day. Then I'd have access to everything I needed without having to touch someone else's germs. I pulled out a package of hand wipes, something I'd brought for exactly this, and began cleaning. I had a thing about using other people's keyboards, and Moira had indulged me at the internet café in Cozumel by doing all the searching for us.

I realized, however, that being something of a troglodyte, I wouldn't have even made it past the welcome screen to set up my new laptop. Each year it got harder. They asked you increasingly obscure things that normal people like myself don't know the answer to—iCloud account info, Wi-Fi password, who keeps this information in their head?

The keyboard clean and smelling of chemical lemons, I logged in to my email account and searched for Susan's email. I scrolled past several from Rick urging me to relax and take a step back. He obviously had no faith in me if he was emailing me. Although the fact that I'd seen them should vindicate him.

In truth, you couldn't convince me that I was launching this investigation to find out who murdered Colin. Although I loved a good mystery, what I liked more, actually, was spending time with Moira. The more we worked together, the more interested I became. This probably wasn't the best time to get involved with anyone, but then again, she probably had no interest in me herself. But if she did, a quick fling on a ship would probably do more for my mental health than taking a stupid cruise vacation.

And there ten down from the top sat Susan's email sandwiched between one from my solicitor and one from Frank, lovely stuff. I hadn't seen him since yesterday. Perhaps he'd finally gotten the hint that I wanted nothing more to do with him. My mental health needed a good vacation from him. When I got back to London, I planned to flog Rick for sharing my travel information with Frank.

I opened and read the first line; however, it didn't appear there would be anything in here that screamed "murder me." She'd attached an article she'd found about Colin making a bunch of Bitcoin from a video game. I scanned the article but didn't find anything useful. I'd print it off and give it to Moira. Maybe she knew more about this Bitcoin stuff than I did.

Just as I swung the cursor up to the red X in the corner, the computer pinged. A new email had arrived in my inbox. I scrolled up to find an empty email with a subject line that read MIND YOUR OWN BUSINESS.

Moira—Wednesday evening: at sea

Alan slapped a USB drive into my hand. "You did not get this from me, and you erase it after you view it."

I smiled as I pocketed the tiny drive and handed him three twenty-minute calling cards. "You are my new favourite human."

Alan grunted but accepted the calling cards. "I'm sure you say that to everybody who does you a favour."

"That hurts you would think that. Not everyone I do a favour for has your eyes."

People streamed past where we stood outside of the crew bar, the night young for most. I had other plans, ones that involved a lot of sleep. After I took the comedian off, something not on my schedule but I couldn't take any chances with Amy's attitude toward me, I planned to sleep for many hours. I'd finally managed to find a comforter, and last time I checked, my cabin wasn't drowning.

"One more calling card, and I would consider us even."

"More? You got an hour for ten seconds of work. You had to drag and drop some video files onto a drive."

"But that drive could cost me my job. The risk means I should have a hundred and twenty minutes to call home."

I huffed, but we both knew I'd cave eventually. "Fine." I pulled another card out of my pocket and handed it over.

Claire—Wednesday evening: at sea

I waited outside the cruise staff office like a stalker, hoping she would eventually show up there. I realized, barring the activity schedule they gave out each day, I had no way of getting in touch with her. I couldn't go to reception and have her paged. We needed to stay inconspicuous, especially now since someone had warned me off.

Someone? Who else but the person who killed Colin would want to warn us off? And how did they know we suspected murder? I needed to talk to Moira.

I stepped back when I saw Amy exit the cruise staff office. She didn't know me, but I didn't want to risk becoming familiar to her in case it got Moira in trouble. She'd mentioned that a lot of rules existed to keep passengers and crew at a distance.

As she left the office, a man broke free from the crowd and began to follow her, or at least it seemed that way. Perhaps he had simply been heading in the same direction.

After another half hour, I spotted Moira coming up the staircase, and I headed her off before she could enter the staff office.

"We need to talk," I said. I didn't want to tell her out here in case the same person who sent me that email was watching us now.

She nodded, searching around the main atrium, as if she'd had the same idea. I felt exposed with so many people standing around. Any one of them could have killed Colin.

"Do you still have that name tag I gave you yesterday?" When I nodded, she said, "Good. Meet me up in Simon's office in ten minutes." She cut me off before I could protest. "I know I said I wouldn't bring you into crew areas, but it can't be helped."

I looked around at the million different elevators and stairs trying to remember how we'd gotten there the other day. "I have no idea how to get there."

"Take the midship elevator to deck twelve and then head forward. On the starboard side near the front of the ship, you'll see a door marked Broadcast Technician. Knock and he'll let you in."

I must have looked at her like she had two heads because she amended her directions. "Go up these elevators, turn toward the front of the ship, and on the right side corridor, you'll find his door."

I gave a small smile, still not a hundred percent certain because I needed to go to my stateroom to grab the name tag before heading to Simon's office.

"Just remember, deck twelve, front, right side." She squeezed my arm and headed into the office.

By the time I made it to Simon's office, Moira had beat me there. She opened the door a crack, like some secret hideout entrance, and pulled me in before anyone saw us. It took me a second to adjust to the bright lights in the office, and I shivered as the cool air from the vents hit me. Simon, who swivelled to greet me, wore a thick black jumper. Goosebumps covered Moira's arms. Like the night before, she wore a small black dress, only this one had only one strap that crossed her chest.

She pulled a small computer drive from some hidden pocket in the dress and handed it to Simon. "Alan gave me this. It's the footage from the elevator camera on the night Colin died."

I noticed she didn't say "murder," even though I now knew without a doubt someone had murdered him. We still didn't know who or why, but I felt closer to an answer than we were a day ago.

Simon popped the drive into his computer and pulled up the first file. "Okay, what are we looking for?"

"Someone heading to the starboard side of the hallway around midnight and then possibly coming back fifteen minutes later."

"And what happens if we do find someone? How can you be certain they killed this guy?" asked Simon. Before I could answer, he added, "Or, if they did, how're you going to know who they are?"

"Alan can flag their face, and the system will run it through a facial comparison algorithm and match it to the picture they took when they came on board."

Simon looked sceptical. "He said he'd do that for you?"

"Not in so many words. It's just a matter of finding his price."

Simon started the first video and we watched the elevator area. The camera covered the four elevators on deck ten and the edge of the staircase. According to Alan, the camera that covered the stairs wasn't connected on the night Colin died.

Not many people came through at that hour. After fifteen minutes, only three people had gotten off the elevator, a couple and a man in his mid-forties, and all three had turned toward the port side opposite Colin's room.

Simon leaned back in his chair and grabbed his mug. "So how exactly does this help you find who killed your guy?"

"The only way to get to Colin's room is from this stairwell. Someone killed him between twelve forty-five and one a.m. because Claire recalls hearing voices in the room at around twelve forty-five. Whoever killed him likely came to his room, maybe even with Colin, and left on their own shortly after."

Simon took a big gulp from his mug. "Hold up, Jessica Fletcher. Sounds like you've got three different jigsaw puzzles you're trying to stick together. How do you know they aren't in his room before that time?"

"Because I heard someone say, 'You shouldn't be here,'" I told him. "You don't say that to someone who's been in your room chatting for several minutes. He sounded surprised. This happened around quarter to one, and then I didn't hear much of anything except a door opening and shutting several minutes later. At the time I didn't think much of it, but when I discovered the cleaner had found him dead the next morning, it took on a whole new context."

"So we think whoever killed him would arrive around twelve thirty and leave around one."

I looked over at the time-stamp on the video, which read 12:36 a.m. The hallway remained empty. I wondered if I should tell Moira about the email now. I'd waited because I wanted to see what came up on this video, but if we didn't find anything, what was our next step? After two days, we had nothing to go on, and the further away from the events I got, the more I began to doubt myself. Had I really heard something, or had I made it up in my head? Was this all just to get closer to Moira or some bizarre need to work myself to death?

12:41 a.m. and still the hall remained empty. We watched through the whole thing up until 1:30. No one else got off the elevator. This didn't make sense. Or maybe I felt like because it made sense in my head, the evidence we'd collected should match my expectations.

"That's it, I guess." Moira flopped her arms to her side. "We have nothing. We have less than nothing."

"Not true." I couldn't let her give up so easily. "We know he had an argument with someone. They found an empty bottle of sleeping pills next to his bed, and at least one of them ended up on my balcony, meaning someone could've tossed the contents of the bottle overboard."

"All of that is pure speculation."

"Yes, but we also know someone broke into his room today to steal his laptop, which must have either evidence on it or the motive for his murder. I also know, and I'm not sure how much help it is because I know nothing about Bitcoin, but there was an article a colleague sent to me about Colin. Seems he'd won about ten thousand Bitcoin from a video game."

"Whoa," said Simon. "Ten thousand? Are you sure?"

"Yes. Why, is that a lot?"

Simon leaned forward, brought up a web browser, and typed into the search field. "Ten thousand Bitcoin as of today would be worth a little over five hundred million dollars."

"What?" I asked. That sounded impossible.

"Wait," said Moira, holding up her hand, her eyes closed, thinking. "The magician made a joke about Bitcoin the other night. Amy was saying nonsense words, and he compared it to his Bitcoin passphrase. And we found a pad on Colin's side table with a bunch of random words in list form."

"Someone had scratched them out, but you could see the imprint."

"Words like 'rabbit,' 'ocean,' and 'quick'?" asked Simon.

"Yes. What does that mean?"

"Sounds like it could be a Bitcoin seed phrase."

"What's that?" Moira asked.

"When you set up a Bitcoin wallet, you get a seed phrase that works like a master password so that as long as you have that, you'll always have access to the cryptocurrency associated with that wallet."

Moira and I looked at each other. "We may have just found our motive," I said.

"Depends on how much is in the wallet," said Simon.

"Can we find that out since we have the password?"

"That's not how it works. And it depends on a lot of things."

"For instance?"

"Well, does the guy have a hot wallet or a cold wallet? If it's a hot wallet, maybe you can access it. If it's a cold wallet, it's stored offline. You said someone stole his laptop earlier today? Maybe that's why. They needed his actual computer to access his Bitcoin account because that's where he stores his wallet."

"So we need Colin's computer to know for sure, and now we have no idea who has it." That set us back a little, but at least we'd made progress. I decided not to share the bit about the threatening email. We needed to keep going, and I knew it would scare Moira off.

Moira pointed to Simon's computer and a list of several other videos on the drive. "What's in those files?"

Simon pulled up the first one. "It looks like this video is from earlier in the evening. It starts at eleven." Simon scrubbed forward to almost the end and stopped when someone exited the elevator.

"That's Colin," I said. We watched him head toward his room, using the bulkhead to steady his walk. "Is he drunk?" The time-stamp read 11:54 p.m.

"So he arrived back at his room alone just before midnight," said Moira. "Bring up the other video again."

We watched again as the mid-forties gentleman exited the elevator a little after midnight, then the couple ten minutes later.

Moira shouted, "Stop!" She pointed to the top of the screen. "Go back." Simon scrubbed back a few minutes. "Look at the top right. Someone came up the stairs and went toward Colin's room."

The footage was of the bottom half of someone's legs. We'd missed it the first time because we assumed the person would come from the elevators. The time-stamp read 12:43.

"Too bad you can't see the face," I said.

Simon and Moira both looked at each other. "It's Amy," said

Moira. She pointed to the screen. "Don't you remember? She wore that hideous skirt with anchors on it for the sail away party."

"And I guess she was still wearing it later in the evening because who else would wear something so..." Simon shook his head, looking like he was searching for the right words. "So...?"

"Hideous. She makes them herself," said Moira.

"Not surprised."

We watched through the rest of the video. At 1:02 a.m., the heels and anchor skirt came back into frame, but instead of going down the stairs, it went up.

"What does this mean?" asked Moira. "Do we think Amy killed Colin?"

CHAPTER FIFTEEN

Claire—Thursday morning: Omoa, Honduras

I watched from my balcony as we pulled into port at five a.m. I couldn't sleep. I kept wondering who had taken Colin's laptop and if they now had five hundred million dollars in their bank account. I didn't even know if they could do that. Imagine the transformation five hundred million dollars would make for someone's life. A pretty impressive motive for murder. I'd written stories with less.

About ten years ago, I met a woman in prison who'd murdered her brother because he wouldn't let her stay with him for a week. She'd recently left her husband who'd beaten her every other day for close to a decade. She landed on her brother's doorstop only for him to turn her away. She pulled out the gun she'd stashed in her purse in case her husband came after her and shot him in the face.

The prosecutors in her trial stated the motive for murder was that he'd turned her away, but for me it never got to the heart of the problem. She'd faced years of abuse, something her brother had to have known, and still he rejected her. For me, the motive only lifted the edge of the carpet to what was really behind the murder.

Thinking about that made me wonder what lay beneath that much money. The story within the story.

I felt my skin go cold and my heart start to race. For everyone complaining about how overworked I seemed, I hadn't had a single episode on this trip. Until now.

I entered my cabin and retrieved my pills. After several visits with Dr. Rajak, he'd diagnosed me with general anxiety disorder, stress-induced high blood pressure, and lots of things. We'd decided medication over therapy, or rather he'd decided. He didn't trust me to do the therapy, and he was probably right.

Interesting that an episode, as Rick likes to call them, started only after thinking about work rather than chasing a possible murderer. I swallowed both pills, one for anxiety and the other for high blood pressure, and stared at myself in the mirror. Perhaps I should think about a career change.

With that in mind, I had some digging to do. I wandered back onto the balcony and pulled out my phone, doing some quick math in my head. Five a.m. here meant eleven a.m. in London. Rick bounced from meeting to meeting, so he could be anywhere at that moment.

He picked up on the second ring. "I hope you're calling me from a beach to gloat at your wondrous view."

"Not a beach, but the view doesn't suck."

"I'll trade you. We've got rain."

"Palm trees and sand don't sound like a great trade-off. But I would give my right pinkie toe to root through your brain about Bitcoin."

I heard a loud sigh through the line. "Any chance this has nothing to do with work?"

"It doesn't actually. Listen, before you get angry, someone murdered my next door neighbour, and we think it has something to do with Bitcoin." Silence. Not even traffic sounds, which told me he was probably sitting in his office watching the rain drench London, with a Diet Coke and a half-eaten strawberry danish sitting on his desk behind him.

"And you think getting involved in a murder investigation is somehow better?"

"Well, they've ruled it a suicide—"

"Of course they have. And you've taken it upon yourself to save the day and set things right. You can't—"

"Someone *did* murder him, Rick. He had five hundred million dollars in Bitcoin. I saw the murderer in his room yesterday stealing his laptop."

"Have you gone to the appropriate authorities and given a description?"

"Well, no. I didn't actually *see* them. But I heard someone in there, and when we went to check out the room, the laptop was missing."

Shuffling and then Rick's voice came back muffled, probably eating the danish out of frustration. "Wait, so you didn't see anyone. You're assuming."

"You've known me how long? When do I usually get things wrong? Assuming and then proving it is more than half my job."

He swallowed and I waited while he washed down the danish with his Diet Coke. "When you say 'we,' I'm guessing you're not referring to the royal 'we'?"

Should I tell him about Moira? It suddenly felt strange. In my mind, it seemed so natural how she'd ended up investigating Colin's murder with me, but having to explain that I'd roped the assistant cruise director into a clandestine investigation all on a whim made it sound inappropriate somehow. And that made me feel like I'd taken advantage of her, which, in turn, made me feel like I had false intentions. I decided to skip over the who and why.

"Another crew member also feels the investigation shut too early."

"Mm-hmm. And who exactly—"

"I need your help, not your judgement." I waited, hoping he'd relent.

"Claire."

Oh, here we go.

"I want you to take whatever you think you've found and bring it to the person in charge. Then I want you to find the nearest beach, throw down a towel, and soak up as much sun as you can."

"And just let whoever did this get away with it? They think he committed suicide."

"Then they have good reason to believe that. Why do you have to get involved and meddle about?"

"Meddle?" My insides began to burn. "Meddle? That's what old ladies do. I've never—"

"Okay, I'm sorry. Wrong word choice. I'm worried for you. This vacation should relax you. You don't sound relaxed."

"It's hard to stay relaxed when people throw words like

'meddle' at you." I almost nearly rung off, but that wouldn't get me what I wanted.

A long silence. I heard his chair creak in the background. He was standing, looking out the window probably, a position I'd found him in numerous times. He had one of the best views of London from his office. It encompassed the Thames, and he would watch the boats and ships drift up and down. He said the slow pace cancelled all the rest of the chaos of London and kept him grounded.

He sighed before saying, "Claire, I can't help you."

"*Won't* help me."

"Exactly. We didn't go to all this trouble of forcing you on a relaxing vacation just so you could get yourself into trouble. Forget about the investigation. Let someone else handle it. You mentioned another crew member, so let them deal with it. I want you to forget about it."

We said our goodbyes and hung up. I knew defeat when I heard it. I would have to get my information elsewhere. It had been a risk calling Rick.

I gazed out at the port of Omoa with its palm trees and sandy beaches. It reminded me of islands I'd seen in pirate movies as a kid, and it wouldn't surprise me if pirates had at one time called this home.

My stateroom phone began to ring. I picked it up on the second ring. "Hello?"

"Get dressed." Moira's voice, low and throaty. "I have something that will take our mind off murder for the day."

Moira—Thursday morning: Omoa, Honduras

I entered the dining hall from a side door leading from the service prep area. The tables sat ready for their next meal. At no point would the tables ever appear empty because empty equaled ugly.

I sipped my second coffee of the day as I entered, in no rush to discover what had Amy in hysterics. She'd called me ten minutes ago, frantic that I meet her in the dining hall, and based on our discovery last night, I had serious qualms about being alone with her.

Could Amy kill someone? The optimist—a quickly shrinking segment of my personality—said no. She didn't fit the type. But the cynical, and let's face it, majority of my personality said yes. If the tourist business teaches you anything, it should teach you that people will do anything to get what they want. Most of the time that means threatening to write a scathing review unless you comp them an upgrade, but threats lead down a winding staircase that could kill a person.

Even if Amy did kill Colin, she had no idea Claire and I knew anything about Colin's death. I felt safer in that fact than in the dining hall.

I found Amy in a far corner trying to unzip the stuck zipper of her dress. When I got closer, I realized a broken zipper didn't even cover a smidge of her problem. Somehow the seams on the back had loosened, so that they spread apart as she walked. The lime green dress she'd put on earlier in her cabin had become the hint of an outfit. What fabric remained in place managed to cover the important parts, but gaping holes made up the majority.

"Did you bring it?" she shouted.

I waved the uniform I'd picked up on the way down here. I'd had questions as to why she'd need a uniform brought to the main dining hall, but nothing could've prepared me for this.

"Could you?" Amy asked in a small voice, her back turned to me, pointing to the difficult zipper.

I stepped around the chair and saw the problem. The zipper had mangled some of the loosened threads, trapping them between its teeth. I grabbed a butter knife from the table and began sawing. I stopped when Amy's body began to shake. I thought I'd hurt her, then realized she was sobbing quietly into her chest.

"Nothing has gone right since I took this job. Everything I do ends up going wrong. All the procedures are different, none of my staff like me, nothing works right. I can't even get off the stupid ship." She turned around, full on sobbing now. "And look at my clothes, the laundry machines here have destroyed them."

No real loss there. I held that thought to myself. I patted her arm, hoping it would quiet her down, but instead it seemed to encourage more sharing.

"I'm thirty-seven years old. Do you know what all my friends back home are doing? They're married and having kids, going to brunch, and Bandini the Great is hypnotizing me for a laugh. It's humiliating." She turned around again and pointed to the zipper. This time I ripped it open, hoping to get out of there as soon as possible. I felt worse by the minute.

"And they all said, go online, you'll meet the perfect guy online, but I'm still meeting the same losers. I invited this guy to come on this cruise. I sent him tickets, and at the last minute he cancelled because supposedly his mom died. I find out his mom *didn't* die, and he came anyway but didn't tell me." She pulled the front of her dress down, exposing a light pink camisole, and stepped out, flinging it to the side.

What if Colin hadn't been murdered for his money? What if Colin had been Amy's date? What if she'd seen Colin during the sail away party and put him on the spot? It would explain why she knew him and why she appeared so confrontational with him. "Maybe you should stop dating. They say women who remain single are happier than the women who get married. To men."

"You only date women, right?"

"I try not to date anyone if I can help it." I thought of a few exes who'd more than torn my heart out. "Doesn't matter the gender. Dating never ends well." But then the image of Claire popped up, and it reminded me of why I still held hope.

Amy pulled the uniform polo I'd brought her over her head, her hair popping back into place once through. "But then you end up alone."

"What's so wrong with alone? Then you never have to fight over mundane things like what to eat, what to watch, cleaning, bills." I'd watched my parents do this, yet they refused to leave each other. I don't think either one of them had felt happy for years.

"You can't really think that? You could also meet the love of your life. And if you don't even look for anyone, you'll never have kids or a home. It all sounds sad." She zipped up the shorts I'd also brought. In the standard uniform, Amy appeared much more approachable, less severe than in her fake corporate polyester outfits. She struck me as one of those hopeless romantics that stayed home on Saturday nights watching the Hallmark Channel eating fat-free popcorn and drinking red wine, hoping one day she'd meet a man in the grocery store making jokes about ripe tomatoes in the produce aisle.

My phone beeped with a message from the shore excursion supervisor. I glanced over at Amy, who had the shreds of her former dress in her hands. A tear ran down her cheek. I needed to go, but I also didn't want to leave her looking so pathetic. I placed a hand on her back. "If you need to talk…" I let the sentence stall because I didn't want to volunteer myself, but also felt I couldn't leave without saying something.

Unfortunately she latched onto that sentence like a lifeline. "How is it so easy for you? Everyone likes you."

I texted Françoise I'd be a few minutes. If this gave me the opportunity to work better with Amy, I'd take it. I sat down next to her. "I've worked for this company for almost ten years. I started as cruise staff and have worked my way up. I've made connections with people over a decade. I'm one of them. You came in already in charge and are drastically changing the way they've done things for years. And I know you mean well, but your attitude about it is all wrong. Instead of letting people get used to you and seeing how we did things, you ran a steamroller over everything. You're the bulldozer that destroyed everyone's houses, that's why they don't like you."

Her hair, surprisingly, still held its bounce, but her mascara had bled out, creating a harsh black ring under her crystal blue eyes.

"Why don't you like me?"

I sighed. Why didn't I like her? Probably because she wasn't Benny—we'd worked so well together. She represented change and new, and I wasn't ready for that. Instead, I said, "Because you cut my paycheque in half when you stopped allowing me to promote bingo. I know you think it's for old people, but you haven't even seen how we do it here."

"It's bingo for Christ's sake, how can that possibly entertain people? Wait, how did that cut your pay?" Her head tilted and then her face fell as realization hit her. "You make commission on it. Of *course* you do. That's how they get you to sell it. So instead of paying you a decent wage, they force you to steal money from people to pad their pockets while they dole out a pittance to you."

"It works like that in every department. The servers and

bartenders don't make their tips unless they hit their quota, and they only hire people from impoverished countries to work garbage so they can pay them garbage, but it feels like a fortune to people who come from nothing. This is how the whole industry works."

"I came from a smaller company that treated us like actual humans."

"Then why did you leave?"

She shrugged. "I wonder that every day."

The one thought I couldn't shake after our conversation: What if Colin wasn't murdered for his money? What if it was love?

CHAPTER SIXTEEN

Moira—Thursday morning: Omoa, Honduras

The five Jeeps sped through the forest of thick, lush vegetation. Palm trees and tropical pines grew in clumps, obscuring the rapidly departing coast. And I welcomed the breeze from the open air vehicle, as it kept the insects and humidity at bay.

I'd convinced Claire to come with me on an excursion Françoise, the shore excursion manager, had talked me into. They didn't have enough crew to cover all the excursions that day and needed bodies for regulation's sake. The bright side? I got to explore Mayan ruins for the day with Claire, who had quickly become one of the best parts of this cruise.

"They built the fortress to defend against pirates, which were plentiful in the seventeenth and eighteenth centuries in these parts." We'd passed the San Fernando Fortress twenty minutes ago, but our tour guide hadn't stopped talking about it yet. He stood in the back of the front Jeep with a microphone, which we could hear through the radio of our vehicle. The short balding man with a beer paunch that made it look like he was about to give birth to twins swiped a handkerchief across his forehead.

We came to a turn-off, and the Jeeps slowed and turned onto a dust-filled side road with old stone markers on each side, decayed and moss covered.

"Here's an interesting story about how they first discovered this site almost three hundred years ago. In the winter of 1762, during the Anglo-Spanish War, pirates kidnapped the captain of the British

Navy ship *Dartmouth* off the coast of Cuba. As the story goes, they hoped to use him as collateral to bribe the Spanish, who were in the process of fortifying the coast of Honduras.

"They'd heard stories of treasure deeper in the mainland, and they figured a navy captain would make a good trade for passage." He paused here, grabbing on to the railing of the Jeep as it swerved to avoid a pothole. "But as the story goes, the naval captain and the pirate captain, who might have both been women, fell in love and escaped into the jungle where they discovered Säq Ya', which literally translates to white water—a strange name since the coast lies almost a hundred kilometres from the site.

"In the years following, gold coins and masks, pendants, and other trinkets began circulating around the Caribbean. Rumours said they'd come from a temple buried deep in the jungle of Honduras, but nobody could prove it. The site remained undiscovered for another hundred and fifty years until 1912, when a British and Spanish team of archaeologists discovered the site. While searching the temple grounds, they found two graves side by side believed to be those of the naval and pirate captain."

Claire raised her hand, which threw him off his game because he looked startled to get a question. "Yes?"

"If they found the graves, couldn't they have determined whether the bodies were female or male based on the skeletons?"

"Ah," he said, sounding pleased she'd brought that up. "The graves were empty. Well, empty of human remains. Archaeologists speculated that when they discovered the temple of Säq Ya' and its treasure, they feared the Spanish would come after them so they dug graves and placed animal bones inside, with the markers to make whoever came after them think they had died. Only no one came after them, and the graves sat for a century and a half waiting for someone to discover them." A large bump in the road made him drop his mic, which clanged about his feet for a few seconds before he managed to grab it. "The story only adds to the beautiful mystery of this temple. Archaeologists have discovered hidden passageways throughout the compound and suspect many more exist. The whole thing is like a puzzle. And as such, there are areas that are off limits to guests. If you see a red rope, it means that area is out of bounds. We are here as guests, so please respect the rules or else they will not invite us back. Thank you." He sat down, his job done until we arrived.

I settled back to enjoy the scenery. Even if the bumpy road made it difficult, I couldn't deny the beauty.

"Quite a life you live," said Claire.

"What do you mean?"

She pointed to the jungle now surrounding us. "You get to go on adventures every week. You get up every morning and see either a new port or the expanse of the horizon."

"It's funny you see it that way. I began working on ships as an escape from home. My whole life, my dad ran one of the most prestigious hotels in Sanremo. As my first job, I would collect towels and bedding from the rooms and bring them to the laundry. Eventually I worked my way up to front desk doing reception work, taking reservations and customer service. I came to loathe the tourist industry." I raised my hands to encompass our surroundings. "And yet I can't escape it."

"You can't escape the responsibility of tomorrow by evading it today."

"What do you mean by that?"

"You must have wanted to escape something—boring job, family drama, who knows—but it led you into an industry you loathe. Perhaps it wasn't the industry you were trying to escape. Because, in truth, you're very good at what you do."

I turned my attention back to the passing jungle, considering what Claire had said. I'd picked ships because I did think it sounded adventurous. Sailing the high seas, a new view every day. It's amazing how fast the same ocean view can become stale after a while. And my job isn't very hard. I entertain people all day. I run bingo, I encourage people to have fun. Nothing boring or taxing about that. Except a lot of times it ends up being the same ports over and over again. I can't tell you how many times I've seen Ocho Rios or Grand Cayman. And I've noticed only four kinds of vacation people exist: the reluctant, the overzealous, the seen-it-all, and the enthusiastic newbie. Once you master how to deal with each, the challenge fades.

We rocked to the side as our Jeep hit a giant pothole, and I slid toward Claire, colliding against her. I pushed myself back but not before I felt the heat of her body, caught the scent of her floral shampoo, and discovered the tiny freckles around her nose. Freckles so subtle, they went unnoticed except by a select few, I imagined. It felt like a frozen moment. When time seems to slow and you think, *I could happily stay here*. Maybe not forever, but a while. Basking in the glow of Claire's smile.

But the moment did end, and I did pull myself back to the other side of the Jeep. Claire fanned herself with the pamphlet they gave us at the beginning of the tour.

"I don't know if I could stand the constant humidity, but other than that, working on ships might prove fun."

"I grew up on the coast, so it reminds me of home a little." We'd get nice breezes in the evenings. And sometimes I missed going up to the roof of the hotel and looking out at the coast and dreaming of what the other side of the ocean held.

"Believe me, London is plenty humid. I can't stand it."

I smiled because I could guess that about Claire. I doubted she put up with very much from life. If something bothered her, she fixed it.

"You're a doer, aren't you?" I asked.

"Meaning?"

"My mom always said there are only two types of people in the world. Doers and dreamers. She always said I was a dreamer. I would go off to my hiding spots and dream of a different life. I sometimes think she's right. I've wanted to leave ships for the past six years, but something always happens, like a new ship, a promotion, more money, and I stick around because it's easier having the dream than actually pursuing it."

Claire leaned forward, her eyes serious as she stared into mine. "Your problem is that somewhere down the line, someone told you that to have a meaningful life, you had to do meaningful things. But what if the goal is to do what you love?" She swatted my knee playfully with the pamphlet. "Can you honestly say you don't love your job? If you had to think about what you loathe, is it the job?"

I closed my eyes for a second to think. With Claire so close, I found it difficult to concentrate, and I wanted to give this question my full attention because what she'd said made sense. Viola, my sister, joined a band in high school and left soon after she graduated to pursue music. I've always envied her because in my mind, she escaped what I hadn't. But did I envy her the escape or that she found what she loved? A truly heavy idea, and yet I felt lighter the more I thought about it.

She squeezed my knee this time. "Something to think about."

"Oh look," said an older woman in the front seat of our Jeep.

I opened my eyes to find we'd arrived. In all the years I'd worked on ships, I'd visited a few Mayan ruins before. Usually a few stones sticking out of the ground. Maybe a pit or two where small temples used to be before previous generations had repurposed the stones into new buildings. Nothing like this. The Maya had hidden a palace within the jungle.

It felt like travelling back in time.

The temple stood in the centre of dozens of smaller buildings, towering over them, next to the palace, just as impressive if not as tall. I could imagine Mayan priests standing at the top steps of the temple, as if they sat in the sky, looking down on the village.

The Jeeps parked off to the side in a cleared spot made for vehicles. As we exited, I spotted Amy getting out of one of the other Jeeps in another group.

Claire—Thursday morning: Omoa, Honduras

Moira nudged my shoulder, pointing to the right of us. I saw a short, balding gentleman help Amy out of a Jeep.

"I think we may have gotten the motive wrong. What if Amy killed Colin because of love?" Moira filled me in on what she'd learned from Amy earlier that morning and I had to admit, it did sound convincing. If Colin and Amy did have a relationship, it would explain how she seemed to know him at the sail away party.

We joined the group queuing to get our maps so we could explore the ruins.

"It doesn't explain the laptop, though," I said.

"What if she'd sent him nude photos, and she wanted to get them back?"

"Wouldn't she find those on his phone then?" Another great

reason not to have a smartphone, in my opinion. Not that I was in the habit of receiving massive numbers of unsolicited nudes.

And that's when I realized we hadn't found his phone. Moira seemed to come to the same conclusion, since she turned to me, her eyes wide.

"She must have taken the phone first, and when she realized whatever she was looking for wasn't on the phone, she went back for the laptop."

It all sounded good, but something still niggled at the back of my mind. I took a map and followed the group through to the centre of the village. Time and weather had worked away at the stone, and as a result, the buildings in the centre hadn't fared as well as the temple and palace.

"Do you want to climb to the top?" Moira pointed to the temple rising above us. I watched as a few dozen people queued for the chance.

"Not right now. Let's head this way." I pointed randomly, anything to get away from the crowds. Even in the open air, my heart pounded, and I didn't want to have any sort of panic attack with Moira watching. How embarrassing. I gazed back down at the map, hoping to orient us, but I'd learned long ago that I might as well try to read Swahili as read a map. "Are you any good with these things?" I asked.

Moira smirked. "These things? You mean maps?" She took mine, turned it—presumably—the right way up, and began pointing out landmarks.

We took a side path and began skirting the outer edge of the site toward what I hoped would bring us to the saunas.

"It says here some sweat baths and saunas predate the Roman baths. These in particular date back almost two thousand years. The Maya obsessed about looks. They would bind their skulls to shape them into points and drill holes in their teeth and set precious stones in them."

Moira rubbed a finger along her two front teeth. "That sounds painful. And extreme."

"Please. Humans are still as vain. Imagine telling a simple farmer from a thousand years ago about someone who voluntarily allowed a doctor to put them unconscious so they could cut their face off to shave the bone underneath. Or suck out their fat? Inject toxic chemicals into their forehead and face? What impresses me is that being vain is an ancient value and universal. A couple years ago I travelled to Egypt for work and while there visited the Egyptian Museum. They used sour goat milk to bathe and various oils and such as cosmetics. I bet if we looked, we'd find every culture throughout history has had its own beauty regimen."

"And you think that unnecessary?"

We stepped across a small stone bridge for a small stream that had long since dried up. As we moved deeper into the structures, the heat bound us in.

"I'm simply pointing out vanity as a universal human trait. We waste so much of our lives worrying about frivolities when essentially we all come from the same place originally." I pointed to a face carved into the stone a few feet from us. Large round eyes stared at us, its tongue sticking out, menacing and yet silly at the same time. "In the UK, women spend around ten billion pounds on beauty products a year. How can our mental health compete with that?"

Moira laughed. "You make it sound like we evolved to feel bad about ourselves."

"I don't necessarily think we evolved that way. I think current societies and cultures use beauty standards as a way to oppress women."

Moira tilted her head at me like I was off my rocker.

"Think about it. Early hunter-gatherers had no concept of science, so women, as the procreators of the species, had a place of honour. At that point they probably had no concept that it took both men and women to create another human. Everyone contributed because the survival of the group depended on it. Somewhere in our past that all changed. This idea emerged that men had to be the providers of the family. I refuse to believe in the inevitability of the patriarchy. It's an introduced concept, not a natural one. Men only started dominating women with the rise of the state. As the ideas of property evolved, men moved women out of a social sphere and into a private one, essentially privatizing their services and using them as commodities. Now, as feminism and equality shouts become louder, men bring women down by telling them they need to look a certain way in order to please men."

"I never thought about it that way."

"And they turn women against themselves by introducing the notion that they need to compete for men's affections, thereby robbing them of their social power again." I clamp my mouth shut and turn away. I have a tendency to preach when I get started on a subject that infuriates me. And nothing infuriates me more than the good ol' boys' club, something I've fought against my whole life.

"I love that these are the topics you think about," Moira said. "I can imagine you daydreaming in some fancy hotel while you're working on a story, thinking about the nuances of female oppression while the rest of us are thinking about what to order from room service."

"More likely I have too much time on my hands."

At the far edge of the site, we reached the saunas, a squat hut made of stones and packed earth. Moira stuck her head inside. "Looks cozy."

A stone bench carved into the rock ran the circumference of the tiny room, fitting three people at most. On one side stood an indentation with a hole in the base. I suspected they built a fire below and placed rocks in the indentation to heat the room. The smaller the room, the less heat one would need. Of course I was only speculating. I had no idea. We squeezed inside and took a seat. I was amazed they gave visitors this much access.

I watched Moira observe her surroundings. She tended to look around like she wanted to take everything in at once. She reminded me of myself, always wanting to know everything all the time.

"Tell me about yourself."

Moira glanced up at me, startled. "Me? I'm not interesting. I want to know about you. I know almost nothing."

"You know lots about me. I'm going through a messy divorce. So messy, in fact, my almost ex-husband followed me on the only vacation I've had in ten years to convince me I should stay with him. At least I assume so. I haven't actually let him tell me since I don't care. The marriage died years ago, and I don't want to revive it." I stood, because suddenly the space felt tighter. As I stepped outside, the sun dipped behind some clouds and a warm breeze scuttled through the trees.

I turned to Moira as she exited behind me. "You do that a lot, you know. You deflect when asked about yourself. Why don't you want to share things?"

Moira shrugged. "I'm boring. I have a sister and a father back in Italy. And I do the same thing every day for months on end. People like to romanticize working on cruise ships, but in reality, we have no personal life. We work and live with the same people, and if you get too attached, your heart hurts every time they leave for vacation or transfer to a new ship." She walked ahead and I followed, not willing to press her. The topic dimmed her usual sunniness, and now didn't seem like the right time.

"Where is everyone?" I asked, realizing we hadn't seen people in at least half an hour.

"All climbing the temple, I imagine."

We both stopped and looked back along the trail. I hadn't seen any red rope telling us not to enter this area. Perhaps people didn't want to visit the saunas as much as climb the temple.

Up ahead stood an elaborate building faded into a hill. Several broken statues, once part of the façade, lay crumbled at the entrance. I wandered in and stopped. Intricate carvings covered the entire wall space. Even the ceiling had sculptures embedded in the surface.

Moira joined me, nudging me in farther. "This must have taken decades to make."

I walked to the far wall where a large statue dominated the entire corner. A man sat on a throne of what looked like heads.

"And some skulls," said Moira.

I heard a tremendous grinding noise behind us and turned to watch all the light in the room vanish as a circular stone door closed us inside.

CHAPTER SEVENTEEN

Moira—Thursday midmorning: Omoa, Honduras

The light from my phone flashlight splashed over the walls. The harsh white glare struck Claire, her face a tableau of shock. It took a moment for my heart to slow enough so I could grasp what had happened.

Claire picked her way toward me, taking care not to trip over any of the rocks strewn across the floor. She held out her hand for my phone. Luckily I'd remembered to plug it in last night, so it had a full charge.

At the door, Claire began to push and motioned for me to do the same. She placed my phone on the ground flashlight up, creating a halo of white around us. I gripped the stone and anchored my foot in a crevice and pushed with everything I had. I strained so hard, my lungs and head felt like they would burst from the pressure. And nothing. Not even a budge.

"It's too heavy," I said.

"Or locked from the outside."

"Maybe we can find another way out." I picked up my phone and began searching the rest of the room. After ten minutes, I noticed my phone had already used twenty percent and shut the flashlight off. "We need to stop and think, give the phone a rest." It felt hot to the touch. I should only use the flashlight for short bursts. I didn't want to break the one good thing we had going for us.

"Can you call someone? Let them know where we are? Maybe they can move the door."

"It doesn't get a signal out here."

"Then why did you bring it?"

"To take pictures. And the flashlight's pretty handy to have in case of an emergency."

"That's why you paid a thousand dollars? For a flashlight?"

"And a camera that's also a mini computer that makes phone calls and has a GPS map when it has a signal." I couldn't see Claire's expression and had no idea if I'd pissed her off or made her smile. I'd hoped to lighten the mood, but getting trapped in an ancient Mayan building with no hope of rescue felt hopeless no matter how many jokes I told. "Maybe in a hundred and fifty years, they'll find our bodies and think we're the pirate and navy captain."

Claire chuckled. "Until they carbon date us and realize we're just idiots who got stuck during a tour."

"You think we got stuck?"

"No, you're right. Someone trapped us here. For whatever reason, I'm not sure yet."

"I think it's obvious. Whoever murdered Colin doesn't want us to find them."

"I noticed Amy getting out of a Jeep."

I leaned my head back against the cold stone wall. I shivered. The Maya knew how to build for this heat. While the temperature rose to forty degrees outside, it felt more like fifteen in here. "Me too." But I couldn't help think about how we got trapped in here. Did Amy have help? She must have. Of course, she might have come here before on a different ship and known the layout. How to find that out now? I guess it didn't matter.

"My brain hurts. All I know for certain is that someone murdered Colin. And I'm fairly certain that whoever did also trapped us in here to stop us from finding out. No other explanation makes sense. I think someone removed the red rope to lure us out of the tourist area and found an opportunity to keep us here."

"But how did they find out we know?" Claire's voice felt far away. Even in the small space, it echoed. She began listing off people we'd talked to. "Dr. Steenbok, Simon, and Alan. Those three. No one else knows we think someone murdered Colin."

I'd mentioned it to Amy, but I couldn't remember if I commented we thought someone murdered him. We didn't know enough. "One thing I do know—whoever killed Colin is also on this tour."

"So all we have to do is figure how to get out, get back to the ship, and look up who was on this excursion today."

"No problem."

Silence.

After a few minutes Claire asked, "Any ideas?"

"Not yet. You?"

"Nothing."

Claire—Thursday afternoon: Omoa, Honduras

At least we wouldn't die of heat stroke. And the room didn't appear airtight. We'd screamed for fifteen minutes with no luck and pushed at the door with equal futility for a few more minutes, but we still had air.

I took a seat in the corner, guiding my way by gripping the wall for support, until I found a relatively flat surface. The blackness of the room had started to enter my mind. I hadn't had a panic attack since, well, since the incident. More accurately, the aftermath. I hadn't had time to panic during.

I tried a couple of breathing techniques, but I hadn't listened too well in therapy. I'd only gone the two times and decided it wasn't for me. Plus I tended to hyperventilate more often than not.

"What's that noise?"

"A breathing technique I'm failing at."

"No, it sounds more like rushing water." Moira's voice moved away to the far corner. "It sounds stronger over here."

"Give me a second, I just need to catch my breath. Can you pass me my bag, actually?"

"Where did you leave it?"

"I don't know." The wave—as I called it—threatened to overtake me. I hadn't had a full-on panic attack in months. When everything clips along, you can't imagine that anything will go wrong. It made me complacent. I guess you could look at my whole life in that context. If I had a mantra, it would be "Everything's fine."

For once, I needed to realize everything was not fine. Through my own actions, I'd managed to trap not only myself but Moira as well in an ancient Mayan ruin where we were certain to die eventually of starvation, or possibly thirst. I guess it didn't really matter what we would die from.

Instead of darkness closing in, bright shapes appeared in my vision, and my lungs felt heavy and useless. The ringing in my ears made me feel like I was standing on the Victoria platform in London, the crowd bustling by, shouting with the screeching of the trains pulling in and the whistles as they pulled out.

And then I felt a calming hand on my back and Moira talking softly at my ear, offering me water. "Drink this."

"My bag has pills."

She placed my knapsack on my lap. "I found your bag." I rummaged through it until I found the bottle of pills and dropped two in my palm. I gulped them down with her water, making sure not to use too much, as if I could hold off dying of thirst by conserving water now.

I slumped back and waited. Her touch, smoothing small circles on my back, had the most calming effect. After a few minutes, I sat up no longer feeling as if my lungs had deflated like sad balloons after a festival.

She didn't ask, but I felt the need to explain. "I have panic attacks."

The laughter in her voice when she answered softened what she said. "I figured with the prescription pills. Did they force you on vacation because of this?"

"Why do you say 'forced' like that?"

"I've seen almost dead eighty-year-olds more excited to travel on a cruise than you. I mean, why book a cruise if you don't like doing any of the things a cruise offers? Plus, you seemed more interested in giving yourself an assignment on your vacation than actually enjoying yourself."

Apparently my dislike of cruises hadn't been subtle. "I'm not good at vacations." Moira made a noise that gave me the impression she didn't buy my answer, but she didn't push me.

She turned her flashlight on and pointed it toward the back wall. "The stone seems damp over here."

I joined her and ran my hand over the surface of the rock. It came away wet and smelled like mineral water and fresh soil. "Maybe there's a natural spring that runs behind the building?"

"Look at this." Moira pointed her flashlight at a sunken indent jutting out from the wall. "What do you suppose…?" She dipped her head down and smelled. "Do you still have that lighter with the…"

I grabbed my knapsack and dug through the front pocket to retrieve the crude lighter and handed it to Moira.

"Stand back," she said and flicked on the lighter, lowering it to the indent. Within seconds, a flame erupted and spread along a groove hidden in the stone wall. We both watched, amazed, as the fire travelled, bathing the room in a dancing glow.

"Holy Madonna." Moira stood, looking at the inside of the structure, which had flamed into view thanks to the ancient light switch. Mayan hieroglyphs, carved on every surface, shimmered. Brought into the light and safeguarded from the elements, they hadn't faded as the stone degraded like many of the others throughout the compound.

I peered down at one such grouping, all in tight lines of two, like tiny ancient comic strips.

"I wonder what it says."

I stood and turned to get the full view of the room which, when lit, appeared bigger than I'd thought. It had an altar-like set-up on one side and made me think they could've used this with the temple, perhaps a prep area before the big show. I didn't know much about the Mayan culture or their history, and what I did know wouldn't help us in this situation.

What I'd originally thought was debris strewn about on the ground was actually stone cylinders, a foot and a half high and the width of a dinner plate. Even these had hieroglyphics on them.

Moira noticed them too and bent down to lift one that had fallen on its side. "God, they're heavy. This must weigh fifty pounds."

Five in total lay about the room. One was on its side, broken in half. I picked up the top half of the broken piece, and inside, the light danced off crystal shards. "What would they have used these for?" I said it more to myself, thinking aloud, but Moira answered.

"I think they sit in these grooves. Look." She pointed to five spots along the floor with tiny indents. She placed the stone cylinder closest to her in the groove in the floor. It slid into the spot perfectly. After a second, it began to sink and we heard a loud grinding noise from below. "Whoa," she said. "What the hell made that sound?"

The noise stopped after a few seconds, and then nothing. We still couldn't hear the outside world, but the rushing water had gotten louder. "Maybe we shouldn't touch anything. What if we break it?"

"What if it's a way out?"

"What if it brings this whole ceiling down, crushing us into smithereens? Haven't you ever seen *Indiana Jones*?"

"A little before my time."

I tried not to let that sting too much. I don't think she meant it in a cruel way. "Well, it's a good cautionary tale about not touching things in ancient ruins." I sat on the first step of the altar and Moira joined me. We rested our backs while contemplating our situation in silence.

After about ten minutes, Moira asked, "Why were you forced on a vacation you didn't want to go on?"

"That's a rather long story."

She spread her arms. "We have lots of time."

I checked my watch. Right about then the excursion would've started rounding up the guests and heading back to the ship, which would sail without us in less than two hours. It didn't feel like we had lots of time. But what else did we have to do? "It started in Tokyo. I'd followed a lead to a story I'd been working on for months about a corrupt businessman who used religious festivals in Japan to launder money from Germany."

"How does that work?"

"This gentleman had several underground businesses on top of his legitimate ones as an IT specialist. His company would send in teams to help companies set up their IT departments. This let him create backdoor access to the businesses he helped, which would feed him information, tips, and endless useful information to help him in other aspects of his business, which included selling drugs and human trafficking. How Japan came in, I still hadn't figured out. All I knew was that he had a contact in Japan who worked to help set up the festivals. I hadn't linked them yet."

I could feel a headache coming on just from thinking about it.

"I'd decided to take a day off to clear my head and come back at it with a clear perspective. While out during one of the Sanja festival days, I got caught up in a mob crush. The only thing that saved me was that I'd been close to the wall. I woke up in hospital several days later. My editor and publisher both ganged up on me, said I'd been working too hard over the last few years, and what with my impending divorce, I should take some time off."

I leaned my head back on the cold stone of the altar. "And here I am, getting myself into more trouble."

"Did you finish the story?"

I shook my head. "They gave it to someone else, who has yet to do anything with it."

"I can see how that might get frustrating, leaving you feeling like you have unfinished business. And so, you load up your time with more work instead of enjoying yourself and getting that rest you need."

The look in her eyes said compassion, not pity, and for once I felt like I'd met someone who might understand. "But don't you feel like sometimes all you have is work?"

She smirked and dipped her head, her eyelashes hiding her eyes. If possible, she appeared even more gorgeous after being stuck in an ancient ruin for hours. "I live where I work, but if there's one thing Italians are good at, it's not letting work interfere with life. Work should be a means to an end, not the end itself." She leaned into me, and I could feel the warmth of her seeping into my arm, spreading down my body. "I can understand your need. Your work helps people. The importance of your work means you view it in a different way than most people. And why shouldn't you? But every now and then, you need to step back and experience some of the things you write about."

I laughed, the sound echoing through the room, because she'd said what I'd discovered earlier in the cruise, when I first decided to walk away from all this. What had stopped me? When she took my chin in her hand and planted the lightest of kisses on my lips, I knew why. As exciting as chasing a potential murderer might be, it couldn't compare to chasing a beautiful woman.

Moira stood, pulling me up with her. My head felt rubbery,

and I steadied myself on the altar. "Let's figure this out," she said. "I don't know about you, but I don't want to end up as a pair of skeletons archaeologists find a hundred years from now."

"I doubt it would take that long. We'd still have flesh on our bones by the time they found us. Unless critters get in."

She turned to me. "Not helping, Claire. Now help me puzzle this out."

"How do we even know figuring this out will open the door?"

"We don't, but I also refuse to sit here and let fate take me." She picked up another of the stones. "This one seems lighter." She placed the stone in one of the grooves, but nothing happened. "Well, huh." She placed her hands on her hips and stared down at the stone.

I picked up one of the stones on my side of the room and noticed that the material didn't match the others. It also seemed to have a different weight. Hieroglyphics etched along the top and the side were unlike the others. I peered around the room to see if I could match any of these symbols with what appeared on the walls. "What if they need to go in certain grooves? Like each one has a specific spot."

Moira picked up the stone she'd recently fit into the indent and turned it over in her hands. "Mine has an angry guy and a blob-like thing. What does yours have?"

I joined her in the centre of the room. Mine didn't match up. She knelt down and scraped away some of the dirt in one of the indentations.

And then I looked up.

Along the ceiling in the same large triangle pattern were markings like the ones on the stones. I pointed it out to Moira, and she smiled like she'd won a game. "Brilliant." She walked a few steps and placed her stone in its place, and more grinding rose up from the ground.

We rushed to finish placing the remainder of the stones. In the back of my mind I worried this might set off some elaborate booby trap that would crush us. No skeletons even to identify, only dust.

As we placed the last stone, a large, round slab behind the altar rolled to the side, creating an opening in the stone. Moira and I whirled to look at each other. Success.

❖

Moira—Thursday afternoon: Omoa, Honduras

The crash of rushing water intensified the moment the door behind the altar opened. Claire hesitated, and I took my lead from her, holding back.

"What are you waiting for?" I asked.

"Bats. There always seem to be bats flying out in these instances."

"Find yourself in these situations a lot, do you?"

She sighed. "In the movies. I try not to get locked into ancient ruins too often."

I laughed, because what an absurd thing to say. I'm sure she had her fair share of scary situations.

I stepped forward and stuck my head through the opening. "Hello?" I yelled into the small cavern. Only my own echo answered. "Think we'll find treasure?"

"I'd settle for dry land and a way out." Claire checked her watch. "Ship sails in less than an hour. What are the odds they'll wait?"

"That depends. They would leave anyone not on an excursion behind. But they make a point of waiting for excursions that come back late."

"So we should be okay. The excursion team would know that we aren't on the Jeep going back to the ship."

"Except that we were a last-minute add and weren't on the list. So if they go by that, they won't notice we're gone."

Her face fell, and I tried to think of something that would cheer her up. "Maybe we'll find a way out and make it back to the ship before it sails. Crazier things have happened."

I stepped inside and found a winding passage leading down into the darkness. The rushing water echoed from far below, which meant there must be a way out. How else could the water escape? It must lead to the sea.

Along the wall next to me, I noticed the same groove running along the passage, and I grabbed for Claire's lighter again. "If we follow this, I think we'll find a way out at the end."

Claire turned back toward the room. "It doesn't look like we have much of an option, does it?"

I sparked the lighter and held it to the indent near the door. Flames burst to life, shooting down the side of the wall, illuminating the tunnel for us.

"This way if you want to live, Ms. Mills." And I pointed the way ahead. She gave me a sceptical, almost reproachful look, but stepped in front of me and began down the passage.

The musty air clogged my lungs, but for the first time since we'd found ourselves trapped I actually felt like I could breathe properly. I hadn't let myself think about what would've happened if we hadn't gotten out of that room. Would someone have found us? Unlikely. It felt strange to still be in danger but feel relief at the same time. It reminded me of the time my sister Viola and I got lost in the city. We'd skipped school and ridden the bus. Viola, who was older, talked me into it. I think she'd had a test that day she hadn't studied for, and classic Viola, in for a penny, in for a pound.

"Why are you smiling?" Claire asked.

"I was thinking about my sister. She used to get us into all sorts of trouble. This reminded me of the time she took us into the city to find…you know, I don't even remember what she wanted to get, maybe just away. We lived along the coast, and she wanted to explore the market without our parents watching. She probably wanted to buy firecrackers or something."

The passage narrowed and we squeezed in tighter together. "She got us lost, and we ended up in this dead-end alley with garbage piled up all around and stray cats trying to kill each other. Her bright idea? To climb the balconies to the roof so we could see our way out from above."

"And that's what you did?"

"Yes, I almost fell right at the top, but Viola pulled me up at the last second. I ended up scraping my knees pretty bad. And the whole way home we tried to come up with some good excuse of how it had happened."

"Did you?"

"I'm not sure. She told my parents some boy pushed me on the way home from school, but since we wouldn't say who, I'm not sure if they believed us. I don't think they knew what we'd gotten up to, but my mother especially said the story sounded fishy."

Up ahead the passage widened, and almost out of nowhere a raging river came from below.

"This must be why they called it white water. They knew about the underground river system."

"Knew about it? I think they built here because of it. It's probably a good fresh water source."

A path ran tight against the rocks along one side of the cavern. An old rope railing, still standing, kept hopeful crossers from falling into the rushing river below.

I stepped onto the path, slick with moss and splash from the river, and gripped both the rope and the rock wall. Our progress slowed after this.

"Can I ask you something personal?" Claire said.

"Now?"

She held tight to the rotted rope along the ledge. "Can you think of a better time?"

I wanted to say *When we're not about to die* but didn't because it might be a good distraction. "Ask away."

"Why did you kiss me earlier?" she said. "Knowing that I had a—"

"Husband? I never pay attention to that stuff. Besides, I saw you checking me out a few times, like the night we went to the morgue." But that wasn't why I kissed her. I couldn't explain it, but it had felt wrong not to kiss her. Sitting there, she'd looked so vulnerable, and in a way I'd wanted to capture that. "I'm not wrong, though, am I? You're bi?"

"I've never used that term, but it probably fits my interests the best. I've always known I liked women. Frank knew. In fact, I think he got off on it a little but never truly believed I would get involved with a woman." She paused to carefully step over a boulder blocking the narrow path. "Last year he slept with a woman in the PR firm I use for my books."

"He cheated on you."

"Yes. That's not the surprising bit. I have a feeling Frank has stepped out more than once during our marriage."

"But he has such a hangdog look about him. Like you could smack him with a newspaper and he'd crawl behind the couch."

"That's just part of his personality. A lot of women apparently find that attractive about him."

I stumbled when the post for the rope I held broke loose and fell. The rushing water swept it away in an instant. "Go on," I said, regaining my balance.

"Well, I took the PR firm lady to drinks, and she didn't appear apologetic in the slightest. The opposite actually. She kept telling me I could do better. I think she saw the end of our relationship coming sooner than I did. After a few drinks, we ended up at her apartment and I got to see what all the fuss was about. I can't really say it was my idea, but I certainly didn't complain. I got closer than I'd expected."

We continued on for a minute or two in silence. "And?" I asked. She couldn't end the story there. "How was it?"

"She wasn't the first woman I'd been with. But it did make me realize that what I had with Frank would never compare. I knew before I slept with her it was over, but that moment, waking up the next morning in my own bed and realizing I couldn't remember feeling that good in a long time, I knew I had to leave Frank and move on."

"He objected, though."

"Not at first. That was the strange thing. He seemed resigned to the whole thing. Then a few weeks ago, he started calling me again. I ignored him and here we are."

"Wow. Your life is much more interesting than mine. All I have to show for it is a persistent ex who occasionally shows up on contracts and insists she wants to get back together."

"Sounds like there's more to the story."

I groaned because anything to do with Gabriela made my throat clog up and my stomach feel heavy. "We met a few contracts ago on another ship. I tend not to get involved with fellow crew members because it can get messy when you go on vacation or get transferred. Sadly that means a lot of one-night stands, but the less drama in my life, the better. Well, Gabriela is very persistent and very needy, so I stopped it almost as soon as it started. Then she got transferred to another ship and I thought that was the end of it. But every now and then, she shows up and insists we're meant to be."

"I don't envy you your situation."

We'd made decent progress, but because it had been a half-hour's drive to the site, I couldn't imagine walking back to the ship in time.

Claire stopped abruptly. "We have a problem."

I peered around her. It looked like a boulder had broken loose and smashed away the rock, cutting off the rest of the path along the ledge. I studied the river. It appeared deep, which worked in our favour because it had fewer jutting rocks to mangle our bodies. "We have to jump."

Claire turned, dread in her eyes. She shook her head. "We go back and wait for help."

"We'll be dead before they find us. The river will carry us out faster than walking anyway."

"I don't swim."

"All you have to do is float. The current will do the rest."

"No, you don't understand. I can't swim, I can't float. I hate water."

"You came on a cruise and you hate water?"

Then it dawned on me that she hadn't chosen the vacation, they'd forced it on her. Who would force a cruise on a woman who can't swim? I guess lots of people came on cruises who couldn't swim. You didn't really need to, but still, it lacked compassion.

Claire tried to push past me in a panic to get away from the edge and head back the way we'd come.

I pushed her against the wall and leaned in, speaking inches from her ear. "No one knows we're missing. Heading back is suicide. It might take days, weeks, even months for them to notice the chamber. We need to keep moving forward."

"We could just go back and see. In a few days if they don't find us, we can try again."

"We need to do this now, when we have the energy and the motivation. If we wait, we'll die." I could feel her heart thumping in her chest, feel her breathing on my cheek. She closed her eyes and leaned her head against the jagged cave. A tear escaped.

"I can't." She shook her head. "I can't do it."

I searched around for something that would help. I spotted the rope attached to the posts along the edge and grabbed a length of it. I tied one end around my waist and held the other up to her. "We'll stay tethered—that way I can always pull you up."

She looked dubious but didn't stop me from tying it around her, making sure the knot would tighten when pulled. We stepped up to the ledge, and I realized what a horrible idea it was. If she drowned, I didn't think I'd have the strength to pull her up or carry her along. What if she pulled me down with her?

She slipped my hand in hers, and I turned to see her wide eyes and pale skin.

"We're in this together," I said. In more ways than one. Even as I projected as much confidence as I could, something I'd learned going up on stage in front of hundreds of people, my heart raced, my blood pumped, and I had a feeling we shouldn't do this.

Before I could second-guess myself, I jumped, pulling Claire in with me. She screamed as we hit the rushing water, surprisingly cold given the climate, plunging into the depths of an angry, whirling river.

I momentarily panicked when I couldn't push up from the bottom. The current contorted my body, confusing up and down. I opened my eyes and by some miracle spotted a bit of light in one direction and began swimming toward that, surfacing with a big gulp of air. I reached for Claire, my hand only hitting water. I swivelled and felt the rope at my waist tighten, and I grabbed for it, pulling the end, and hopefully Claire, toward me. She surfaced with terror in her eyes and latched on to me, pushing me under the surface.

On ship, they make you go through weeks of training when you start, and every now and again, you get a refresher course. I knew I had to turn Claire and get her into a hold from behind so I could keep her above the surface and use my other arm to steer us to safety.

Before I could do any of that, we smashed up against the side of the cave, and Claire lost her grip on me. I bobbed to the surface in time to see her flail and sink. I pushed off the wall and dived under, searching. I got hold of her shirt before the momentum of the river changed, curving around a bend and ripping the fabric from my grasp.

And then the rope squeezed, yanking me to a stop. The rope had caught on something in the river. I almost succumbed to my instinct and panicked, but something deeper kept me focused. I took hold of the rope and pulled myself toward where we'd snagged. A large outcrop of rock in the middle of the river had caught us. I'd gone along one side while Claire had gone on the other. I found Claire clinging to the rock, sucking in breath.

We stayed like that, breathing heavily for a few more moments, then I quickly put her into the rescue position, snaked my arm around her neck, and dragged her back into the river, this time with both our heads above water.

The river did most of the work, propelling us along at tremendous speed until I spotted what looked like a little underground beach area and began swimming toward that. The sandy bottom came upon us suddenly, and I shoved Claire onto the beach ahead of me. She crawled up and collapsed, her face half in the wet sand.

I followed and lay on my back, eyes closed, getting my breath back. What a colossally stupid idea. For someone who's supposedly had training, if any of my trainers had seen that, I'd have failed in an instant.

After what felt like an hour, I opened my eyes. A shot of light, a crack in the rock above illuminated a small section of the beach enough to get my bearings. I found Claire sitting up and staring at me. I couldn't gauge her expression, but I could guess when I sat up and she slapped me hard across the cheek. A moment later she pulled me in for a searing kiss, the sting from the slap disappearing. She dug her hands into my back, a desperate grip in a desperate moment.

As the kiss slowed, the heat building in the pit of my stomach, I felt the tension in Claire's body lessen. She pulled back, holding me in an intense stare. "You almost killed us." She took my face in her hands. "You are no longer in charge of the entertainment."

I laughed. "I suppose almost getting your date killed is counterintuitive to dating."

I pulled her wrist up and checked the time. Her watch no longer worked but it had stopped at 5:45 p.m., fifteen minutes after the *Summit* would've sailed. I didn't know how to feel about that. Who would believe that someone had tried to trap and ultimately kill us? A few days ago, I would've believed Amy capable of this. Now I wasn't so sure.

CHAPTER EIGHTEEN

Claire—Thursday evening: Omoa, Honduras

"You can forget about getting me back into that water. Never going to happen," I said from my sloped position on the beach. The dark brown sand stretched several metres in both directions, ended abruptly on one side by a smooth cave wall and on the other with the end of the original path. At one point, the Maya must have travelled from behind the altar to this beach without the heart-pounding swim.

Moira stood, wandering to the far edge of the beach, refusing to answer. That didn't bode well for keeping me out of the river of death.

While she explored, I lay back on the sand and closed my eyes, willing my heart back to a normal rate. I'd survived worse, but today it didn't feel like it. From as far back as I could remember, I had nightmares of drowning. Both Frank and Rick have told me to go for swim lessons as a proactive way to rid myself of my fears. But I can't. I actually signed myself up once and got as far as the change room. Standing in my brand-new swimsuit—I'd had to rip the price tag off before putting it on—the humidity of the pool surrounding me, the smell of chlorine invading my nostrils, I felt paralyzed. By the time the class had ended, I still hadn't moved. I watched the bathers, my fellow classmates, also all adults, wet from their first class, stream past me with hopeful faces. I never went back.

I wish I could share some childhood trauma that led to this fear, but it doesn't exist. All I have is this image in my mind from as far back as I can remember of seeing a grey stormy sky from below the water as my lungs burn and I sink into oblivion.

Most days it doesn't bother me. I don't live near water and make a habit of avoiding the Thames. I think this is Rick's way of getting me to face my fear. Or he doesn't realize how terrified I am.

I only let Moira pull me in because she was right. Going back we certainly would have died. At least going forward we had a chance.

I dug my hands into the sand, feeling grounded for the first time in days, and felt the spiky fibres of rotted rope. I looked down as I lifted the rope from the sand. One end led to a metal spike buried deep into the ground. I followed the other end to the far side of the beach, where a mishmash of stilted vegetation grew.

I found Moira digging in the underbrush. "Look what I found," she said. A rickety raft, hidden behind the brush, stuck out of the sand, a broken makeshift mast on its side. "Help me dig it out. Maybe we can use this to get down the river."

The moment she said it, I balked. "This thing must be ancient."

"Ancient doesn't mean it isn't seaworthy."

I backtracked to the wall with the crack in the top. Maybe we could climb through the opening? I examined the fissure, a tiny crack wide enough to filter light down, but no wider than my hand.

"It still floats," Moira called, and my heart plummeted. She'd dragged the raft, made from four once-solid trees, into a calm pool of eddies. Still tethered to the spike, it bobbed with the motion of the water. My stomach roiled.

Moira took my hand and waited until I looked at her before speaking. "I can't pretend to know how terrifying it is to get on a raft when you can't swim."

"Rickety. A rickety, barely floating raft."

"It's made of wood. It'll float."

"As individual logs, I'll grant you."

"I've checked the rope holding them together. They'll last for the rest of the ride."

"We don't even know if this river goes to the sea."

She took my face in her hands. "I know. All of this is a risk. And I'm asking you to because we don't have another option. If you want to get out of here alive, you need to get on this raft with me. I will try my best to keep you safe."

She warmed my cheeks with her hands, and I felt a bit of my fear dissipate. I could do this. I *had* to do this, what other option did I have? "Okay." But even after making the decision, I shivered. Adrenaline shot through my system, numbing a lot of my fear. Imagine people willing to jump out of a plane with a little knapsack strapped to their back. The nerve it must take to do that. I could get on a raft and ride it down a fast river to safety. How long could I live on a few metres of sand?

I followed her back to the raft and sat in the middle where she pointed, gripping the remnants of the broken mast with both hands.

"I don't have anything to steer with," she said, "so this will get bumpy. Hold on tight."

"You don't have to tell me that."

She pushed us into the flow of the river and jumped on at the last second. We lurched into the current, dipping sideways. I scrambled to grab the other side to stop from flipping us into the water. We spun around once and then the raft righted itself, propelling us along at a stomach-dropping speed.

"Oh bugger." I closed my eyes, not wanting to watch any longer. I felt Moira wrap an arm around me, anchoring us to the raft.

She pulled me down flush and then, all of a sudden, the darkness lifted. I opened my eyes. We'd exited the cave system. I glanced back to see the tiny hole in the side of a towering cliff. We'd made it out with centimetres to spare.

I watched the expression on Moira's face change from anxiousness to one of absolute joy. We were flying down the river, the expansive sea a few kilometres ahead. We just had to hold on for a few more minutes, and this might all end.

As we neared the opening, the river slowed and the unmistakable scent of salt water engulfed us.

Moira—Thursday evening: Omoa, Honduras

The antiseptic stench of the medical bay washed over me as I sat waiting for Dr. Steenbok to release me. I knew he'd find nothing wrong. Besides a few scratches, our terror-filled ride down the secret Mayan river hadn't caused any permanent damage. I worried about Claire, but more for her mental health. I couldn't even remember not being able to swim, so I couldn't fathom the idea of jumping into a rushing river without any way of keeping myself afloat.

Viola and I used to bet tourists we could beat them in a race around the first buoy. We'd make a killing because it didn't look far from shore, but when you actually started swimming, you'd find that the current and waves worked against you, and it became twice as far. It wasn't dangerous because the shore didn't drop off until past the buoy, and at any time they could stand up and touch the bottom.

I was the ringer. They'd take one look at me and think they could out-swim a small eleven-year-old without any problems. I always made it around the buoy by the time they admitted defeat, standing to watch as I swam past, my spindly arms and legs slipping through the water like a well-placed oar.

The summer I turned twelve, my father found us out. Furious, he confiscated our money. That was the summer I started working at the hotel. He said if we wanted to make money so badly, we could do it legally. Not that Viola and I thought betting gullible tourists was illegal. Quite the opposite. What person comes to another country and thinks they can outsmart the locals? Obviously we wouldn't be betting we could do something if we hadn't already done it a million times. With age, I've come to realize it was misogyny that pushed them to do it. No way a girl could whip them in an endurance contest.

Viola refused to work at the hotel with my father. I often wonder if that decision defined our paths in life. Here I am, still working in the tourist industry, and Viola, who got a job as a bike courier, now makes music, her true passion.

The ship jerked, and I felt the familiar vibrations below as the thrusters started up to push us away from the pier. Still docked in Omoa hours after our intended departure, the *Ocean Summit*, down one engine, finally began its journey toward Belize several hours late.

I felt relief we weren't sitting in an overpriced hotel room at the moment. And the only reason we weren't was because one of the ship's engines failed to start. It had delayed the ship long enough for us to make the sailing.

They'd had to lower the gangplank for us, having removed it assuming everyone had already boarded. I also felt relief because I didn't want to lose my job. That surprised me. For years I've told people I wouldn't come back after vacation, every contract my last, and yet, I felt worried we'd missed the ship's departure. A sure way to get fired. Had I finally come to terms that I worked on cruise ships for a living?

"How goes your investigation?" Dr. Jan asked, entering the waiting room.

I debated how much to say, but since we still didn't know for sure how we got trapped in that room, I decided to play it safe. I shrugged it off. "I suspect we won't find anything else. He probably did commit suicide, and we need to step back from it."

He nodded, his blond hair bobbing with the motion. "Probably for the best." He pointed behind him. "You are free to leave. You seem in good health, but may I recommend a good night's sleep? Drink lots of water as well for the next few days."

"How's Claire?"

"She has a few deep gashes in her leg I'd like to suture, but she'll make a full recovery. Not to worry."

I nodded, understanding that I wouldn't get a chance to see Claire. Maybe just as well. If it were me, I'd be furious. I almost got her killed.

Jan put his comforting hand on my arm. "You did a marvellous thing. She didn't drown, and you both made it out alive. Who knows what would've happened if you hadn't."

When we made it back, we'd explained what had happened. Françoise, the shore excursion manager, had confirmed we'd left on the excursion, but they'd left us behind because we weren't on the official list of participants. They were looking into how we got trapped so far off the main path.

I stood—still a little shaky, the result of massive amounts of adrenaline coursing through my system—and walked toward my cabin, hoping they'd finally gotten to the inch of water covering the floor.

I entered my cabin to discover the good news that they'd

removed the water. Unfortunately, they'd also removed the toilet. Only a forlorn hole existed in its place. I didn't have time to call anyone from maintenance. Amy had me taking off Bandini the Great, and I needed to eat something. I really needed a shower after my ordeal but didn't have the time. I wet a face cloth and did my best to clear any visible dirt. My hair, crusty with dry salt water, would have to go into a stylish, messy bun. I examined my face and determined that no amount of makeup would make me look rested, so respectably tired would have to do.

I threw on a dark blue suit and affixed my name tag to the pocket.

Before heading to the mess to eat, I visited Françoise in her office to get a list of excursion guests. As soon as I entered, she jumped up from her chair, knocking it back against the wall.

"I heard what happened. Moira, I'm so sorry. I never thought they'd leave you behind."

I waved my hands to try to slow her down, but she barrelled ahead.

"I've spoken to the manager of the site, and he confirmed someone removed the red markers. They are still working to remove the stone placed over the door."

"So it was put there on purpose?"

She nodded vigorously. "Oh, yes. They confirmed that the stone door would not have moved without help, and it wouldn't have accidentally rolled into that position."

"Is it possible to get a list of all the people who were on that excursion?"

"Why? You think someone on the excursion did this to you?"

I tilted my head from side to side. "I'm not sure. But it would help in case something else comes up."

Françoise glanced at her computer sitting on her desk. "What else do you think will come up?"

I decided to weave a plausible lie instead of telling her the truth. "I suspect someone played a practical joke that went wrong. I want to check with security to see if they've noticed anything. I'm sure if any damages occur, it would help to have names."

I could tell she didn't want to give me the list. Françoise played by the book, which struck me as odd for a French woman. Like the Italians, the French had a relaxed view of formal rules.

I didn't know much about Françoise. We'd only worked together once before. A lot of people thought she was rude, but I think it had more to do with people mispronouncing her name. They called her François, which was the equivalent of calling her Frank. I'd have a chip on my shoulder too.

I needed her to give me the list since only she could access it. Maybe I should've told her the truth, but the fewer people who knew what we suspected, the better. We stared at each other for a few moments before she said, "Okay, but you must promise you won't tell anyone I gave it to you."

"Of course. This stays between us."

She took a seat at her computer and typed in a few commands. A few seconds later, the printer behind her started up. She handed me the sheet, which also listed cabin numbers. This was even better. I could cross-reference anyone on this list with people who had a cabin on deck ten. I folded the paper up and stuck it in my inside pocket.

I bumped into Amy on my way out of the office, dressed in a knee-length pink dress. She looked at my suit, complete with skinny tie, and then back up, a disapproving look on her face, but she didn't say anything about it. Instead, she said, "Can you meet me in the cruise staff office after you're done taking Bandini off? I have something important to talk about." Before I could ask what, she stalked off in the direction of the elevators.

I didn't get my hopes up because this could concern anything from my outfit, to what we'd talked about earlier that morning, which felt like a million years ago, to something else I'd done to piss her off. I hope it didn't have anything to do with her dating life.

When I climbed the stairs at the back of the stage, I found it more packed than usual. All the stage techs and several dancers and crew milled about watching the show from backstage.

I asked the first tech I saw why everyone had crowded backstage, and he simply pointed to Bandini strapped upside down in a contraption with a curved sword halfway down his throat. "Next he's doing a bullet catch."

"What?" I asked. "He can't do that. The cruise line would never allow that."

The tech shrugged and walked off, squeezing through a group of people to get a better view. I went to look for the backstage manager.

Out of all the magic tricks in the world, the bullet catch held the title of the most dangerous. Dozens, possibly more, had died over the years trying to perform it. I couldn't imagine the cruise line allowing something so dangerous on ship. The last thing they wanted on their hands, besides a murdered passenger, was a dead performer.

I found Jen in the back control station quietly relaying directions into her headset.

"Did I hear correctly? Bandini's doing a bullet catch?"

She smiled indulgently. "It's fake. He had to sign a million waivers swearing he wasn't actually firing a live gun onstage in order to perform the trick. He walked me through it, and everything checks out."

I scrunched up my face. Call me cynical, or call me experienced, but I still had reservations. The trick requires the magician to mark the bullet, then place it in the gun and have someone fire it at them. Then they catch it, usually in their teeth, and show the audience the bullet has the same mark they have just placed on it. Obviously magicians fake it because who wants to die onstage, but other magicians would know and your reputation would suffer.

"He doesn't actually mark the bullet. He shows a clean bullet, pretends to mark it, switches that out for a pre-marked bullet, and then places that in the gun. The gun makes a lot of noise and smoke but doesn't fire, and then he reveals an identically marked bullet in his mouth which he's placed in there sometime before the trick begins. It's all very safe and approved. Don't worry."

I groaned. The last thing I needed was another dead body.

As we spoke, he'd set up this last trick, choosing a member of the audience to come up onstage and assure everyone that the bullet and gun were real. Jen assured me this person, a plant, wouldn't fire a real gun at anyone. I watched, mesmerized, waiting for someone to drop dead in front of me.

But the trick came off without any problems.

As soon as he took his last bow, I entered stage left, mic in hand, big smile on my face. "Wasn't that amazing?" I asked the audience, who roared back with enthusiasm, half of them more than a little drunk at this point in the evening.

Before I could continue, Bandini stopped me. "Wait." He turned me to face him, my side to the audience. Then spun me around the other way. "What is this? No. My mistake. I thought I saw something behind your ear. Happens a lot in my business." The audience laughed, and too late I remembered he'd done something similar with Amy. Years ago I'd learned never to wear watches when dealing with magicians. One in particular, James the Magnificent, loved randomly taking people's watches while talking to them. Even though you knew he'd try given the chance, it still ended up a surprise when he did.

"Could you be a doll," he said, "and hand me that box on that table there?" He turned to the audience. "My assistant has a strict hour-and-a-half work limit."

I retrieved the box, dreading what would happen a little. Intricate with inlaid diamond shaped onyx, it felt heavy and solid.

He opened it to reveal an old-fashioned pirate blunderbuss pistol. "Now, when you came onstage you had a folded piece of paper in your inner breast pocket." My heart sank. "Would you retrieve that for us?"

With growing dread I reached in and checked my pocket to find I had nothing there. "It's gone," I said.

"Maybe the audience can help you look for it." He flickered his eyebrows at me as he lifted it out and aimed it above the heads of the audience and pulled the trigger. A burst of what looked like confetti shot from the gun. A second later, the lights cut and darkness pervaded the auditorium. Bandini seized my arm and pulled me from the stage, but not before I'd bent down and captured a scrap.

By the time the lights came back on, we both stood stage left, Bandini breathing heavily, a grin and sweat plastered to his face. "That went well. That last trick doesn't always work."

I looked down at the scrap of paper I'd managed to grab. Sure enough, it contained part of the list. "I needed that," I said.

He shrugged. "It looked like a printed list. Just print another one."

"I can't just print another one."

An assistant and a few techs swarmed him, and he turned away, attention on something else. I looked out at the stage, now littered with my best piece of evidence, stark white against the blackness.

Claire—Thursday evening: at sea

I knew from prior experience that the numbness of the stitches would fade, replaced by incessant itching. Back in the safety of my cabin, a vodka tonic in hand, I could breathe for the first time since this ordeal began. I replaced the bandage on my leg and strolled to the balcony, where the wind played with my bangs. The moon dispersed its illuminated trail in the waves created by the slow passage of the ship.

I let the vodka tame the edges of my nerves, surprised I didn't feel more on edge since I'd almost drowned earlier in the day. I worried that meant something about my life in general. What did it mean if this felt like an average day? My work hadn't always gotten me into trouble. When I'd first started with the *Evening Standard* I couldn't imagine ever investigating anything that would leave me for dead in a hospital halfway around the world.

In those early days, a man named Bruce Doyle once told me that until people began shooting at me, I wasn't doing my job well. Being shot at comes at the top of a slippery slope. It never starts there. It starts with angry letters to the editor and snowballs into lawsuits. After that, ninety-nine percent of the time, violence gets involved.

I'd had shots fired at me on at least three different assignments. Had my brake lines cut on my vehicle and now could add drowning and the possibility of suffocation to the list.

Standing on my balcony watching the moonlight play with the waves, I felt lonely for the first time in ages. I almost called Frank only because I knew Moira would be working. I needed someone to talk me back to Earth, and with no one around to do that, it put a lot of choices I'd made into perspective.

For the first time ever, I knew why my mother did what she did. Loneliness has a way of creeping inside your soul and expanding until nothing feels real or right anymore. I'd turned five the day before she committed suicide, ten when told the truth of her death, and now at the age of forty-five, I finally understood it. Not that I'm contemplating the same fate. I don't have the same loneliness inside that she must have.

Looking down into the water, from this height, I could imagine jumping would do the trick.

Death on the water.

How many corpses did this ocean hold? Thousands? Millions? More?

I suspected someone on board imagined they'd gotten away with the perfect murder now.

Did they know we made it out? Did they trap Moira and me in that chamber with the hopes we'd die or miss the ship? Was it the same person who'd sent me that threatening email to mind my own business? I still hadn't told Moira about that and now felt even less inclined.

And what did we really know about Colin's death? We had no idea how he died, although I suspected poison since we couldn't find any markings on his body. How did that poison get administered? Before the killer confronted him in his cabin? Or during dinner earlier? In a drink at a bar? Would we ever know?

We didn't know how, and we also didn't know why. The motive for Colin's murder still eluded me. Did Amy kill him because she felt jilted? Or did this involve his Bitcoin fortune? A fortune we couldn't even confirm because someone had stolen both his phone and laptop. If Amy had killed him, would she have come back for his laptop? Perhaps, but wouldn't emails and messages exist in other places like a computer at home? If he was a gamer, he'd have a much better setup than a laptop, I imagined.

And if Amy hadn't killed him, why was she on the eleventh floor that night? Why did she appear to recognize his name, but not necessarily him? That's what had been nagging at me. It was only after Colin spoke his name that Amy reacted. If she had expected Colin on the ship, wouldn't she have recognized him?

And how did the killer know we were on to them?

The quiet broke as a loud shout came from a man in a cabin a few doors down. I peered over the side and saw a man speaking on his cell having an argument with the person on the other end. I could hear his conversation plain as if he were standing in my room.

I turned suddenly remembering the conversation I'd had with Rick that morning, which felt like a million years ago. I put down my drink, grabbed my keycard, and rushed out of my cabin. I had to find Moira.

Chapter Nineteen

Moira—Thursday evening: at sea

I bent and snatched another scrap of paper from behind the first row. Luckily Bandini only did one showing, and I didn't have to worry about guests grabbing seats for the next show.

I flipped the paper over. It showed the cruise line's logo, confirming Bandini had indeed blown my one lead into smithereens. What kind of jerk pickpockets someone, and for entertainment destroys it? I found a few more scraps under a seat. It had a few names on it, but without the room numbers, it didn't mean much. I'd have to recover every piece. I looked toward the back of the house where hundreds of tiny pieces of paper lay in various positions. The task seemed impossible.

Would Françoise print me another one? I shook my head before the thought even cleared. I'd barely gotten her to print this one.

I checked my watch. I didn't want to piss off Amy by showing up any later than I already was. I would figure this out later. I couldn't think about it now, but I could guarantee that jackass Bandini had it coming to him. I didn't know what yet, but he definitely needed a sorting out.

But when I got to the cruise staff office, I only found Brad and Noah lounging around Amy's desk.

"Is Amy back yet?"

Noah took his feet off her desk and sat up while Brad, still leaning back in the admin chair, said, "I haven't seen her since 70s night." Both wore polyester suits with bell-bottomed pants. Noah still wore his fake hair, while Brad had taken off his wig and tossed it on Amy's desk. It resembled a dead rat.

Theme nights were one of many things I hated about working as cruise staff. It depended a lot on the cruise director you had, but chances were good you'd spend the night in humiliating costumes doing fad dances from bygone eras. I'd spent more nights in a poodle skirt and pigtails doing the hand jive than I could count. No amount of money seemed worth that kind of humiliation.

Benny was one of the better cruise directors to work under. He'd banned wigs a few years ago because they were racist. Even if the cruise industry's labour ideals were stuck somewhere in feudal Europe, it didn't mean he couldn't at least try to elevate his department to the twenty-first century. Amy didn't have the same standards. I could write her off as racist and insensitive, but that only touched on part of the problem. She seemed to have a lot more going in her life, and I could give her the benefit of the doubt. Next meeting I would bring it up and see if she too would ban them.

I checked the schedule. They held 70s night in the top lounge at seven and it ended at ten, over an hour ago. Where the hell could she be?

I pulled out my ship cell and hit the shortcut for the cruise director. It rang several times before it clicked over to voicemail, and I heard Amy's fake excitement at receiving my message. I hung up.

"If you guys see her, tell her to give me a call," I said and began to leave when Noah stopped me.

"Did you see the numbers for bingo yet?"

The absolute glee on his face told me I wouldn't like them. He handed me a sheet, and the number at the bottom should have totalled five times what it did. I dropped it on the table and left the two of them to go get out of these clothes. I didn't have anything more scheduled until tomorrow morning at nine. I wanted nothing more than to go back to my cabin, take another long shower, and fall into bed.

When I got to my room, the hole in my bathroom floor still gaping, not only did I still not have a toilet, but I also had no water. One blow after another. I knew many crew had similar problems in their rooms, which made it feel even more personal somehow.

I didn't have any way of getting into Kaitlin's room without her keycard, so I trudged up to deck nine to find her behind the bar at the nightclub. She looked severe with her hair slicked back into a tight bun at the nape of her neck. She always wore black with dark lipstick, which added to the aesthetic.

"I need your keycard."

"I'm going to start charging you rent." Kaitlin turned, grabbed a bottle of Beluga vodka from the premium shelf, and poured a generous shot over ice, topping it with a spritz of tonic. She slid the tumbler over to me.

"They shut my water off, and I need to shower."

"I didn't want to say anything, but now that you've brought it up, you do look like hell. What happened?"

I raised the glass to her and took a sip. "It would take many more of these to get through the story, and I don't have the energy." I didn't want to worry Kaitlin with the details of my adventure today. Even to me, it seemed surreal and impossible that I'd almost died. To say nothing of getting trapped in an ancient Mayan temple and barely making it back to the ship before it sailed. So, why did I keep thinking of it as an adventure? More like an ordeal.

Despite her outward appearance and attitude, Kaitlin would worry about me. And lecture me, and it was fear of the latter that held my tongue. I did want to talk about Claire, though. I'd kissed her today on impulse. And for some reason I didn't fear getting fired over fraternizing with a passenger.

I took another large swig of the vodka. "I kissed someone today."

Kaitlin cocked her head and leaned her elbows onto the bar, her full attention on me instead of the man in the ugly brown suit trying to catch her eye. "The journalist you mentioned the other day? Well, well. I can't say I approve, but I do enjoy gossip."

I nodded. "Why the disapproval?"

"She'll get you fired. Not on purpose, but if anyone sees you..." She didn't have to finish her sentence. We'd both seen first-hand what happened when a crew member got too close to a passenger. Our friend Ian slept with twins while on a contract several years ago and got escorted off at the next embark day by security. One person recounted that he'd said it was totally worth it as he passed.

Kaitlin and I had debated about this for years. While we could both agree sex, even good sex, would never outweigh a good job, this had never been a good job to me. The hours sucked, the pay sucked harder, and you had no personal life. So if Ian wanted to throw that away for a threesome with twenty-year-old twins, I wouldn't hold it against him. I wouldn't cheer him on either. Did I think Claire was worth throwing away a job I hated? Maybe. A big maybe.

I held out my hand. "Can I please have your keycard so I can shower off my dirt?"

She rolled her eyes, the Coles Notes version of her lecture, unclipped her card from an extendable pull on her belt, and handed it to me.

"I promise no one saw a thing," I said to appease her. No one possibly could have since it happened in a hidden cave kilometres underground.

As I turned to go, in the corner of my eye, I spotted that jackass Bandini sipping a drink at the end of the bar. I pointed him out to Kaitlin and asked what he was drinking.

"Chocolate martinis."

"Gross."

"I know. Why?"

"He's a dick."

She nodded. "Leave it to me."

Claire—Thursday evening: at sea

I'd searched three venues before realizing I should've checked the schedule to find Moira. All the day's big events had already happened, so she might have retired for the night. Despite my ordeal today, I felt energized. We hadn't gotten any closer to discovering who killed Colin, but in my mind we had confirmed one important detail. Someone had murdered him. Why else would they try to kill us? Who would go into his room after a suicide and steal his laptop? No, Colin Avery had not committed suicide, and no one could convince me otherwise.

I also had an idea of how to possibly find out who had killed him, but I needed Moira's help. It could probably wait until tomorrow and would have to, it seemed, except my body didn't want sleep. It wanted to move forward, to figure this out now that we were so close.

"Claire?" I turned at the sound of that familiar voice. I'd wandered up onto the pool deck. Frank looked aghast as soon as I faced him. "What happened to your face?"

My hand went to the cut on the side of my cheek, a souvenir from when the river swept me into the cave wall. Or from landing on the sandy beach. I didn't know for sure. "A mishap during an excursion today. Nothing to worry about."

"Can I buy you a drink?" he asked. My default response was no, but since I didn't feel like heading back to my room, I said yes. He guided me to the pool bar at the back of the ship. The one that only allowed guests twenty-one and older in. It stood dark when we passed through the sliding glass doors, but a sign said the upstairs bar would stay open until midnight.

Frank guided us to a table near the edge overlooking the pool, which glowed orange and purple, flicking between the two. Beyond, the atrium lay dark, cordoned off with rope and caution triangles. The kind that warns you about slipping on wet floors.

Frank ordered a double scotch and I a vodka tonic. Such creatures of habit. It made me sad—so much so I almost went up to the bar to change my order, but in truth I wanted a vodka tonic and to change it only to do something different seemed counterintuitive.

When our drinks came and the server had gone, I said, "Why did you really come on this cruise, Frank?"

He took a small sip of his scotch, turning the cheap tumbler around in his hand. They'd bought everything in plastic for all the bars around the pool. "I got an interesting call from an old friend a few weeks ago. I thought it best to talk to you in person, and since you haven't responded to a single thing I've sent you in over six months, I thought this the best way to get in touch." The ambient lights from the pool made the frizzy hair on the top of his head change colour every minute or two.

"Booking a room on a cruise last minute? How did you even get one?"

"I got lucky. Someone cancelled last minute, and I pulled a favour from an old contact who works in the industry."

"I don't believe any of that."

He leaned forward. "I needed to talk to you, Claire. This is important."

"Than why haven't you spit it out yet? You keep stalling."

He shrugged and gazed down into his drink. "I got the renewal form for your subscription to the *Times* a few weeks back. The bright thing to do is chuck it in the bin, but I pinned it to the fridge like old times, like you might spot it one day and remember that you needed to take care of it."

I let that sentence fall away, drowned by the steel drums playing by the main pool. Our bar sat empty save for a few guests enjoying the music without having it jammed in your ears. I started wishing Moira sat across from me.

"Do you remember the time we rented that car in San Clemente and we ran out of petrol on the way to that little castle outside of the city, what was it called?"

I shook my head not because I didn't recall the name, but more that I didn't want to travel down memory lane with him.

He waved it off. "Anyway, we had to flag down someone to take us to fill a jerrycan, and we both couldn't speak enough Spanish to get anyone to understand? We got stranded by the side of the road for most of the day and didn't end up finding the castle."

I took a sip of my drink and waited for him to get to the point. With Frank it might take a while.

"Well, last month I had a meeting near there and had an afternoon off. I decided to take a car up and finally see it."

I gave him a weak smile, now sorry I'd agreed to a drink. He still hadn't told me why he'd followed me halfway across the world on a cruise.

"Turns out it was nothing more than four walls shaped in a square, just this piddly little thing in the middle of nowhere. Imagine, we wasted an entire day on the side of the road but hadn't missed a thing. I remember you'd felt terrible we hadn't made it."

Loneliness so profound and aching wrenched my heart at that moment. Not for myself but Frank. I suspected he hadn't come to bring me any important news. More likely he wanted to hold on to those last dregs of wine in our marriage. It was me who'd moved out of our flat, leaving him to wander the empty rooms like a ghost.

And here I felt unscathed because I had work to fall back on. The one thing he'd railed against our entire marriage saved me from ending up a lonely sack.

A scream broke the relative calm on the pool deck below, and I stood to see what had happened. From that vantage point, I could see people gathered around the hot tub hanging off the back of the ship. As the crowd parted, the field of view cleared. A dead body, face down, floated in the overheated water.

Moira—Friday morning: at sea.

I pulled out a cushioned chair so new it smelled faintly of factory chemicals and took a seat around a large conference table. I was lost in a sea of men. The only other woman was the food and beverage manager, a short stern woman who reminded me of my second grade teacher, Mrs. Gorski. When she caught you doing something she didn't like, she would lower her gaze until you met her eyes and incline her head toward the corner, not speaking a word. The quiet disapproval was more threatening than all the screaming and howling my parents did combined.

Selena Vogel turned her accusatory eyes on me now. Gooseflesh rose on my arms. Usually Amy would've attended this meeting, a weekly occurrence of department heads to discuss issues. Noah said he'd heard Amy complain all this week that they'd had one every sea day because they couldn't cover everything in one meeting.

I, of course, knew the main reason for this meeting, but it appeared not everyone had heard yet, because the first officer and the purser came in laughing, their heads bowed together in shared mirth.

Jan nodded sombrely when he entered and took a seat to my left. He leaned in and whispered, "Stick around after the meeting. I have something to share with you. Regardless," he fluttered his hand around, indicating the room, "of what they have to say about what happened."

Interesting. So the official report and what really happened wouldn't necessarily coincide.

As everyone took their seats, the staff captain and the captain entered from a separate entrance. The table, a large oval made of teak, fit twelve people. Floor to ceiling windows emphasized the swath of navy blue stretched before us. It amazed me how the colour of the ocean could denote its mood. Today it said "Don't piss me off."

The captain, a man in his late fifties, with blond hair no longer his real colour, stood tugging at the pockets of his pants. Captain Haugen nodded to the group before he spoke. "For those who haven't heard, we found Amy Dabrowski, our cruise director, drowned in the hot tub late last night. We'd closed them off earlier in the day because some of the jets had malfunctioned. We have concluded that she tripped, hit her head, and as a result, drowned. A tragic accident, but an accident nonetheless." Jan gave me side-eye. "Moving forward, we have installed Moira Andolina as our acting cruise director until we get word of a permanent replacement."

A few pathetic claps later, he continued. "We ask that you don't discuss this with passengers. We will continue as usual. Moira will take over Amy's duties, and if anyone asks, you can say Amy fell ill. Starting next cruise, Moira will assume the cruise director position, and we will wait to see if head office makes the change permanent." He looked at me with his watery blue eyes as if to say he didn't have much hope of that. He turned to the staff captain, who rose as Captain Haugen sat.

Peter assumed a much more jovial air. "Hello. We are almost done with our inaugural cruise." He even raised a fist and shook it in a hurrah kind of way.

My hand shot up before he even finished his sentence. It caught him up and he almost got halfway through his next before he stopped. "Yes, Moira?"

"That's it? She's dead, let's move on? This is the second death that's happened on this cruise. The first of which, I might add, got dealt with much too quickly, if you ask me."

Jan grabbed my hand under the table and squeezed.

Peter managed to hang on to his smile for a whole minute before my meaning finally drove itself into his brain. "You think the gentleman found with an empty bottle of sleeping pills next to his bed didn't commit suicide?"

Jan squeezed harder. I thought his fingernails might have drawn blood. "Did you know Amy knew that gentleman?"

Peter looked at Captain Haugen, obviously surprised to learn this fact. This meant we'd stumbled onto something they hadn't. A sense of intense superiority smacked me hard in the face. I wondered if Claire felt like this on a regular basis. My euphoria didn't last long with two dead bodies at the other end, though.

The head of security spoke. "So you think someone from the entertainment department has a better understanding of investigation than our security team?"

Jan had already given me up for dead. He'd dropped my hand and scooted his chair farther away from me. I shot him a look. "No, sir. I'm concerned for the safety of our passengers. I think the coincidence of two deaths is too much to dismiss. And furthermore, I'm concerned about the death of my former superior. I talked to her earlier in the evening and she asked me to meet her at the cruise staff office but never showed up."

"Well, she obviously couldn't meet you in the office because she'd tripped and fallen in the hot tub."

I pursed my lips closed. No, they wouldn't investigate further, and it had nothing to do with knowing what happened but saving the cruise line's butt. If word got out about both deaths, sales would drop.

The meeting moved on to other things. I tuned out most of it because it didn't have anything to do with catching murderers or running the entertainment department. My interest piqued when they mentioned Hurricane Gert. Who named these things anyway?

"We're keeping an eye on it. As of right now, Hurricane Gert will not affect any of our ports of call. We will have to skirt farther north than normal to avoid it on our way from Belize back to Florida."

I'd weathered a few bad storms but never a hurricane. The beauty of modern radar and weather reports was that ships rarely let themselves sail into dangerous storms. The meeting began to break up, but I raised my hand again. This time, several people gave me a death stare. No one wanted to be the person to extend the meeting, but I felt I had a rare opportunity to advocate for the crew. I didn't usually get to have this many department heads in one room as crew welfare ambassador. I needed them to know how mistreated the crew were.

"One more thing," I said. "The crew party that got cancelled? I think we should seriously think about putting it back on and also work on fixing a lot of the issues creating problems with the crew's working conditions."

"Excuse me?" said Peter. He frowned as if he had no idea what I was talking about.

"Many of the crew have voiced concerns over safety issues causing them to work longer hours, as well as maintenance issues with their cabins. I myself have experienced problems. They are working very hard to keep this ship together, and I think the least we can do is show our appreciation for them."

"They can't have a party back there—the aft pool deck lights aren't working. We need to block it off at night for safety reasons."

"The pool lights still work. All we need to do is bring in some of the spare stage lighting and secure it. I can guarantee you if you ask the crew to make it happen, they will."

"And instead of doing their job, they'll be working on giving themselves a party?"

"Some people don't even have running water or toilets in their rooms." I assumed if it was true for me, it must be for others.

Instead of answering me, Captain Haugen and Peter stood, ready to move on with their day and effectively shutting down the rest of my questions.

CHAPTER TWENTY

Claire—Friday morning: at sea

I awoke with a dreadful feeling flopped in the pit of my stomach. It followed me up to breakfast, where I could only manage a piece of toast and a cup of tea. Unaware of the dreadful things happening on board, everyone around me laughed and smiled, gorging on the overflowing trays of food. The sight made me even queasier.

I dropped my unfinished toast in the bin and headed to the computer lab with a cup of tepid tea, the night before still fresh in my mind.

Frank and I had watched as the ship's security swarmed the area. They completely closed off the lower pool deck, but it took them a few minutes to realize they had an audience watching from above. After that, crew members came around asking everyone to vacate the bar area as well. Before they forced us to leave, I got a good look at the scene. I'd heard someone say they'd closed them off yesterday because the jets no longer worked. One woman said she'd gone in anyway. As long as they were still warm, who needed the jets? She now mentioned she wished she hadn't. I thought that silly. It wasn't like she was bathing with the dead body.

I asked Frank to take a few pictures with his phone. He didn't have the same qualms about technology as I did. I had him email the lot just in case I missed something.

My first heart-stopping thought was that they'd killed Moira, but looking at the pictures on a bigger screen in the computer lab, I could see blond hair. We didn't see the removal of the body, and they hadn't made any announcement regarding the finding of a second dead body.

As a journalist I, of course, thought it atrocious, but Frank had pointed out the need for secrecy to stop a widespread panic. It didn't matter, though. People had seen. Soon everyone would have an opinion about what happened.

"Oh, my goodness," a woman exclaimed behind me. I turned to see that she'd spotted my screen. "Is that the woman they found in the hot tub last night?"

"I heard she drowned," a man to her left chimed in.

I closed the web browser and smiled politely, excusing myself before they tried to suck me into their gossip.

I didn't know who they found in the hot tub, only that it could have nothing to do with Colin Avery's murder. After all, they'd cordoned off those hot tubs for a reason. Maybe they'd found something dangerous and had restricted access for the safety of passengers.

One thing I did know for certain: I needed to find Moira.

She was in the main atrium speaking with an officer in a white uniform. I waited off to the side until she spotted me. Eventually the officer frowned and stalked off.

"What was all that about?" I asked.

She looked around us, like me probably paranoid someone might hear. "They've temporarily promoted me to cruise director."

I blinked a few times. "Why?"

"They found Amy drowned in the aft deck eleven hot tub last night."

Moira—Friday morning: at sea

I pulled Claire through the doors leading outside on deck. To our right lay an expanse of ocean and brewing storm clouds. Hurricane Gert, no doubt, wreaking havoc on the other side of the Caribbean Sea. We sped past the few people brave enough to be out in this wind to the aft of the ship, where I knew we would have privacy.

"Amy wanted me to meet her in the cruise staff office, but she never showed up. At the time, I thought she wanted to speak to me about the dress code, but what if she had something else to tell me?"

"Like what happened to Colin?" Claire asked.

"We assumed already that if she hadn't killed Colin, she was probably involved. I'm not sure how yet, and maybe that's something we'll never find out."

"Have they ruled it murder?"

"Accidental drowning is the official verdict, but they're half-assing the investigation because they don't want it to come back on the company. But after the meeting, Jan told me he found bruising on her arms, like maybe someone pushed her into the hot tub and held her down."

Claire took a seat on a large rope. "Well, if the investigation has gone cold, why would the killer need Amy dead? Killing her just brings more attention to Colin's death. We need to find out what she knew."

"We need to look at it from the point of view of the killer. Let's take Amy out of the equation for a second. Say they killed Colin for money. They lure him on with a contest, then kill him by making it look like a suicide. As far as they know, security isn't looking for them. Why come after us unless they knew we knew something? Which brings us back to how did they find out? I know I didn't tell Amy. I haven't told anyone about our investigation except Kaitlin, but she wouldn't repeat it. And Simon knows, but again, who would he tell?"

"I haven't told anyone either. Well, except..." She paused, and the silence spread. I could hear the wind whipping through the anchor holes in the front of the ship.

"Except who?"

"I told Rick, my editor. I'd hoped he would help me out with some information. And I was standing on the balcony when I had that conversation."

"Which means anyone on a nearby balcony could've overheard."

"Exactly."

"Okay, wait. Let's think about this as plainly as possible. Let's assume the people who know haven't told anyone, because who would they tell? And let's assume we did stray from the tourist area—"

"We know we left the tourist area. All the buildings in the pictures on that pamphlet have roped-off areas so you can't touch the walls. They've cleared the floors of debris and kept them swept. That place felt like a death trap."

"And the sauna. We walked right in. I'm not sure when we left the tourist area or if someone planned it ahead of time. It felt more like we gave the killer an opportunity."

"In order for the murderer to know we were on to them, they would have to have a room close to yours." I smacked Claire on the arm. "They have the room next to Colin's. The door between the two rooms. That's how they got in to get the laptop. You didn't see them in the hallway because they never used the hallway."

"Wasn't it locked?"

"It could've been, from the other side. If this person had the door unlocked here, they could lock it from their side and keep Colin's side open. They never entered the hallway, even to kill him. All they had to do was go back to their room and wait for Colin."

"That doesn't explain Amy. What was she doing in the hallway that night?" said Claire.

"Maybe she doesn't have anything to do with this at all. It looks like she knows Colin, so maybe she went to visit him. He didn't answer the door and she left."

"He could've been dead already."

"But it doesn't explain why Amy drowned in a hot tub." I sat next to Claire on the rope, utterly confused.

"How can we find out who has the room next to Colin's?"

Water sluiced along the ropes. The cover overhead saved us from the light rain that fell. The storm front must be expanding farther than originally thought.

I stood and motioned for Claire to follow me. "I have an idea, but I need to go to my cabin first. Wait for me in the main atrium."

Once I'd zipped down to my cabin, I came up to find that the ship had already found calmer waters. The sun had even poked out, giving us angel fingers in the distance. I found Claire leaning against the wall, and I nodded toward reception.

Maria, in her mid-twenties with a family back in the Philippines, sat behind the desk, with a vacant but pleasant look on her face and the posture of someone appearing attentive.

"Hello, Maria. I'm hoping you can help me." Her face shifted from boredom to excitement to clouded in a few seconds. Maria looked over at her co-worker, also sitting behind a sweeping desk that encompassed the entire middle pillar in the centre of the atrium, and then back at me. "I'm sorry, Moira. I can't help you."

"I just need the name of the man staying in cabin 1025."

She shut her lips and folded her hands on her lap. "I'm not allowed to help you."

"What? I'm not asking for anything out of the ordinary. I have two twenty-minute phone cards with your name on it."

Her sad gaze sank to her lap. "They told me not to help you anymore."

"Who told you that?"

Her colleague, a new face, stood and leaned in to our conversation. "You're on notice. No more favours until we get what we want." She gave me the shoo gesture and stalked back to her station.

I felt my face flood with anger or embarrassment—I couldn't be sure, as I felt both at that moment.

"Come on," said Claire, and I followed her to the other end of the atrium out of sight.

"Well, there goes that plan."

"And what was that?" asked Claire.

"I wanted Maria to call the person down to reception to fix his credit card. But that's not going to work now. I don't understand." I felt betrayed. That was the dominant emotion at that moment. For some reason, they'd shut me out.

Claire walked over to one of the courtesy phones and picked up the receiver. "Do I just dial the number?"

"No, you need to dial 43 first."

She dialled the room number and waited. Then, in the most prim voice I'd ever heard, she said, "Hello, this is Elizabeth from reception. May I please speak to Ms. Chapman?"

"Wrong number." The voice growled so loudly I could hear it from where I stood.

"Oh. And who am I speaking with?"

"You called me, you should know."

Claire rolled her eyes for my benefit. "Is this room 1025?"

"Yeah, but I'm no lady."

"Are you perhaps Mr. Chapman?"

"No."

"Oh. Well, that's a shame, but now things are starting to make sense. We have had some rather large purchases made to this room, except the credit card information does not add up. I believe these charges are on your account. We—"

"My account?" he screamed. "You take them off."

"We apologize for the mix-up, sir. If you come down to reception we can provide a list and remove the erroneous charges."

He slammed the receiver down before Claire could get any further.

She turned and smiled impishly at me. "I believe he's on his way down, whatever his name is. Now. How did you plan for us to get in his room?"

"With this." I pulled out Perlah's access card and hoped desperately it still worked.

We took the elevator up. One of the perks of being cruise director, or at least acting cruise director, was that I now held the rank of an officer and could use the passenger elevators. I knocked at the door. "Room turnover," I called, just in case he hadn't left yet. I waited thirty seconds, and then I slipped the keycard into the reader. We both sighed with relief when a green light appeared.

I shut the door behind us quickly and looked around the messy room. The unmade bed held a pile of clothes as well as a heap of used towels. Glasses and empty plates covered every surface. It looked like he'd holed up in his room since we left port in Florida.

We separated, each taking a section of the room. I went to the couch, a treasure trove of clothes, and lifted them aside to find a knapsack. Inside the first pouch, he'd stashed a Clive Cussler novel, *Inca Gold*, a Dirk Pitt adventure. I'd never read any, but the name sounded familiar. I opened to the middle where a slip of paper kept track of his progress. It was a ticket stub for the excursion we'd gone on yesterday.

"Have you found the laptop yet?" I asked.

"Not yet. But his name's Jack Kerne," Claire called from her side of the room.

I replaced the book in the front and kept digging. No point in letting on that we'd broken into his room. The next flap held some pens and old receipts. I pulled out a couple to see what they were for. Nothing interesting—a Walgreens receipt for sunscreen and Gravol. One for the Clive Cussler novel, and another for Popeyes. I shoved them back in and opened the main section. Deep at the bottom, I found a bunch of pill bottles. One had clear liquid it in.

"You seem to know about medications. What does gamma-hydroxybutyrate do?" I turned to Claire and showed her the bottle of liquid.

Her eyes widened in surprise. "That's also known as GHB, the date rape drug." She took it from me and held it up to the light. "And this definitely wasn't obtained legally. Probably over the internet. Back in the 90s they used it as a diet supplement."

I took the bottle back and replaced it with the pill bottles. He didn't have anything else in the bag, so I hid it under the clothes trying to make it look like it had when we got here. "Do you think that's what killed him?"

"It could be, but we won't ever know for sure. I think our best chance is to find out why he killed Colin. That's where we'll find the evidence."

"And what exactly are we going to do with the evidence? The cruise line won't want any trouble from this. It's easier for them if he committed suicide."

Claire shook her head and sucked her lips in. "I haven't figured that out yet." It seemed to pain her to admit that.

We found Colin's laptop wedged under the mattress, and for the life of me I couldn't understand why he'd tried to hide it. The sign on the outside of his door and the general upheaval of his room told me he hadn't let the cleaning staff in. Had he been expecting us?

The laptop had a password, but a pink Post-it next to the track pad gave us a clue to what it was. I assumed Jack had stuck it there.

We scoured his internet history and confirmed he'd been in Colin's Bitcoin wallet. Neither of us knew enough about this to make much sense of it, but it was all we'd found that could help us decipher what Jack had done and why. I wanted to take the laptop, but Jack would know it was us. Just then we heard the handle of the connecting door jiggle as if someone was having problems opening their door.

We both stared at each other in terror. I pulled Claire toward the balcony.

We scooted behind the blind, ducking out of sight, and waited. For what, I wasn't sure. It had to be Jack. By this point he'd gone down to reception to find no one had called him. Would he notice someone had been in his room? We hadn't messed it up much, not that you could tell. He kept it like a teenage boy expecting his mom to clean it for him. Any second he would find the laptop missing, still tucked under my arm.

I watched from a slit in the balcony curtains, but no one came through the door. Instead we heard a commotion coming from Colin's room, and I peered around to see a shadowed figure searching it—tearing things off the couch and the table, dumping the suitcase. I looked behind us, the balcony to the left leading to the room beside Jack.

I nudged Claire and mimed climbing over to the next balcony.

She leaned in and whispered, "You told me never to climb the balconies."

"Except in life or death situations."

"You never mentioned that part."

"Well, I am now."

I handed her the laptop and swung a leg over. The railing felt rough and sticky from the constant salt the ocean spit up. I stared down at the waves buffeting the ship.

And then, as I put a toe on the balcony next to us, my watch began to beep—an alarm to remind me I needed to get to deck twelve to host the Mr. Hairy Chest contest.

Claire and I both froze, eyes wide. Had he heard that? A second later we heard a scramble and then the door slammed shut.

We waited for over a minute before moving. But nothing moved in Colin's room.

❖

Claire—Friday morning: at sea

"I think he left."

"Do you think he noticed Colin's laptop missing?"

I shrugged.

Moira stood beside me with the laptop clutched to her chest. We'd done it. We'd gotten out of there with the biggest prize of this investigation. Never mind the evidence was now useless because we'd removed it, and Jack could now deny he'd ever taken it. In fact, if anything, we'd set ourselves up for a number of dangerous allegations.

Not to mention, Jack knew we'd taken the laptop and also knew where to find both of us.

For some reason, none of that worried me. I'd won a small victory, and I wanted to enjoy it for the next few seconds before reality bonked me on the head.

I'd known for some time that wherever our investigation led, it wouldn't help to go to the ship authorities. Moira had basically confirmed that earlier. We were on our own for now, until we could find truly damning evidence and take that to the authorities in Florida.

"He knows where your cabin is. You can't stay there."

"I know." I sighed, because I'd figured this out as well. "I know someone who I can stay with. Although I can't say I'm happy about asking him for a favour." The idea of going to Frank made my skin crawl, but I didn't have any other choice. The more pressing issue, though, was to find out what this laptop could tell us.

"Do you know anyone who can help us figure out how to trace what Jack's done on this laptop?" I asked.

"I do. I'm loath to deal with him, but luckily he owes me a favour. Unfortunately, I'm late to host the hairy chest contest." She handed me the laptop. "When you think it's safe, take the laptop and get some stuff out of your room. Don't stick around."

CHAPTER TWENTY-ONE

Moira—Friday afternoon: at sea

I grabbed a mic from the stand behind the stage. The sun, beating hot down on the deck like we hadn't spent the morning in rough seas, had reached its apex. I shrugged off my sweater and dropped it over the stand.

Jamie and Austen already had the crowd ready for some hairy chest action, even though I hadn't scheduled Austen for this event. He waved when he saw me.

I took a deep breath and then turned on the mic and held it up to my mouth. "Who's ready to win some prizes?" Already riled up, the crowd shouted, some hoisting signature drink glasses. I jumped off the stage to mingle with the gathering crowd of men swarming to show off the hair on their chests. Of all the events we did on board, I loathed doing this one. I know I wasn't the target audience, but I still found the idea of flaunting part of your body to win prizes in poor taste. But people loved it for some reason. Probably because half the audience was already half in the bag, and watching blindfolded women run their hands over hairy chests seemed like the best entertainment on offer.

I stepped back to where Austen stood. He leaned over and asked, "You want me to take this over for you? I know it'll be a sacrifice on your part, since it's your favourite and all."

"You deserve a promotion."

He nudged my arm. "Well, not to be morbid, but I heard a spot opened up recently. Maybe put a good word in for me? I'd make a great assistant cruise director." He looked sheepish saying it.

The job opening, of course, all depended on whether I held on to the new position or not. I climbed back onstage while Jamie and Austen took over the duties of choosing the contestants for the show and replaced the mic in its spot.

"You know, I warned you this would happen."

I turned to find Jimmy, his ever-present heavy leather smile pointed toward me. "What would happen?"

"The crew has turned against you. Well," he said, pausing to contemplate the sun and the clouds drifting overhead, "some of the crew. I heard you had a rough go in your cabin."

Wait. My cabin issues were because the crew had a vendetta against me? "They're taking their frustration out on the wrong person. I brought their concerns to the captain and the staff captain, and they didn't care. Jimmy," I leaned against the bulkhead and crossed my arms, "you and I have worked here long enough to know that every single one of us is expendable. They don't give a shit because they know that recruitment office is going to pump out a bunch more suckers next week. This doesn't mean I condone how they treat the crew, but I'm also powerless against it, because I'm like you. I have no power."

He nodded to my name tag, which still said assistant cruise director. "You're cruise director now. You have a lot more say than you think you do."

"Acting cruise director, and not a single department head gives a crap about what I have to say. You're wrong. You have the power. The crew outnumbers the officers like twenty to one. If you wanted to make a statement, you could." I grabbed my sweater and left the heat and cheers of the crowd behind.

Claire—Friday morning: at sea

I found Frank in the casino. Frank has a gambling problem. Not in a terrifying way that I worried he would gamble away all our money. No, Frank's problem has more to do with the fact that he rarely wins. But to his credit, he knows when to stop.

He once said he treats gambling like a fun game he has to pay to play. And I attribute this to Frank's father, Wallace, who first introduced him to gambling when he was about six or seven. Wallace used to play bridge for money. He'd even considered going pro, but then Frank's mother got pregnant and told Wallace he needed to get a real job.

Frank never got the hang of bridge. Instead he liked to play craps and roulette, two games full of chance and very little skill. But the love of games came from an early age.

I heard a cheer go up at one of the craps tables in the back of the casino, full of people, smoke, and noise. There sat Frank, several people collecting winnings from the table. Frank smiled, but I recognized that smile. He'd not won as much as they had. He picked the dice back up, moved some chips to a different position on the board, and rolled the dice again, an optimistic determination slathered all over his face.

I'd only ever gone to a casino once before I met Frank. My father viewed gambling with distaste. He said it wasted money and time, two things he never joked about. In my experience since, I can't blame him for feeling that way. Even as this is the *Summit*'s first voyage, the casino already feels shabby. Dark and dingy with the gaudy carpets and flashing lights. I've never gone to Vegas, nor can I ever see myself going.

Frank shook the dice close to his ear, then with a flick of his wrist, sent them skipping down the table, and again, the group cheered where his face fell. It brightened as soon as he saw me. He collected his chips, wished his fellow players good luck, and strode toward me.

"Ahead?" I asked.

He peered down at his chips, doing the mental calculation. "Not too bad today."

"Can we get out of here? I can't breathe properly."

"No worries, let's head up to the atrium and find a bar." He pointed to a set of stairs hidden behind a row of slot machines that led one floor up to the atrium.

"Why do you have a bag with you?" He'd noticed the smaller carry-on I'd lugged with me.

"Got into a bit of a pickle, and I need a favour, Frank."

"What sort of pickle?"

I decided I'd need a stiff drink to get through this. Before packing my bag, I'd made up my mind to tell Frank the whole story. I needed him on my side, and he'd hardly believe anything normal if I made it up.

We parked ourselves in a café table at the pub much closer to the waves on deck five. The dark clouds brewing in the distance waited, ready to ruin the fun like a parent who'd shown up early to a birthday party. I slipped my bag under the table, and we both ordered a pint of beer.

The pub had a decent selection of beer, unlike the rest of the bars, which carried mostly watered down American beers that tasted more like piss.

As we waited for the first round, I filled Frank in on the basics, and of course his first question nailed me to the wall.

"Does Rick know?"

"Of course. He helped a bit." The problem with sharing things with someone you've lived with for over a decade? They know all your tells and tricks and secrets. Frank knew I couldn't resist a mystery. He also knew I couldn't keep secrets very well, especially from Rick.

"Had you met him before?"

I shook my head and signalled the server for another drink.

"Did you see anyone on the balcony?"

"No, but that doesn't mean he couldn't hear me."

"I'm curious how they'd know what you looked like if they weren't watching and you hadn't bumped into them before. If he did go on the excursion, which you said you took last minute, how did he get on it? That's one hell of a coincidence."

I frowned because I hadn't even thought of that before. We'd assumed he'd heard my conversation, which was how we found Jack in the first place, but what if that had been a massive coincidence as well? After all, he had the room next to Colin's because it had a connecting door which allowed him to slip in without going into the hall.

"Then who tried to kill us?" I explained how we'd examined the site. "Someone purposefully removed the red markers and pushed the stone door in place. Why would someone randomly do that if they weren't trying to get rid of us?"

Frank wiped foam from his stout off his lips with a napkin. "Now, hear me out. I think someone has put out a hit on you."

"That's absurd. Who talks like that?"

"Remember that German businessman using Japanese religious festivals to launder money? Even though the article didn't get published, word got out that you were looking into his business dealings."

"What source are you using for this?"

"A reliable source, Claire. How many times have I told you, how many times has Rick told you? Eventually your recklessness will get you in trouble."

"Wait. Why did you wait until now to tell me this?"

"It never seemed the right time."

"There's always a right time." And then it occurred to me, Frank might be trying to pull one over on me. I sat back, trying to muster a calm I didn't feel.

"It's ridiculous you think someone's trying to kill me."

He set down his drink, agitated. "You literally sat down and told me someone is trying to kill you."

"That's different."

"How?" he practically screamed. "You are on this vacation because you had an 'accident'"—he put the word in finger quotations—"while working on a story trying to expose a man's illegal business dealings. You think that's a coincidence? Rick sent you off to get you out of the way, let it cool off. But you gave your story to someone else to work on because you're insane, and now you're surprised they want to take you out? Your story could put him in prison for a very long time, not to mention shut down his business, and you don't think that someone who does illegal things on the regular is willing to have you killed? You're delusional." He took a deep gulp of his stout, finishing it off.

"Take me out? Where do you come up with this stuff?"

Could Frank have it right, though? Either way, someone wanted me dead, maybe several someones. The difference, though, if Jack didn't know Moira and I, specifically, were on to him, then I didn't need to ask Frank to stay in his room. I would, however, have to watch myself in the next port. No doubt, if the German had hired someone, they would know the ship's itinerary and know that we docked in Belize first thing tomorrow.

At no point did I feel sorry for handing the story off. This man deserved to go to prison, especially if he intended to kill me. The only thing I did find myself regretting was bringing Moira into this. I hadn't at the time thought it would get dangerous. I sighed inwardly at myself because this sort of thinking was why Rick had sent me here in the first place. My father used to call me reactionary. Impulsive too. And I am all those things.

Frank signalled the waiter. "I'll pay for the lot." He pointed to my drinks and his, had his card swiped, and stood, giving me a stare I couldn't interpret. "You know, this is the first time I'm happy things ended between us. I don't think I could stand by and watch you...well." He pocketed his card and turned and left without a backward glance.

I took a swig of my pint but replaced the glass on the table, pushing it away. It tasted bitter. I don't know why that should sting. Perhaps I thought if Frank still wanted me, I wasn't all the bad things I thought about myself?

Moira—Friday afternoon: at sea

I found Bandini in the crew bar surrounded by smoke. Not his, but a group of crew members crowded around him. Groupies? Did magicians have groupies? I stood back listening, not eavesdropping on purpose, but I couldn't help but overhear. At this time of day, devoid of the sounds and smells of off-duty crew, it echoed with stale smoke and stray conversations.

"Stay away from gold right now. You'll never get the returns you want." The fake Italian had disappeared, replaced by something much more Midwest American. Word had spread that Bandini knew a thing or two about money, what to invest in and whatnot, and he didn't mind sharing his advice.

Watching him hold an audience gave the impression that he

craved one even without the stage or auditorium. As soon as he spotted me, he waved off the other crew members, like some mob boss in one of those old Italian restaurants in American movies.

He uncrossed his legs and sat forward, taking a sip of coffee, the chip on the side of his mug telling me he'd gotten it from the mess. He put it back on the knee-high table. "Moira, right?"

I nodded and took a seat across from him. His cologne cut through the lingering smoke, musky and strong. I crinkled my nose. His black pants and turquoise polo screamed expensive, since they fit like a glove and didn't have any logos on them.

I placed the laptop on the table between us. "What do you know about Bitcoin wallets?"

He leaned back and stretched his arm along the back cushion of his seat. "Why do you want to know about Bitcoin wallets?"

"Hmm." I nodded, grabbed my laptop and started to stand up.

I got two tables away before he asked, "Is it your wallet or someone else's?"

I turned. "Does that change the answer?"

"No, I'm curious."

"Well, then it shouldn't matter if the wallet belongs to me or not."

He shrugged and held out his hand for the laptop, beckoning with two fingers impatiently. "Let's have a look, then."

"Bandini—"

"It's Chuck." He opened the computer and navigated through the open web tabs.

"Chuck?"

"Bandini the Great fills the seats better than Chuck Baxter."

"Understood."

"As soon as I changed my name and adopted the accent..." He paused, then added with a wry smile, "Yours of course is better."

"Mine's real."

"Sounds it, too. Well, let's say I stopped having to do kids' birthday parties and started getting invited to the big boys' table."

"That's an image." I didn't think doing magic shows on cruise ships equalled the big boys' table, but then anything would beat doing kids' birthdays.

I watched as he frowned at the computer screen. Not as young as I'd thought. In the harsh daylights of the crew bar, visible lines appeared on his forehead and the corners of his eyes.

After a few minutes, without looking up, he picked up his empty coffee mug and wiggled it at me. I snatched it from his hand, loath to gopher for him, but if he gave us something useful, it justified the degradation.

I stomped off to the crew mess, not realizing my mistake at the time. I headed to the coffee dispensers and found my way blocked by a large man in a white uniform. "I'm sorry, miss, we closed the coffee station after lunch."

"Since when?"

"Since now. We need to refill them."

I tilted my head sideways and sighed. Jimmy had warned me the crew had turned. I spun around and exited. I knew where to find coffee at any hour, and in places I wouldn't get turned away. It meant a longer trek, though.

By the time I returned, Chuck still had his head buried in the laptop screen. I set his coffee on the table and took a sip of mine. I felt less like a servant getting myself one as well.

"What have you found?"

He blinked a couple of times, then sat up, crossing one leg over the other and cradling his coffee in his lap. "Well. I would guess that whoever owned this laptop doesn't have it in their possession anymore. And whoever took it transferred five hundred million dollars in Bitcoin to a numbered account in Belize."

I almost spilled my coffee. "Belize?"

"Belize City, more specifically."

"All of it?"

"So you know there was five hundred million in Bitcoin in that account?"

"I had a guess."

We both sipped our coffees, eyeing each other.

A group of servers on a lunch break crowded into the bar, taking a seat a few tables down, cigarettes already in hand and lit by the time they scraped their chairs around the small tables.

"I found a few interesting emails as well."

I raised my eyebrows. Maybe I shouldn't have left him alone with the laptop. Would he choose not to share everything?

"What kind of emails?"

"What are you planning to do with five hundred million dollars?"

I set my coffee on the table in front of me. "I don't give two craps about the money. I want to find evidence against the person who transferred the money to the bank."

He sat staring at me for several minutes, sipping his coffee. Occasionally, he glanced over at the other table when they laughed at something, their voices large in the small, smoke-filled room. I didn't know what he expected of me, so I sat watching him back.

"Okay. Whoever transferred the funds was smart enough to use a bank no outside government could request any information from that might identify the individual account holder. But they left a trail. There's an email exchange between the individual and the bank. A lot of people assume a numbered account makes you anonymous, and it does to an outside source, but the bank still needs to know who you are. Belize in particular has a rigorous screening process. They need to know the funds you're depositing were lawfully gained. Bitcoin makes that difficult. It appears, however, that hurdle was conquered by your individual. But he has to go into the bank to get a bank card and produce valid ID to do so, and he's arranged to do that tomorrow at eleven."

"What kind of ID?"

"Usually a passport and government-issued photo ID."

"But all our passports are held with the ship's pursuer."

Chuck shrugged. "He'd have to have first-class fake IDs to fool bank officials."

"Would they even care?"

"You'd be surprised."

"What was the name used on the email?" she asked.

"Jack Kerne."

"So he is using a fake ID."

"Or more likely he gave the cruise line a fake passport. Easier to fool."

"All the passports go through customs agents."

Chuck laughed. "You think they're scrutinizing each one? They don't care about these Americans trailing through their souvenir shops."

At that moment, I felt exhausted. I didn't know what to believe. "Are the emails enough to implicate this guy?"

"Nah, it's all circumstantial."

Which would mean we'd need to find something else to prove he killed Colin.

"How do you know so much about all this?"

"I don't plan on performing for the rest of my life. I have retirement plans that a magician's salary won't fulfill."

"Why do it if you don't love it?"

"Oh, I didn't say I didn't love it." He paused for a moment, then said, "I grew up with those puzzle boxes as a child and became fascinated with magic contraptions. Sadly, it barely pays the bills, so I diversified." He spread his arms as if highlighting our surroundings. The dingy bar, already stale after a few weeks, could hardly sit in as anyone's ideal.

"What are you going to do now?" he asked.

"I don't know."

"Chances are, he gets that bank card, you won't see him again. He'll disappear with a fortune."

I accepted the laptop back and stood. I needed to find Claire and fill her in. As I left, Chuck called, "If you need help, let me know." For some reason, that offer didn't seem entirely genuine.

Chapter Twenty-Two

Claire—Friday afternoon: at sea

Moira found me at a bar aptly named the Crow's Nest on the very top deck of the ship. I'd moved from the pub, still with my bag next to me on the floor, to this out-of-the-way spot. A strategic glass wall stopped the wind from blowing the few of us brave enough to drink here into the sea. I liked the view and the feeling of overlooking everything as I sipped my very expensive vodka tonic.

I still didn't know whether to believe Frank or not. On one hand, I doubted he'd lie about this, although he might have gotten a few things mixed up. The question I kept asking myself was did I trust Frank. It had taken me two vodka tonics to realize that no, I didn't. That's why I'd divorced him. But I also didn't think he'd lie about something so serious. This felt like a good place to hide until I figured out what to do.

"How'd you find me?" I asked when Moira spotted me.

"I bumped into Frank. He said to try the most out-of-the-way bar on the ship."

I might not trust him, but we knew each other well enough after over a decade of marriage. I spread my hands as if to say, "Here I am." A slightly dysfunctional, almost middle-aged woman with a few bad habits that might get people killed.

Moira slid into the seat across from me, waved over the server, and ordered a drink.

I leaned forward. "Are you allowed to do that?" She gave me

a slightly affronted look. "I didn't mean that in a rude way," I said. "You mentioned you couldn't use the elevators, so…"

Moira smiled, and for a second I forgot everything I'd come up here to drink about. "As long as the bar isn't busy, and I have my name tag on, I can. As cruise staff, I'd never drink during working hours, but as the cruise director, it's almost expected." She checked her watch. "And it's just come five, so I don't feel bad."

Far-off whitecaps dotted the horizon. I knew enough about sailing to know those meant waves. Not the calm, undulating waves we'd experienced in the relative calmness of the Caribbean Sea. If we could see them this far off, they must be giant.

I closed the notebook I'd written a few ideas in while I sat contemplating my next move. Moira nodded toward it. "Did you always want to become a writer?"

"I didn't really have a choice. My family's full of them. My mother wrote fiction. Important stories, now that I look back on it. Books for housewives, my dad used to say. They reflect a certain life that no one talked about, and I guess we should've seen it for the cry for help it was. She wrote about women who felt stuck in life.

"My dad's first book won the Author's Club Best First Book award, and as always happens with men, they turn a small success into the world's greatest accomplishment. Even though he didn't do much else after that, and most of his books got mediocre reviews, he made it appear like he'd won a Pulitzer.

"I used to spend my summers in the country with my aunt, who's also a writer. She's the real reason I think I became one. She truly loved all aspects of writing, even the editing. She used to say it lets you step back and see the piece as a whole. You can't do that when you're still in the middle, writing.

"I remember spending most of my summers roaming the English countryside, finding shady trees and reading. I miss the simplicity of it sometimes."

A server brought Moira a bright orange cocktail with a splash of red running through it. "Your Malibu Sunset."

She smiled at the server but picked the drink up and turned it around as if looking for something hidden in it.

"Anything wrong?"

She shook her head and took a sip. "When you're working on your stories, do you ever worry you've not done enough?"

"Sometimes. Why?"

"No reason."

"You know, when we first started this…investigation, you had serious reservations. Now you're full in."

Moira shrugged. "I don't know. It's more fun than I thought— minus the almost dying thing." She twirled her glass around. "I like outsmarting people. Not the best quality to admit to, but true." She waved at the ship. "Most of this comes with a lot of baggage. We work long hours for very little money. When higher-ups try to take it, I tend to fight back the only way I know how."

"How did you end up working on ships?"

The last of the other patrons got up, leaving us the only people there. Moira picked the umbrella out of her drink and closed it, aligning it on the table with her napkin. "I grew up doing this. My dad wanted me to take over for him running a hotel on the coast of Sanremo. He even called when he retired, hoping I would come home. I didn't want to get stuck reliving my parents' lives, but I essentially did. I have no life, and instead of a hotel on the coast, mine floats."

"What about siblings? Couldn't they have taken over?"

"My sister Viola went her own way from the start, refusing to even work at the hotel as a kid. While I got stuck delivering towels and cleaning rooms and helping guests find the nearest gelato place, my sister was off living her life. It's hard being around her. Every time we talk about our lives, I feel like I haven't moved past my early twenties."

"I'm sometimes glad I didn't have siblings. No one to compare myself to. It's hard when you have different choices. But I think you've sold yourself short."

"I've tried to quit several times now, and every time I do, I get a promotion. It makes it harder to leave."

"Maybe you can't leave because you're so good at what you do? When you're onstage, I can't take my eyes off you."

She smirked. "I doubt others have the same thoughts you do."

"I wouldn't be so sure about that. But it goes beyond the fact you're gorgeous. You have a presence that people want to be near."

Moira's cheeks reddened. "Thank you for saying that." She said it like she didn't truly believe me. "I've always felt I could do good things. I cater to frivolous people. My life has no meaning. What you do changes people's lives."

"Or gets them killed." I didn't know if I'd tell Moira about Frank's theory that the person who tried to trap us might be a German businessman from an earlier story I'd worked on. I had my opportunity at that moment. In retrospect, I should have told her then. Things would've gone a lot better for both of us if I had. But I still felt I had, if not infinite choices, enough that I could hold on to that information a little longer.

"I had someone take a look at the laptop. How did you know his name was Jack Kerne?" asked Moira.

"I found his passport in the safe. Which means either the ship has a fake one or that's fake."

"The guy I talked to said that one's probably real. We can easily find out what name he's using on the ship. The other thing I found out, Jack transferred all of Colin's Bitcoin out of the account to a bank account in Belize. My guy thinks as soon as the ship docks, Jack will get off and disappear with the money."

"So we have less than twelve hours to figure out how to either keep him on the ship or—"

"Steal his passport. No passport, no ID, no bank card. Plus he'll have to come back on the ship or else get stuck in Belize without a passport."

"But how do we do that? He won't fall for the billing scam again."

Moira took a sip of her Malibu Sunset while gazing out at the pool deck below. "We could send him up a gift package with a free entry to tonight's blackjack tournament. We couldn't be certain he'd use it, but it would give us a chance." The phone on Moira's hip began to buzz. She had two clipped to her waist. Before answering it, she flipped it over to check a label on the back that said "Ass. C. Dir."

"Hello?" I watched as she listened to the person on the other end, then asked, "Where is she now? Okay, I'll come down shortly. I'm just wrapping up something."

She hung up and slipped it back on her belt, still frowning.

"Is everything okay?"

"That was someone from housekeeping. They've asked me to come down and speak with Perlah, the woman who found Colin. Jack has accused her of stealing his laptop."

"Why do they want you to go down?"

"I'm crew welfare ambassador. They want me to comfort her. This is a firing offence."

"She doesn't get any recourse? They can just fire her?"

"Yes. Her keycard was used to enter Jack's room right before he reported it missing."

"The keycard we used."

"Correct. Incidentally, they've disabled that card, so if we do get Jack out of his room tonight, we'll have to find another way in."

"What's going to happen to Perlah?"

"She obviously didn't use the card. I'll instruct her to tell them she lost it, and hopefully she'll be able to prove she's been using a different card to get into the rooms to clean. I'll sort it out either way. I'm not going to let her get fired because of something we did."

I nodded, breathing a little easier as the recklessness of what we'd done slammed home. For the first time I actually thought Rick might be right. I rarely thought through all the implications of my actions.

Moira—Friday afternoon: at sea

It didn't take long to clear Perlah's name by pointing out the inconsistencies in their logic. It helped that they had her on camera in the main crew corridor when the supposed theft took place.

Going head to head with Nigel and Peter felt good, but of course they didn't offer Perlah an apology. I suspected Nigel still assumed she'd done it, or at least that she'd done something wrong. He assumed the worst in everyone. Which meant he must have gotten extreme pressure from the head office to declare Colin's death a suicide and Amy's an accident. And I bet if he had any decent proof, he would pursue it himself. But as Chuck had mentioned, all we had was circumstantial evidence. And stolen property.

The most interesting bit of information to come out of this was that Jack didn't suspect us of stealing his laptop. What if he didn't know anyone had figured out he'd killed Colin? Then who had tried to kill us in Cozumel? I didn't believe that was an accident.

That mystery would have to wait. I entered the casino from the spiral staircase leading from the main atrium into the cacophony of sound and lights. It was more packed than usual, but I steered my way through the crowded tables until I reached an office hidden in a panel of mirrors. I rang a discreet doorbell and waited.

Behind me a woman and man cheered at the sound of a winning slot machine. Before I could turn to see, the door opened and Marlise, the casino manager, stood in front of me. She smirked at the celebrating couple. "Doesn't matter if they win five dollars or a thousand, you'd think they won a million."

She led me down a narrow hallway to an office with three desks each pushed up to a wall. The other two sat empty, cleared of any paper or personal effects. The one on the far wall lay scattered with several manuals and three skinny monitors, one full of cameras showing the casino floor.

She saw me look. "I know they have security watching them like a hawk, but I've always liked to keep an eye on my own floor."

I always imagined if Marlise had lived in 1940s Vegas, she would've scared mob bosses into submission. You didn't bet against Marlise because she always won. Petite and occasionally demure, she had a no-nonsense attitude that came with extreme confidence in her abilities.

"Do you have any room left in the blackjack tournament tonight?"

"Of course. I love stragglers."

"Do you have a free entry ticket?"

She tilted her head. "Did you already grab all the bingo prizes?"

"It's not for bingo. I have a VIP guest that hasn't really gotten out and joined in."

"And you think getting them to come lose at blackjack will make them feel like joining in more?"

"A free entry ticket means he won't spend his own money, but it gets him out. Maybe he'll have fun?"

"Maybe he'll buy in for another round? Which is why we give out free tickets."

"Don't you ever feel guilty? Tricking people to spend more money than they should?" They design every aspect of a casino, down to the hideous carpets to the mirrors on the walls, to manipulate you in some way. Somehow I didn't think that bothered Marlise.

She opened a drawer and pulled out a bunch of tournament tickets. "If you don't know that chances are against you when you come into a casino, you're stupid, and we deserve to take your money."

I juggled that in my brain for a second. "Harsh."

She pulled a free ticket from the bunch. "Maybe we should put a disclaimer on the entrance? 'Let the money-burning ceremony commence.'" She handed me the ticket and smirked again. "I mean, we could, and they'd still think they could win. You know how many conversations I overhear about the odds of roulette and how you have to play both black and red at the same time? People are idiots. Everything is luck, mostly our luck."

"Doesn't make it luck then, does it?"

I noticed one of the cameras on Marlise's screen pointed to the forward observation deck instead of the casino. I pointed it out, and she said, "Oh, a glitch. They haven't fixed the system yet, so I can recall most, not all, of the cameras on ship. For the size of this ship, that's not many."

"I heard they have someone coming in on embark day to sort that out. Some of the wiring didn't get threaded properly. Hey," I added, getting a thought. "Can you access the passenger list system?"

"Of course."

"Can you look up to see who has cabin 1025?"

Marlise took a seat and swivelled to face her bank of screens. "Let me see here." She brought up a program with a search bar and entered the room number. Jack's picture, name—he was going by Miller on board—and latest purchases popped up on screen. "Looks like you've made a smart choice offering him a free ticket into the tournament."

"Why?"

She pointed to a string of purchases. "He joined us last night for several hours and spent a considerable amount on chips."

"Did he win?"

"It doesn't show a chip buyback, so my guess is no. It's unlikely they hold on to them to use another day. Oh, and he came in on the first sea day as well. Didn't spend as much, just a few hundred, but yesterday's loss was close to ten thousand."

"Ten thousand? That's a hell of a lot of money to lose on vacation."

Marlise shook her head. "Not for casinos. The wives come for the beaches, massages, and cocktails. The husbands come to gamble. I used to work for a company that had several cruise ships in Asia. They cater to people exclusively on board to gamble, and some will lose millions in a week. Nine thousand and some change wouldn't make a dent in most of those men's pocketbooks."

Good Lord. I couldn't imagine losing a hundred dollars, let alone a thousand. I realized this might offer a better motive than simply money. What if Jack had a gambling problem with heavy debts? Many would kill for five hundred million dollars, but what if Jack's life depended on it? That didn't excuse murder, but went further into explaining why someone would kill.

"Well, this is interesting."

"What?"

"Amy Dabrowski used her comp tickets for Jack Miller's adjoining room. Jack Miller put his credit card down for Colin Avery's cabin next door, but Mr. Avery hasn't purchased anything since the first day."

I wasn't sure if that clarified or confused things more. I thought fast. "You heard about the suicide victim?"

"That was Avery?"

I nodded.

"Does this have something to do with that?"

"I thought it might be a nice gesture considering he knew the victim."

"I guess everyone has their own way of grieving. Mr. Miller likes to drown his sorrows in expensive gifts. He's bought some jewelry and other expensive items from the gift shops in the last few days."

❖

Claire—Friday afternoon: at sea

"That makes sense. If he's using a fake identity with a fake credit card, why not max it out before disappearing into the streets of Belize City?"

Moira and I stood in the atrium watching as the gift basket she'd spent the last hour putting together made its way up the glass elevator to Jack's room. With this new information, it seemed likely he would take the bait.

In ten minutes, Moira would start hosting the singalong in the pub, which gave us both a good reason to stake out the atrium elevators. From my table in the atrium patio and Moira near the entrance, we could see all four glass elevators leading to the casino. He could take a different route, but this was the most direct. If we didn't see him arrive, I could always pop down to the casino and try to spot him that way. Once he was out of his room, the plan was for me to go in and take his real passport from the safe. This, we hoped, would have a twofold outcome. One, he would reboard the ship at Belize since he wouldn't have a passport to escape, and two, he wouldn't have necessary ID to confirm his identity and take possession of a bank card for his numbered account.

It might all come to naught, but at least we had a working plan.

The tournament started at the same time as the pub singalong. In five minutes, we'd know if this would work. I looked back at Moira, speaking with a tall cruise staff member with a blond bob and someone setting up a microphone.

Apparently, the pub singalong was an Amy thing. She liked to sing and could play guitar. Moira could do neither, so she'd recruited someone from her staff who could.

"Hi, I'm Jamie, from Canada," she said into the mic. "Can everyone hear me?" She looked toward the rear outside patio for confirmation. "We're going to start in a few minutes, so now's the time to order a pint, find a good seat, and warm up your vocal cords." A small cheer rose up from a table right in front. One of the group shouted, "We love you, Jamie."

"Oh, look at this, you already have fans." Moira leaned into the mic. "They haven't heard you sing yet."

Jamie laughed. "They're lucky you didn't decide to sing for them." The gathering crowd cheered, entertained by the light teasing between Moira and Jamie. They worked well together, and even if I hadn't known they'd worked together on other ships, I could have guessed by the easy back and forth between the two.

Jamie pulled out an acoustic guitar and began to tune it, the noise and laughter pulling people in from the atrium. I might not have had the best seat to see the performance, but I had an unobstructed view of the elevators.

It also allowed me a great spot to observe the goings-on of the ship. I used to love to find a spot at a café back home and watch the interactions between people on the street and in the shops. Especially when people didn't know someone was watching.

I checked my watch. Five minutes before both events started. The one downside to sitting there was that while Jack might be visible, so was I. Would he recognize me as he came down the elevator? I had a suspicion that if I saw him, if he took the bait, then Frank was right. He hadn't clued in that someone had figured him out. On the other hand, it meant that Emil Fuchs had hired someone to kill me. This presented a larger problem I couldn't walk away from at the end of the cruise.

Not for the first time since this started, I questioned my driving need to always get to the bottom of a mystery.

I turned to see one of the technicians hand Moira a mic. She smiled at something they said. One of her real smiles; her face lit up, her eyes sparkled, and it made you feel like you'd achieved something great to witness that smile. My heart tugged a little because I knew why I'd ended up so far down the rabbit hole. I'd followed that smile.

At the same time as Moira introduced herself, still using her assistant cruise director title, I spotted Jack in one of the glass elevators. I swivelled in my seat to hide in case he did recognize me.

As soon as he disappeared below the atrium level, I got up and headed toward the stairs. The first part of our plan had worked, although now that Perlah's missing card had gotten scrubbed, we couldn't easily gain access to Jack's room. I'd told Moira I had an idea for that, and it would work out. In fact, my plan probably could've used some more thought as I found myself back in my cabin balcony, looking at the sizeable waves pummelling the ship.

Sitting in the pub amidships, it hadn't felt as rocky as deck ten forward did. I took a deep breath and swung a leg over the side, holding tight to the rail. I'd done this before. Of course, the ship hadn't felt so wobbly at the time. I'd changed into sensible trainers and pants. The wind whipped at my jumper, and for a brief second my heart leapt out of my chest and my stomach somersaulted overboard. I held tight to the rail and waited for the feeling to pass before swinging my other leg over.

I kept an eye on the nearby balconies. I didn't want anyone watching. Which in retrospect wouldn't work so well in my favour. What if I fell in? There would be no one to sound the alarm *if* I survived falling from this height. Regular people might stop and rethink at that moment, but if I didn't do this, Jack would get off the ship tomorrow and walk away with five hundred million dollars of Colin's money. He didn't deserve to get away with murder.

Once I reached Colin's balcony, I swung my leg and clambered over as fast as I could, breathing deeply. I entered his room and tried the side door but found it locked. I turned back toward the balcony, the night sky hiding the height of the waves. I had a chance right now. I could leave out Colin's door and no one would know. I could take the elevator back down to the pub and enjoy the rest of the show.

I placed my hand on the balcony and stared out at the abyss. Far in the distance I saw the lights of another ship gleaming off the water, and it reminded me of that Dionne Warwick song, "Two Ships Passing in the Night." And that made me think of Moira. What would happen when the cruise ended? Would we each go our separate ways, or would this become something more? Did I want it to?

I couldn't imagine a world in which our lives made sense. Even if she did quit ships like she wanted, surely she'd go back to Italy.

Laughter came from the hallway, and I refocused my attention. I only had a finite amount of time. Neither of us knew if Jack was any good at blackjack. What if he lost the first few games and was out of the tournament? He'd likely come back here, which put me on a timer.

I took a deep breath and scrambled over the side of the balcony, holding on to the edge with stiff fingers. Two things happened before I could stop them. My leading foot hit a slick spot and slid out from under me. At the same time, the ship dipped like finding a pothole in the ocean. As a result, both feet slipped from the rail, and with a cry, I found myself hanging by my hands from a balcony rail not my own ten decks up.

Wind rushed through my hair, tangling with my legs, a testament to how much faster we were going than earlier in the day. I made the mistake of looking down, the drop a dizzying sight while midnight waves spurred us on.

I could smell the hurricane—the one on everyone's lips today— barrelling toward us. The spray from below tasted salty and left my skin sticky.

I bit my lip and pulled, willing all those missed gym sessions with my trainer to magically have strengthened my arms in the last few seconds. It didn't matter. No amount of training could've pulled me up. For a second, I wondered if I could drop to the balcony below, but I didn't think I'd drop at the right angle. I pictured my body smacking the side and spinning like a pinwheel as I plummeted into the ocean.

Instead, I tried to hook my leg back onto the ledge and give myself some leverage. The first few times I tried, I missed, and with each try, my fingers lost strength.

Tears gathered in the corners of my eyes as panic invaded my mind. I started to worry I might actually fall. Of all the strange life and death situations I'd found myself in the last few months, for some reason this one felt the most personal. The most real. I'd put myself here. I had no one to blame but myself. No outside force had willed me onto this balcony. If anything, Moira and the other crew had warned me off.

This was dangerous.

And for the first time in my life, that sank in. All my truly insane decisions flooded back, and I could finally see through Rick and Frank's eyes. I put myself in these situations, then brushed them off as nothing. But I could so easily slip into the ocean and no one would know where I'd gone. They'd report me missing and eventually dead, but no one would know for certain what happened to me. I took some solace in the fact that they wouldn't know the stupid decision that got me killed.

For one brief moment, I let all that self-doubt and hate in. Then I took a deep breath, shook it off, and worked my left foot onto the ledge. I wedged it under the glass panel and pulled with everything I had until I'd righted myself. I leaned over and let my muscles take a moment. Then I inched toward Jack's balcony, swung my leg over, and collapsed into his room.

Moira—Friday evening: at sea

Sitting in Amy's chair in the cruise staff office felt strange. Any second I expected her to enter and give me that stern look she used to communicate a novel of disapproval.

The office usually swarmed with cruise staff, but it sat silent as I woke the computer from sleep and typed in the cruise director's admin password. The generic background with the cruise line's logo popped up and I opened Outlook to complete the least fun part of this job, responding to head office requests and complaints.

The first email, from IT ashore, prompted me to change my password and not share it with anyone else. I decided that could wait. I checked to see if any of the items in the inbox were urgent. Next week we had several new entertainers coming aboard on embark day. A new comedian and magician would sign on. We also had a B-list band from the 70s signing on tomorrow for the next month. I'd never heard of them but clicked on the YouTube link provided and immediately shut it down again as a poor man's ABBA began some wretched disco theme.

I opened a web browser, navigated to Gmail in order to check my personal email, and found it still signed into Amy's. I didn't mean to pry into her private life but couldn't help notice more than half of them came from dating sites. How morbid and disrespectful to be snooping through a dead person's correspondence, although I supposed history books would've been very different if people respected the privacy of the dead.

I was about to sign out when I noticed an email from a Jack

Miller, Jack Kerne's on-board alias, near the bottom of the page. I clicked on it and saw twenty more. I scrolled back and read through them, discovering Amy had unwittingly given Jack the idea to kill Colin on board because the cruise line had failed to get the cameras and other safety features ready before the first sailing. I had no doubt that she felt she was innocently griping with someone who she assumed had taken a liking to her but in reality had used her to get on board with Colin, who he said was his nephew.

I couldn't be certain if they were really related, the way lies seemed to come so easily to Jack. I had a fairly good picture of the lead-up to Colin's murder.

Jack had randomly met Amy on a dating app and, through their correspondence, come up with the idea that killing Colin would be easier on a ship with more than half its cameras not working. Amy even described a similar incident. Looking through the emails, it appeared Jack was really interested in Amy. But I doubt that was true in the end. He used her to get free tickets as her guest and then lied saying he wouldn't be able to make it. A ship this size, he probably thought he could avoid her, kill Colin, and steal the Bitcoin, and with Amy unaware he was on board, there would be no one to connect him to Colin. When Amy learned by accident that Jack had come and brought Colin, she was understandably furious. Jack must have thought she was too much of a liability to keep around and killed her.

I forwarded all the emails to my personal account. We could use this. It might not equal hard evidence, but at least it helped create a narrative of possibilities.

I checked my crew ambassador email next and found hundreds of the same emails I'd gotten all week. Water and sewage issues with crew cabins, as well as issues in the crew mess. An electrical fire had forced them to close it, and now we only had one mess because the officers had refused to open theirs to crew members.

I forwarded some of the more alarming cabin issues to maintenance and marked them urgent. And then I sent a scathing email to Peter telling him he had to either fix the crew mess issue before breakfast or open the officer mess. I explained how dire the situation was and informed him the crew would take drastic measures if this didn't get resolved. I also mentioned my earlier conversations with him to reiterate how many times I'd brought it up. Now I had it in writing, so if anything went wrong, it wouldn't be my butt on the line.

Before I logged off, a new email notification dinged. It was from Dean, a former cruise staffer who'd transferred to head office to stay close to his family living in Miami. He'd attached a news article about finding James the Magnificent dead in his apartment. Cause of death was unknown, but they suspected a heart attack. It would explain Bandini's last-minute hire.

Poor James. He'd already worked a lifetime by the time I joined ships. I'd worked with him on my very first contract, and he'd given me a good piece of advice: "Don't worry if the guests are having a good time or not. Make sure you're having fun, and everything else will follow."

That explains my longevity in this job. Even if I claim I'm going to quit, I'm still having fun. The promotions help, but that doesn't make up for the long hours, crappy pay, bad food, cramped quarters, and entitled guests. And then I'll stop on the top deck after finishing a game of pool volleyball, my skin warmed by the bright sun, the sea a blue spectacle laid before me, and realize if I quit, I'd end up in a dark, gloomy office somewhere.

I logged out and checked the clock on the wall. Half past eleven. Was that too late to call Claire? I decided to risk it. I needed to know if she'd gotten into Jack's room and stolen his passport.

Claire—Friday evening: at sea

I didn't feel safe in my cabin after I'd broken in and stolen Jack's passport. I also felt shaken after dangling along the side of the ship. The pub singalong had ended and passengers dispersed to other bars around the ship.

I wanted to get in touch with Moira. We needed to work out a plan for tomorrow, but I had no idea how to contact her, so I left a message at reception.

A wave of exhaustion hit as I took a seat in the champagne bar off the theatre. The shows had ended and now the bar sat empty except for me, the staff, and a cozy couple in the corner.

Stepping in felt like time-travelling to the 1930s with its lavish art deco style. I got the impression the cruise company wanted you also to feel expensive when you walked in. The space gave you permission to indulge your more extravagant tastes.

At one end a bar wrapped around a large glass case holding hundreds of champagne bottles, the space also host to several low tables with wide chairs you could sink into. One wall had floor to ceiling windows overlooking the casino below, like a crow's nest where patrons could watch other people lose piles of money.

"As I understand it, you and Moira need a little help."

"Excuse me?" I turned to find a blond man with tight curls gripping his scalp like vines climbing a building. He smiled with his teeth and took a seat opposite without asking.

"Moira told me you needed help tomorrow."

I suspected I'd encountered Bandini the Great. The one Moira had gotten help from with Jack's laptop. I doubted she'd asked him for help without telling me. Five hundred million would draw a lot of people in, so I couldn't fault him for trying.

He called over the server and ordered a glass of champagne, apparently the only thing they served. I refrained from ordering anything, claiming I still hadn't decided. I didn't want to give this man an edge. He radiated danger the same way plutonium-238 radiates heat. I leaned back and used a tactic that had worked well for me over the years: Let them do the talking. "What did she tell you?"

"Well, there is a gentleman who has transferred stolen funds from a Bitcoin account to a numbered account in Belize, and you'd like to stop him from getting access to those funds."

"She told you all that?"

"Mostly."

"And what do you get out of helping us?"

Moira walked in the second I asked that question.

"Chuck, what a surprise. I had a feeling you'd come sniffing around."

He leaned back in the opulent chair and smiled for Moira.

"Come now, you can't expect me to hear about five hundred million dollars sitting in a bank begging me to take a piece of it and walk away?"

"The money doesn't belong to us and has nothing to do with what—"

"Then let me have the money, and I'll help in whatever way you want."

I leaned forward and flicked his knee so he'd turn to me. "That money doesn't belong to any of us. It should go to Colin's family."

She planted herself in the third chair so that we formed a triangle. "Chuck, this has nothing to do with you."

"But it could if you'd bring me in." He took a sip of his champagne, the rings on his fingers glinting in the overhead lights.

"What do we need your help for?" asked Moira. "We've already arranged it so that he won't have enough ID to claim the account, and if he leaves the ship, he'll have to return or risk getting stranded."

He smirked. "What did you do? Break into his cabin and steal his passport? How do you know he doesn't have other forms of ID? Even if he doesn't have a passport, five hundred million can buy you anything you want. This isn't something you want to leave to guesswork." He leaned forward. "This guy gets off the ship tomorrow, he's not coming back. I'm not sure exactly why you care if he comes back on board, but I know your plan has massive holes in it. You've never needed me more, ladies."

"He killed someone for that money," said Moira. "We want him charged."

Bandini laughed with great joy, as if we'd shared a delightful story with him. "You can't be serious. And you're what? Playing detective?"

"That money belongs to his family," I said.

"No, it belongs to whoever controls that bank account. And if we play our cards right, it could belong to all of us."

"And what is your plan?" I said. The best way to deal with Bandini was to play along.

Moira shook her head, possibly regretting going to Bandini in the first place.

"What if I could guarantee he would serve time in a Belize jail while we all walk away set for life? Hear me out." He signalled for the server and proceeded to order a round for all of us. Moira got a call at that moment and stood up to take it outside.

By the time Bandini finished talking, I thought I might be going crazy because it didn't sound half bad.

Chapter Twenty-Three

Moira—Saturday morning: Belize City, Belize

It felt so good watching Jack getting handcuffed and stuffed into a police car a few blocks from the port. Spectators gathered as they manhandled him into the car. He even looked guilty. I wondered if they'd told him what they wanted him for or he assumed.

He might not serve the time he deserved for murdering Colin, but we could correct that later. Right now, watching him as he pulled away from the curb in the back seat of that cruiser felt like a win.

As soon as he turned the corner and pulled away, I sat on the nearest bench, exhausted. I hadn't slept much last night as we'd used most of it setting up today's adventure. And with everything that had happened in the last week—murder, mayhem, and mutinies, or at least the threat of them—I didn't think I could take much more. I needed more than a night's sleep. I deserved a week off to get my head around everything. And yet, once this was over, I'd be the new acting cruise director.

I felt squeezed by the oppressive heat. Breathing hurt. And according to our plan, we still had so much more to do.

Witnessing Jack getting hauled away meant we'd already accomplished a large part of our plan. Or more specifically, Chuck's plan. When Claire filled me in, she assured me the first part included putting Jack in jail. Chuck called in a tip that a known drug dealer would enter the port sometime before eleven that morning. He'd somehow managed to plant enough drugs on Jack to make it look legitimate when Jack got searched when arrested.

The next part of the plan relied on Chuck. He would impersonate Jack, intercept the debit card, and obtain the required information to transfer the money from Jack's account. This next part relied too much on Chuck, in my opinion.

Claire and I stood, ready to find Haulover Bank in the north side of Belize City, no easy feat since the ship drops anchor and the locals tender us ashore on the south side. It's the only port I know of that doesn't allow ships to use their own tenders.

Belize City has a history where the ownership and naming volleys back and forth between several different nations. Originally a Mayan city known as Holzuz until English settlers looking for good lumber landed, at one point it was the capital of British Honduras, which changed in the early seventies. It's still part of the British Commonwealth, and whether that's a benefit or not I'll never know.

If working on ships has taught me one thing, it's that colonization takes many forms, and nothing good ever came of strangers arriving purporting to have better ways of doing things.

Claire and I hopped in a taxi and found our way to the bank. I had the driver stop a block away because I didn't want Chuck seeing us.

I checked my watch as we stepped out of the cab. Ten thirty. That gave us half an hour before Jack's appointment. I wasn't entirely sure I'd recognize Chuck, who swore he could disguise himself to look like a balding, middle-aged man with a beer gut.

"You think he'll stick to the plan?" I asked Claire as we headed in the direction of the bank looking for a cafe or something we could take up watch from.

"Not for a second."

"But how do we stop him from taking off with the money? You know he wouldn't help unless he thought he could get at least most of it."

"I have an idea about that," said Claire, but she wouldn't tell me any more. We found a good spot across the street and down a few stores at a café specializing in bright-coloured smoothies. We took a spot at a table under a green umbrella. A breeze swept through the café, bringing relief from the humidity and heat. Storm clouds massed like an army waiting to strike, billowing up to block out any trace of blue sky. I ordered a cortado and Claire asked for a tea with milk but no sugar.

As we waited for our order, we watched three ships' worth of tourists passing by. I'd seen paintings of what Belize looked like before the English got here. While still tropical, it no longer resembled the paradise of those romantic paintings.

"What's that look mean?" asked Claire. The server placed our drinks in front of us, and I watched Claire stir milk into her tea.

"I worry sometimes I'm making things worse by being complicit."

"You mean by facilitating this?" She pointed to a couple with matching windbreakers, hats, and fanny packs picking through a bargain bin in a shop next to us.

"Sometimes it feels like I wade through the worst part of humanity."

"I can relate. I often find myself associating with individuals who, for whatever reason, are at a low point in their lives. But it doesn't mean you have to let them bring you down. I remember doing a story about a woman who'd turned to sex work to earn enough to care for her three kids. She'd gotten caught up in a scandal because one of her clients happened to be a prominent politician. Everyone thought the story was about how horrible a person she must be to subject her kids to that. And I didn't want the world to see her like that. I wanted the world to see her like every mum who gets a job to pay the rent. It's not like she brought her clients home with her. She had a babysitter. And whether people want to believe it or not, sex work is honest work.

"Well, the story didn't go down well. I'd sung this woman's praises instead of going along with the established plot that this perfectly honest family man got hoodwinked by a woman who wanted to use her power over him to influence things.

"Things got a little out of hand. Some gentlemen from the government came to talk to me about the story I'd written, asking me to reword it. As if I could go back in time and unwrite it."

"Doesn't it scare you?"

"What? My job? I'm not going to let people intimidate me away from the truth."

Claire spotted Chuck first, dressed in a drab grey suit, but he hadn't come alone. Beside him, looking rather grim, trailed Jack. Chuck gripped his forearm firmly as he pulled him through the streets, both sweating in the hot sun.

"That didn't take long," I said, referring to Chuck double-crossing us. He must have bailed Jack out and brought him along, likely at gunpoint, to transfer the money. This wasn't the plan Claire had relayed to me. "What should we do?" I asked.

"Well," said Claire, taking a sip of her tea, "I think we should see what happens when they leave the bank. It'll give us a moment to regroup and think more clearly."

I'd gotten pulled away during the plan reveal to deal with a crisis in the crew bar. Apparently the ship had run out of certain types of alcohol in the passenger bars and pulled supplies from the crew bar, which they had absolutely no right to do because the alcohol belonged to the crew account, which remained separate from the cruise line. I had to sort that out before we had a real mutiny.

As a result Claire had filled me in on the plan after Chuck had left. After getting the information, we'd planned to meet up after and figure out how to transfer it to a bank account we could hand over to the authorities. Both Claire and I felt Chuck agreed to hand the money over far too quickly. And here he'd already deviated from the plan.

"Why would he bring Jack with him?" I said.

"Maybe he didn't think he could impersonate him and he's figured out a way to coerce him to hand over the money," Claire said.

"If you'd already killed someone for that money, would you give it up so easily? I couldn't imagine anything that would make Jack give it up."

We decided we couldn't know for certain what had happened, so we'd follow them once they left the bank. I took a sip of my drink and wished I'd ordered something cooler. The air crackled with the impending storm.

They spent more than an hour inside the bank, and when they left, Jack looked even more dejected than when they'd arrived. Chuck still had hold of him. We stood, leaving money on the table ready to follow, but a black private hire car pulled up, and Chuck shoved Jack in.

Claire grabbed my arm and tugged me toward the road. "Quick, we can't let them get away." She hailed a taxi, and we fell inside with Claire instructing the driver to follow the black car.

He put an arm up on the seat and turned, slow. "This isn't a movie."

Claire pulled out a couple hundred American dollars. "We'll pay."

He grabbed the money, threw the car into drive, and sped off after the black car, cutting off a tour bus as he re-entered traffic.

The few hundred Claire had paid turned out to be a good motivator. The driver had us two cars behind the black car in less than a minute, tailing them as if he'd done this before.

The shops and hotels gave way to factories, industrial buildings, and residential homes as soon as we crossed Haulover Creek. Vegetation crowded us on both sides as we got farther away from civilization.

The driver looked in his rearview mirror back at us. "Not much past here except ruins and abandoned buildings. You sure you want to keep following?"

"I'm sure," insisted Claire.

Fewer and fewer cars passed us, making it easier for the black car to spot us as we now shared the road as the only cars heading in this direction. I turned to Claire to ask if maybe we should head back. I wanted no part of the things you could do with someone in a place full of ruins and abandoned buildings. Why else would Chuck bring Jack out here? But as I considered the possibilities, the car pulled off the road down a side road almost obscured by brush.

Our driver slowed and pulled over, then swung his arm back over the seat to face us. "I don't think you should follow any farther. This road will not lead to anything good."

I agreed with him, but the look of determination on Claire's face stopped me from speaking up.

"Let's give it a few minutes, and then we'll follow."

He sighed, heaving his giant shoulders, and turned back around. "Okay, it's your life. Usually it's the Americans demanding stupid requests."

"I don't think any one nation has the monopoly on stupid."

"You can say that again."

He waited two minutes, then pulled onto the side road that looked more like a long driveway. He pulled over again before reaching a dilapidated building surrounded by trees.

"I'll wait. If you like."

Claire started to shake her head no, but I stopped her. "Thank you. That's very kind." We'd never get a car to come back out here.

We climbed out, and I pointed to a path along the side of the building we could use to see inside before announcing our presence. Claire didn't seem worried at all, and more than anything, that terrified me. She might do this all the time, but I could say for certain I didn't want to ever do this again. What kind of person puts themselves in this situation?

As we neared the back of the building where a huge tree had fallen and taken out most of the back wall, Claire pulled me close and said in a low voice, "I don't want you to worry, okay? I know what I'm doing."

"What does that mean?"

"I can see how frightened you are." She tucked my hair behind my ear and kissed me softly on the lips. "This will all work out."

"How can you be so certain?"

She smiled and shrugged one shoulder. "Experience."

As we slipped around the side, I accidentally stepped on a branch, which acted as a doorbell announcing our presence. From our vantage point I could spot Jack and Chuck in the empty space, talking about something in hushed tones. Before Claire or I could react, Jack grabbed for something at Chuck's waist and aimed it at us. We both ducked as we heard the shot.

When I looked down, Claire lay at my feet and Jack had taken off running. No one went after him.

I dropped to my knees and shook Claire. And that's when I saw the blood pooling under her shirt.

CHAPTER TWENTY-FOUR

Claire—Friday evening: at sea

I waited until Moira left to take her call, then leaned forward and asked Bandini, "Who are you?" Besides the server behind the bar, no one else could hear us, but I still kept my voice low. This seemed the type of conversation to whisper.

"I'm Bandini the Great, also known as Chuck Baxter, magician extraordinaire."

"That's a lie. Or only part of the truth. When you came in here, you knew who I was, and yet, Moira hadn't mentioned me. Why would you know me?"

"Who wouldn't know Claire Mills, the great investigative reporter?"

I leaned back. "No. As much as you think you can appeal to my ego, you can't. So don't try."

Moira stepped back in at that point. "I'm sorry, I have to go. We have a slight"—she tilted her head from side to side—"emergency, and if I don't take care of it right now, it will snowball into a mutiny."

I promised I'd fill her in on the plan later.

Bandini leaned back and toasted me with his champagne glass. "As it so happens, we may have someone in common. Do you remember Emil Fuchs?" The second he said the name, I stood, ready to leave, but he wrapped his hand around my wrist and pulled me down into my chair. "Listen, I don't mean you any harm. At least, not anymore."

"So it is true he hired someone to kill me." I paused, lost for words. "Why…"

"We can't all be David Blaine." He chuckled. "Look. I'm about to offer you a serious way out of your predicament. In exchange, I get to make enough money to retire and live the kind of life I've always wanted. And you'll get Fuchs off your back and have enough money to live comfortably for the rest of your life in some tropical paradise. If we do this my way, we both get what we want."

"And what about Jack Kerne and Colin Avery? Jack killed him for that money, and we owe it to Colin's family to make sure they get closure."

Bandini huffed at this. "I can't compete with your moral compass, and I don't even plan to try." He leaned forward, capturing my attention. "I don't want to have to compete with it. I'd rather you get on board. Otherwise, I'll have to carry out Fuchs's contract, and at this point, it'll get messy. And I hate messy. Claire, let's make this easy on both of us and assume you'll go along."

I took a small sip of my champagne and put it down on the table. I really wanted a vodka tonic, something with more bite than the sweetness and bubbles. I was shocked to be sitting across from a man hired to kill me. And yet still alive, so that gave me reason to hope.

"Okay," I said. "What's your plan?"

"I'll phone in a tip to the authorities in Belize that a man matching Jack's description will be entering port carrying drugs."

"How do you know he'll have drugs?"

"I'll plant them on him."

"Like a reverse pickpocket?"

He frowned like I'd asked a stupid question. "No. He's going to a bank to finish stealing five hundred million dollars. He doesn't plan to get back on board, so he'll need some clothes for the next couple of days, and maybe he plans to take some cash out with him. Either way, guaranteed he'll have a bag I can plant drugs in."

"How will you get drugs?"

"I'll use baking soda. It looks enough like coke to pass a visual inspection and hopefully we'll be long gone by the time they test it and figure out the truth."

He'd thought far more about this than I'd given him credit for. "What's next?"

"I'll present myself to the police as a CIA agent on Jack's trail. I'll go in and convince him that it's in his best interest to turn the money over to the CIA in exchange for a lenient or possibly non-existent sentence. Then I'll lead him to the bank and get him to sign the money over to us."

"Nice use of the word 'us.' Before we even get to that part, let's backtrack on all of that. And go through it one step at a time." I looked down at my champagne and realized I'd need something stronger to finish this conversation. "Also, I'll need a real drink. Let's switch to a different bar."

He spread his arms along the back of his chair. "I like this bar. It's fancy. Makes me feel rich already."

"You want my help? You'll get me a vodka tonic."

He shrugged and stood. For someone planning a list of illegal acts, he didn't appear fazed one bit. Then again, he'd practically admitted to being a hired killer, thereby proving he'd do a hell of a lot for money.

The next bar had a tropical tiki feel with three different levels overlapping. The geometric shape of the glass behind the bar made it feel splintered. I followed Bandini as he went up to the top and picked a table in the back next to a living wall. I ordered a double vodka tonic and watched as Bandini spent several minutes sorting through every specialty drink before choosing a screwdriver.

"Okay, so walk me through how you're going to get the police to release Jack to you."

"I'll tell them Jack will show me his base of operation, which I will then share with them."

"Aren't you worried they'll want to come?"

"I'll tell Jack to say he'll only show me."

My vodka arrived, and I took two gulps. "That sounds suspicious as hell."

"I'll make it sound unsuspicious. My whole job is getting people to believe in illusions. You don't think I can convince some cops to let me have a small-time drug dealer?"

"What if they're listening in while you question him?"

"You think Belize City will have surveillance in their interrogation rooms? If they have interrogation rooms."

"Belize City has one of the highest murder rates in the world, and is a leading tourist destination, which means they have the need and the money for surveillance in their interrogation rooms."

"Okay, I'll make sure I talk to him in a jail cell." He took a sip of his screwdriver.

"How are you going to get Jack to hand over all that money? What if he likes his chances of going to court better?"

"I'm going to go at him as if I'm crooked, his freedom for the money. If he wasn't open to the deal, he wouldn't have stolen the money in the first place."

"How do I know you're not going to screw me over for the money?" I didn't really care about the money, but if I wanted him to think I was serious about the job, it's a question I had to ask.

"I'm going to tell you where I'm going every step of the way. After the bank, I'm going to take him to a deserted hotel out in the middle of nowhere. I've hired a car to pick us up so it strengthens my story that I'm CIA. I'll show you on the map where we're going, but it'll look better for you if you follow us in a cab."

"Why?"

"Have you told Moira about the whole contract out on your life? Might make the ruins in Cozumel hard to explain."

I took another sip of my drink and leaned back in my plush chair watching the other patrons. The clock had now passed us into the next day, and yet the crowded bar didn't seem to notice. I wondered how many other interesting conversations were going on at the same time. I shifted my gaze back to Bandini, with his smug smile and insouciance, as he lounged in his chair owning this moment with triumph. I knew for certain I didn't trust him. I also knew if I didn't follow along, I'd never get a chance to make Jack pay for murdering Colin or make sure the money didn't end up with this troll.

I ignored his earlier comment. "And what happens when we get to the abandoned hotel?"

"Jack will see you, take my gun, and shoot you."

I scoffed at the absurdity of the comment. "Telling me kind of kills the surprise."

"You're not actually going to get shot. I'll put a squib in, and it'll look to Jack that he shot you."

I waved my hands in the air. "How can you guarantee it will play out that way?"

"A magician never reveals his secrets."

"This sounds bonkers to me. I have no reason to trust you. How do I know you won't shoot me—and Moira, for that matter—with a real gun after I've so graciously led us to the middle of nowhere?"

"Have the taxi driver stick around. When he hears a gunshot, he'll investigate."

"That's crap. He'll do a runner the second he hears that gun."

"Claire. You have to trust me. You have no other choice. Either you say no, I kill you in some imaginative way and take a picture to send back to Fuchs, Jack gets away with murder, and the world is a sadder place without your stories in it. Or you extend a modicum of trust toward me, we make Jack think he's killed you with a CIA agent's gun, and he takes off into the bush with no money or ID and the cops on his trail. He'll either die in the woods or get arrested. Either way, he gets what he deserves. But only if you trust me."

"Why do you need me? Why can't you just fulfill your little plan yourself?"

"Ah, the one hitch in my brilliant plan. I have no idea what happened to Colin. If I'm to convince Jack I'm on to him, I'll need to know all the details. Details only you and Moira have."

"So once I'm on the ground bleeding, you take a picture and send it to Fuchs, wire me money, and then what?"

"And then you ride off into the sunset with your millions and disappear forever."

"And the ruins? How did you plan to get proof of my death?"

"The headlines would've taken care of that for me: 'Famous Writer Goes Missing in Mexico.' Not unique enough to rouse suspicion, but enough to prove to Fuchs I'd fulfilled the contract."

We both sat with our drinks as the noise of the bar washed over us.

After a few minutes, Bandini said, "I get it. Why should you trust me? As far as you know, I'm the guy trying to kill you, and here I am asking you to put yourself in harm's way and take a bullet."

That wasn't what I'd been thinking about. My first thought had to do with Moira. Should I tell her the truth? I would have to come clean eventually. It would be a hard conversation to have.

The second thing I'd thought about was how did someone slip so seamlessly into performing magic shows to killing people?

"Okay," I said. "I'll tell you what I know about Colin's murder, but on the condition you tell me how you got hired to kill me. Is this something you do often? Kill people?"

"My mom was a prostitute and my dad used to beat me. I turned to drugs really early to numb my daily life." He laughed. "Something like that? Is that what you want to hear? How does anyone get into anything? They fall gradually. There's no real revelation to any of this. I owed money to the wrong people, and surprisingly, no one pays any attention to the magician when they're not onstage. It gave me access to places others couldn't even dream of."

"And no one suspects something when suddenly a murder occurs every time you perform?"

"Well, that's the fun part. I make it look like an accident. Or sometimes I set up something that may take weeks to happen. So, no. As of yet, no one has ever suspected me."

That all sounded a bit ludicrous, also like a lot of possible failures. No contract killer—not that I knew many—would leave so much up to chance.

I sighed because I didn't have any more objections and I still hadn't thought of a way to turn this around on him. For now, I'd have to go along with it.

"One more question." Something had nagged at the back of my mind since we discovered Jack had no idea anyone was on to him. "Did you send me that 'mind your own business' email?"

He threw his head back and laughed. "I wish I could've seen your face when you saw it."

We hammered out the last few details before leaving the bar in the early hours of the morning. As I took the elevator up to my room, I wondered if Jack had discovered his passport—nestled between the pages of one of the many books I'd brought—missing. Would he call security? How would he explain it if he did?

As I lay in bed, the gentle rocking of the ship lulling me into that in-between state of dreaming and wakefulness, I finally came up with how I would take care of both Bandini and Jack.

CHAPTER TWENTY-FIVE

Moira—Saturday morning: Belize City, Belize

I watched as everything unfolded in front of me like a TV show I couldn't switch off. Jack stumbled out of the building, pausing long enough to throw the gun into the bushes before disappearing.

Chuck took his phone out and snapped a picture of Claire on the ground at the same time I knelt down next to her.

"Out of the way for a sec," he said, nudging me. "Come on, Claire. You're dead, slump your face a bit more."

I pushed him away. "What are you doing? She needs our help." But as soon as I pressed my hands to the wound, I felt a little pouch under her shirt. Claire's eyes popped open, and we stared at each other for a few seconds before she sat up like a zombie raising from the grave.

"What is going on?"

Claire took my hand. "It's fake. We staged it to look like Jack killed me."

"But he shot you."

"With a prop gun," said Chuck. "It's the gun I use in my final act in the first show. Only shoots blanks. But he thinks it's a CIA agent's gun." He helped Claire stand. "You okay? You did great." He turned the phone around and showed her. "You look really dead. Fuchs is going to love this."

Claire took my hand and turned me to her. "I will explain all this later, I promise. For now please trust me." There was something else behind that plea, and I decided to trust her because so far she'd never given me a reason not to. As much as I didn't like this surprise, there was probably a good reason Claire set it up this way.

"Well, that was a hell of a ride. Once Jack thought we'd caught him, he wouldn't shut up. Thought somehow playing extra cooperative would help his case."

"What did he say?" Claire asked.

"What didn't he say? Apparently, Colin was his nephew. Jack had asked him for a loan to pay off some gambling debts, but Colin refused. As Jack put it, Colin never wanted to spend the money. He never thought of it as real money. And this ate away at Jack until this situation fell into his lap. He met the cruise director who—oh, and he also confessed to drowning her in a hot tub—gave him the idea when she started complaining about how horrible the security was on the ship." He wiped a pool of sweat from his forehead. Dark patches seeped from the pits of his light grey suit. "If this guy ever gets arrested for real, he doesn't stand a chance. He'll just puke his confession on the table in front of him. I thought he was going to piss his pants."

Chuck handed her an envelope. "Everything you'll need to access those accounts is in here."

Claire slipped the envelope into her knapsack.

"What about Jack?" I asked.

"Hopefully he'll get eaten by the local wildlife." Chuck saluted us and walked off as Claire and I stood alone in a crumbling hotel strewn with garbage, rotting vegetation, and probably several mysteries I didn't want to know about.

I stared at Claire, waiting for her to share. But instead of saying anything, she gave a brief striptease as she pulled her stained shirt over her head, discarding the device that held the fake blood on the ground. She wiped some of the red off her stomach with her shirt. It occurred to me that I should look away, but I was mesmerized. The freckles that lightly peppered her nose ran rampant over her shoulders like the sun had dusted them in colour. She wore a practical white bra that did little to cover her ample breasts. I shoved my hands in my pockets and turned away as she threw a clean shirt over her head. If she'd noticed me watching, she didn't say anything.

"So are you going to tell me what's going on?"

She hooked her arm in mine and pulled me through the opening in the wall toward the front of the building, where, hopefully, our taxi driver waited for us. "Let's find a good restaurant and enjoy this story over a meal. I think you're going to like it."

Claire—Saturday afternoon: Belize City, Belize

I let Moira choose the restaurant since she knew the area better than probably even Tripadvisor since, as she pointed out, she'd tried every restaurant worth eating at more than once. She chose a tiny Indian fusion place on the water, tucked away from the rest of the tourist spots along the coast.

I'm not one for fusion food in general, but I couldn't find anything to complain about.

"I found this place because of the view. While on the way back from an excursion a few years ago, the boat swung close to the shore to show us some of the local places to eat. No doubt they get a kickback for sending guests to the right restaurants. This one looked all alone and I liked that." Staring across from the table with a mojito halfway to her lips she asked, "So, this magician, Chuck Baxter, is actually a hired killer?"

During lunch I had filled her in on most of what had happened, surprised she'd let me finish my whole story before asking questions.

"It appears that way."

"And in exchange for Colin's millions, he's helped you fake your death and given you a portion of that money to disappear for the rest of your life?"

"I'd like him to think so."

She finally took that sip. "Good. Because that jerk deserves prison time. In a very lonely cell. With bigger cellmates who don't like him. Oh my God." She thumped her drink down on the table. "Does this mean he killed James?"

"Who's James?"

"James the Magnificent, the originally scheduled magician. They found him dead in his apartment, not sure what killed him."

"I think that's very likely. It gave him an in. He probably had Fuchs or someone else pull some strings for him."

"So what is the game plan? Why did you let him leave the hotel?"

"We have one very important factor on our side. You can't jump ship midvoyage. He mentioned he'll perform his last show tonight to keep suspicion down. Once on the ship, he can't leave, and that means we still have time."

"Time to do what? You're supposed to be dead. Won't that look suspect if someone claiming to be dead signs on board?"

"I have no intention of playing dead for Bandini or Emil Fuchs. Not when I can stop them both."

Moira reached across the table and grabbed my hand, forcing me to look at her. "Let's think about this. He's given you a chance to escape with your life. What happens if we do get Chuck and Jack? What then? This guy will only go and hire someone new to kill you."

"If my plan tonight works out, I won't have to worry about either of them again."

At the sound of thunder, we both looked up into the sky and watched the approaching storm looming over us. "Perhaps we should head back to the ship before we get caught in the rain."

I looked worriedly at the sky. I'm used to rain. We get a lot in London, but never anything so gripping as a tropical storm or, thankfully, a hurricane. Moira must have seen the worry on my face because she took my hand as we left the restaurant and said, "We'll be long gone before it arrives." I let that thought ease my worry. After all, she'd worked on ships for years. And at that moment, it felt more important to focus on the details of her eyes and the way strands of her hair escaped her messy bun. We had one more day together after this, and who knew what would happen after that. I would head back to London and my job. I had full confidence we'd sort out the mess with Bandini and Jack and Fuchs.

And then what?

What did I want to happen? What could possibly happen beyond a quick physical relationship? As much as Moira protested about her job, I could see the joy she took in it. And I would never ask anyone to give up what they loved in order to please me.

And then a strange, revolutionary thought entered my head.

One that I'd felt in the back of my mind since the start of this cruise. What awaited me back in London? I loved my job, but as this week progressed, few of the ailments that plagued me on a daily basis back home materialized. As much as I loved my job, it was slowly killing me. I was working myself to death.

And yet, I had still worked this week, in a way. But I'd also taken time for myself and done more than work. I'd slowed down, and that's what Rick and Frank and my doctor had told me to do for years. What if everyone was right except me? Another revolutionary thought I wasn't ready to hold on to.

CHAPTER TWENTY-SIX

Moira—Saturday evening: Belize City, Belize

I stood on deck watching the ship roil with the ever-growing waves. According to our schedule, we should've left port over an hour ago and yet we still hadn't pulled anchor. The land sat bathed in grey, with its yellow lights aglow the only colour, poised to accept the onslaught of wind, waves, and debris that would rip into it within the hour.

The sky, at the precipice of dusk, shocked to life with lightning. I knew then something had gone wrong. We shouldn't have let the storm get this close. The danger of running aground in a storm surge was too high.

To my left, two crew came charging down the deck toward the bow, one of them shouting into a walkie-talkie, and the other zipping up a life preserver.

Behind me someone shouted my name. I turned to see a crew member calling me toward the atrium. "We're locking down the outside."

As I entered the arctic blast of air-conditioning, an announcement on the main system blared through the ship. "For your safety, please keep all balconies closed and locked until further notice. We will close all outside decks, pool areas, and hot tubs for the duration of the evening."

A growing crowd had gathered around reception, shouting questions at the increasingly harried crew.

I threaded through them and into the cruise staff office, where I found Jamie and Noah. "Have you guys heard anything about why we haven't left port yet?"

Jamie shook her head, taking several bingo packs out and shoving them into one of the cloth souvenir bags we gave out as prizes. Mostly we used them to transport materials from different venues.

I logged onto my computer to see if I'd received any emails about cancelled events. Depending on how bad the storm is, they usually won't cancel shows unless we lose power—which felt a little sadistic. We could list thirty degrees to starboard, but as long as we still had power, no need to inconvenience the passengers.

Noah, who usually didn't offer up anything for free, said, "I heard a rumour the deck crew quit."

"Quit?" If this was true, it explained why we hadn't left port.

"They can't do that." Jamie slung her bag of bingo supplies over her shoulder. "Can they?"

"Why not?" Noah said. "About time. You can't expect people to work in crap conditions for no pay for that long without rebelling."

"Because how will we get back to Florida?" asked Jamie.

"There are other people who can get the ship ready to leave port. Most of it is automated from the bridge anyway," I told her. There must also be some engine crew who quit as well. They wouldn't wait much longer before leaving port. They had no choice but to leave.

I opened my drawer for the USB drive I'd come in for but found it empty. "Noah, did you grab the highlights reel from Simon yet?"

He grimaced. "Crap. I forgot."

"We need it for the final. Can you go get it?"

He held up one of the bingo bags. "I have bingo in five minutes."

I checked my watch. I needed the drive to give to the stage crew before Chuck's final show. The last thing I wanted to do was head up to deck eleven where the swaying of the ship was the strongest.

❖

Claire—Saturday evening: Belize City, Belize

My stomach did another somersault as I clutched the dresser in my room for support. The lights of Belize City grew faint and small as the ship put distance between us and land. More than two hours late. From what I'd learned from Moira earlier, they'd never put us in serious danger, so I decided not to spend my energy worrying that something would go wrong.

Bandini's last show started in forty-five minutes, and I had a few more things to set up before that happened. The only thing I got snagged on was Jack. Without money or ID, I didn't think he'd get far, and if we could convince authorities of what had happened, I knew they'd catch up to him.

I popped out a couple of Gravol pills into my palm and washed them down with water. Anything to get my stomach settled. I slipped my phone and keycard in my pocket and headed out into the night, ready to take on a hired killer.

In the corridor, I swayed back and forth with the ship as it listed from side to side. The rain hadn't started yet, so maybe we would outrun the storm before it really hit. As the elevator filled on the way down, I noticed many shared my optimism.

The splendour of the atrium came into view as we descended into crowds of people milling about. Music from the pub filled the space as the doors of the elevator opened. I headed to the aft of the ship where I was supposed to meet Moira at a bar outside the theatre.

Moira—Saturday evening: at sea

I lurched down the hall, swiping at one of the guardrails along the side to stop my fall, missed, and smacked into Simon's office door.

"It's open," he called.

I stumbled in and rested against the door, letting my body sway with the ship. You get used to bad seas, especially if you've ever done Alaska in the late or early season. The swells can get up to five metres. I'd experienced worse.

"Hey, I came to grab the highlight tape."

"Sure thing." He slid his chair across the floor and pulled a small hard drive from a stack. "Let me make sure I updated it for this week." He plugged it into his computer and pulled up a video file. The tape began to play the same opener we saw every week and then a couple of the shots from sail away started. He clicked stop as soon as it switched to the variety show and was about to eject the drive when I noticed a detail on the screen.

"Wait. Can you play that segment?"

Simon hit play, and we watched as part of the welcome variety show started. Every week the cruise director would welcome performers on board, and some would give a sneak peek into what they had to offer that week. I'd forgotten Chuck had done a short segment for it. But Colin was standing next to him onstage. We both watched as Chuck walked Colin around as if he were a pet dragon on a leash. Then Chuck clicked his fingers and Colin came back to life.

I stood stunned. Why hadn't Bandini mentioned he'd met Colin? Perhaps it was just a name? "Do you have the full thing recorded?" Something about this seemed too much of a coincidence.

"Maybe. Let me check." He pulled up a project file and brought up the clip. Chuck invited Colin onto the stage. Colin refused at first, but then Chuck leaned in and asked Colin his name, then shouted into the crowd, "Let's give Colin some encouragement." Within a few seconds, the entire auditorium started chanting Colin's name. He gave a sheepish grin to the crowd and followed Chuck up onto the stage. It struck me that in two hours he'd lain dead in his cabin. He didn't look like a man contemplating suicide.

Chuck brought him centre stage and then turned him around three times before yanking him to a stop by his shoulders. "Okay, here we go." Chuck pulled out a handheld mic from somewhere on his person and held it up to Colin's mouth. "For everyone in the back, what is your name?"

"Colin." The audience cheered.

"And where are you from, Colin?"

"Michigan."

"Big place, Michigan. Whereabouts?"

Colin leaned into the mic. "Bay City."

"Great place. And what do you do in Bay City?"

"I'm a freelance coder."

Chuck turned to the audience, and in essence, the camera and smiled. "That sounds super fun. Have you ever dreamed of being anything else?"

Colin shrugged and shook his head.

"Well, let's see if we can make some dreams come true." He stepped to the side. "I want you to plant your feet shoulder length apart and straighten your back."

Once Colin had done that, he said, "Great. Now hold out both your arms, make them as strong as you can, and I'm going to push down on them. I want you to resist me." It took a couple of tries but eventually Colin had his arms out straight and strong. "Now, I'm going to take your hand and turn it so you're staring at your palm. I want you to look at all the lines on your hand. And listen to my voice. Hear what I'm saying. I want you to focus your eyes on those lines, and as I move your hand closer, they'll begin to blur."

Chuck moved Colin's hand an inch closer, continuing to talk in a soothing voice. "And as it moves closer, I want you to relax your eyes…listen to my voice…and when I tap you on the shoulder, I want you to drop your chin down to your chest and sleep."

As soon as Chuck tapped his shoulder, Colin dropped his head to his chest. Chuck guided Colin's hand down to his side while saying, "I'm going to ask you a few questions, Colin, and I want you to give me the truth, with confidence and enthusiasm. So when I count to three, I'm going to tap you on the shoulder and wake you up. One, two, three." He tapped Colin on the shoulder. "You're awake and refreshed. Hello."

"Hello." Almost a completely different person, Colin smiled at Chuck.

"How are you tonight, Colin?"

"I'm feeling lonely and embarrassed."

Chuck turned to the audience. "Why is that, Colin?"

"I'm on this cruise by myself, and I'm not really sure what to do. I also don't like being the centre of attention."

"What's one thing you can tell us that you don't normally share about yourself?"

"I have a little over ten thousand Bitcoin in a wallet account."

"Wow. Lucky guy."

"Wait, go back," I said.

Simon scrubbed back a minute, and we watched Colin share how much Bitcoin he had. The absolute shock on Chuck's face was visible if you knew what to look for, and he covered well. He'd probably done a quick calculation, and even if in that moment he didn't know how much ten thousand Bitcoin was, he did after the show.

The show played on. "Okay, one last question," Chuck said. "Have you ever dreamed of being something other than a coder?"

"I've always wanted to be a dragon."

I leaned forward and hit the spacebar to stop the playback, I'd seen enough. "Holy shit."

"What?" asked Simon.

James the Magnificent had also used hypnotizing in his act, and part of his schtick was that he could approach passengers he'd hypnotized earlier in the cruise and say one word to put them under his control again. I suspected that would be the same for Chuck, and the implications of what that could mean began to mount in my brain.

"Hey, I know we told you to scrap it, but do you still happen to have the footage from the elevator from the first night?"

Simon turned to me, his face scrunched up, thinking. Then he pulled open a drawer full of loose USB drives. "Do you remember what it looked like?"

I shrugged. I hadn't given it much thought. "Orange?"

He pulled one at random and plugged it into his keyboard. He brought up the contents, scrolling down, and rejecting it. We went through three before he found the one he wanted.

Again we watched the static shot of the elevators, this time, looking for something different. I spotted Chuck coming out of the elevators at 12:15 a.m. I hadn't noticed him the first time around because he'd gone to the opposite side. But he could still get to Colin's room, because it looped around at the bow of the ship to the port side.

"There. Pause it."

Simon and I both stared at the image of Chuck walking toward the camera.

"Holy shit," Simon said. "That's Bandini. You don't think

he killed Colin, do you? Twelve fifteen. That's almost forty-five minutes before Colin was murdered, right?"

I nodded.

"So he had time to leave."

Or a really long time to get Colin to share his Bitcoin passcode. He must have taken Colin's phone thinking that's how he accessed it, and when he realized he couldn't get in, he came back for the laptop. That's why we heard the commotion in Colin's room. He must have taken Colin's keycard, and maybe forgot which room it was. But by that time Jack, taking the opportunity presented to him, took the laptop and transferred the money to an account in Belize.

So if I had never gone to Chuck for help, he'd have never known about Jack, and we wouldn't be in this situation. Then again, Claire might be dead somewhere.

CHAPTER TWENTY-SEVEN

Claire—Saturday evening: at sea

I watched Moira enter and spot me, her face registering relief for some reason. Tonight, she wore another tight suit with a dark camisole underneath. I watched her body sway as she walked over to my table. What I wouldn't have given at that moment to have met Moira under normal circumstances. Then again, do you ever meet anyone under the right circumstances? If anything was out of my control, it was this.

"We need to find Chuck," she said. "He's about to start his show, and I want to catch him before he goes on."

I followed Moira as she led me out and up a twisting flight of stairs leading to the theatre above. "I don't think Jack killed Colin."

My foot almost slipped off the second stair either because the ship listed or because of what Moira had said. I latched onto her arm and turned her to face me. "If not Jack, then who?" I couldn't think of anyone else who had a motive, especially after finding out he'd arranged for Colin to come on board with him in the guise of a contest.

"Five hundred million sounds like a perfect motive to me."

"But who else would know he had that kind of money?"

"I just watched a recording of Chuck hypnotizing Colin in the variety show where he shared he had ten thousand Bitcoin, which Chuck would know was a lot."

"But everything fits with Jack. He got the room with the connecting doors next to Colin."

"Exactly. I have no doubt that Jack intended to kill Colin, but I think Chuck got there first. I think he used hypnotism to get Colin to let him in his room."

For the first time since I'd met her, I worried Moira had left the shallow end of the pool. "But he told us Jack confessed."

"Did he, though? We have no idea what Jack told him. For all we know, he hypnotized Jack in the police station. He could've told him anything, even planted the idea to shoot you in the first place."

Of course. Again, he'd done a switch. He told us the lie we wanted to hear while diverting our attention from the truth. "But why would he need us to steal Jack's money? He could've done this on his own unless he decided it would be easier to fake my death than actually kill me, and this way he gets Fuchs's money for doing the job. The question is, what do we do now?"

"We confront him."

Moira had her hand on a door with a sign that read "Back Stage, Crew Only." She turned and said, "He'll deny it."

"I might have a way to make him tell us what happened. Two can play the illusion game." It might not get a confession out of him, but I certainly wanted to see Bandini's face when he realized he hadn't gotten away with it.

Moira stopped midway up a short set of stairs and leaned in close. "I don't know if this is the best idea. This is a man hired to kill you."

I took one step so that we stood on the same stair, evening our height difference slightly. "I have something he wants. He won't kill me, I promise." I closed the space between us, leaning in as I kissed her on the lips. I expected her to pull away, but instead she pushed into me, wrapping her arm around my waist.

We stood feet away from any number of people who could catch us. Even in the darkened stairwell, it lent an urgency to the kiss. This need built from the pit of my stomach like a heat wave spreading throughout my body until it reached my fingertips, which gripped her silky camisole under her suit jacket. I felt enveloped by the smell of jasmine and fresh laundry and an elusive floral scent she used on her hair.

As she deepened the kiss, I opened to her and melted into this moment of heat and passion. She skidded her hand up my back, gripping the back of my neck and holding me in place as she devastated me with her mouth.

And then the ship listed.

We broke apart, out of breath. I looked around, getting my bearings staring up into her golden brown eyes.

"Thank you."

I laughed. "For what?"

She shook her head and her hair fell forward. "I'm not sure."

An announcement that the show would start in five minutes came over the auditorium speakers, breaking the moment.

The light from a lone lightbulb cast a red glow on everything in the backstage area. We found Bandini leaning against a ladder in the back flipping aces out of a deck of cards every few seconds and shuffling them back in.

He paused the second he saw me and turned toward us. We'd passed several crew on the way in rushing to finish the stage setup before the show started in five minutes. But we had this area to ourselves.

"Bold move signing onto a cruise ship when you're supposed to be dead. I've already messaged Fuchs that I finished the job." He shuffled the deck once more, then dropped it into his suit pocket. Again he wore a garish silk suit, bright orange this time. He exuded menace in the red glow, like the devil come to collect his reward. "Did you already discover I stiffed you on that money? The envelope I gave you obviously held false information."

I waved him off. "Oh, I never cared about the money."

"Everyone cares about money."

I ignored that comment and steamrolled ahead. "I think you should worry more about the money you think you have."

He shook his head, confused. "I've already transferred the money I know I have, to a number of different anonymous accounts. I never put all my cards in one deck."

"Wow, that was fast."

"You think I wouldn't have this all planned out? I did this at the bank."

"Are you sure?"

"Of course. I watched them do it."

I smiled because this was turning out to be far more enjoyable than I thought it would. "What's the first thing you learn to do as a magician?" I asked. "Distraction, right? You want people looking over here, say." I held up my left hand and waved it. "While really all the good stuff is happening over here." I then waved my right hand.

He shook his head, confused. I also noticed he'd begun to sweat. "I don't know what you're getting at."

"You hired a car to pick you up at the port to take you to the police station and then over to the bank and then over to the abandoned hotel?"

He tilted his head. "Yes."

"The same car for all three?"

"Why would I hire three different cars?"

"You may have hired a car, but I cancelled it and hired one for you."

"No, that's impossible."

"Why, because you used your real name, Brantley Klimek? Don't look so surprised. I'm an investigative journalist, and you gave yourself away in the champagne bar last night when you mentioned your proclivity for setting up accidents."

"How did you know I'd use my real name?"

"You told Moira Jack would most likely use an alias on board and save his real passport for when he escaped on board, and when I learned about your other name, I assumed you'd do the same."

"So you guessed?"

I shrugged. "Essentially."

"And why should it matter if you hired the car or I did?"

"Do you know where the Haulover Bank is?"

He paused for a very long time as his mind caught up to what had happened. Once I'd left Bandini, I'd called Rick and asked him to look into accidents or unexplained deaths that occurred around the time of a party that hired a magician. That's when I'd discovered that sometimes Bandini the Great went by Cristo or Brantley Klimek. I'd set in motion the car hire and asked Frank to pull in some favours for me, and we set up a false front. Banks today look nothing like they did even half a decade ago. They automate everything now, they don't even need tellers. So when Bandini walked into what he thought was the Haulover Bank, he was really walking into an office building where he met a man who fulfilled all his needs—at least, that's what Bandini thought. Really it was a man creating false bank receipts on a computer.

Bandini must have been comparing what he thought he saw with what he actually saw, which was not much of anything.

As realization hit, his face contracted in anger, and before he could lunge toward me I held up a hand. "If you tell me what I need to know, you have a chance to get Colin's money."

A crew member came up to us. "We're ready to start. Are you good to go?"

"Can you give us a moment, Brad?" asked Moira. She turned to me and winked. "Let me take care of this." And she walked away with Brad.

"It's very simple, Claire. You don't have the power here."

"How will Emil Fuchs feel when he finds out you lied to him?"

I could see him pause as he contemplated that, but recovered quickly. "You'll be dead before he finds out."

"And Moira? Are you going to kill her as well? Or Frank, my ex-husband? Or Rick, my editor? I've told a lot of people about you."

"No one will believe them. I've covered my tracks too well."

"For the others, maybe. But Colin wasn't planned out as well as the others, was he?"

"Colin? I didn't kill him. Jack did."

"I don't think so. I think he planned to kill Colin. He set him up on this cruise, with a connecting room. But then you pulled Colin up on stage that first night and found out he was sitting on half a billion dollars in Bitcoin and couldn't help yourself. It was everything you'd worked toward your whole life. Except you made two mistakes."

"And what are those?"

"What's been bugging Moira and me was why you needed us involved in your plan to steal the money. Why not go to the police station yourself? You didn't know about Jack. Moira never mentioned his name or what he looked like. You needed us to fill in those details so you could tell the Belize police. You know exactly how Colin died that night, and now I want you to tell me. Then I'll give you the information you need to transfer the money."

"Really? You think I'm going to fall for that? You've got a phone or something hidden on you that you're recording from."

I raised my arm and turned around. "I don't own a phone I can record on. And despite what my editor, publisher, and ex-husband think, I don't walk around with a recording device with me on vacation."

He leaned back, contemplating my proposal. Did he really think I'd give him the money? Maybe he thought he could get it from me some way and figured why not tell me. Regardless of his reason, he dropped his guard for a moment. "It was all too easy. I didn't use the end phrase 'Let's finish this,' before he got off stage, which meant I could put him under again any time I wanted. As I walked him offstage, I covered my mic," he pointed to the tiny mic wrapped around his ear and pointed at his chin, "and asked him what room he was in. Then I showed up later that evening after most people had gone to bed. At first he argued that I shouldn't be in his room, but the second I told him to sleep, he became docile. Even swallowed the sleeping pills himself."

"So he did die from an overdose."

"He was out before he even got halfway through the bottle. I threw the rest overboard. You said I made two mistakes, what was the other one?"

"It's possible you made more than two." He took a step toward me, and I held up my hands. "You took his phone assuming that's how he connected to his bank but then, realizing he must be using a laptop, came back for it. At first we thought it was Jack, but it was you that afternoon looking for the laptop."

He looked so pleased with himself. "And then Moira brought the laptop to me without me having to do anything. It was like the world telling me I should have this. I deserve this."

I shook my head, smiling sadly. "The only thing you deserve is jail."

"Well, that's going to be hard to do, isn't it? All you really have is circumstantial evidence."

I tilted my head. "We have you impersonating a CIA agent with the Belize police."

"Do you, though?"

"We have your confession."

"Your word against mine? Without proof? I don't think so."

I pointed behind him. "What about five hundred audience members?"

He whipped around and spotted Moira next to the audio booth. She motioned to the mic he was wearing. While we'd been talking, Moira had Brad make his mic live.

He ripped off his mic and made a run for the stairs into the hallway below. Moira walked over to me. "He's on a ship in the middle of the Caribbean Sea, where does he think he's going?"

Two large security guards blocked his way, ready to stop him, but he pivoted and rushed back up the stairs and passed us onto the stage.

Instead of the applause he usually received, the audience sat in stunned silence. Then, somewhere in the back, a lone clapper began and a smattering of the crowd joined in as if this were part of the act. But it died quickly as the panic seeping from Bandini became apparent.

He rushed to the edge of the stairs and jumped off, running up the aisle to one of the exits. Before anyone could stop her, Moira rushed after him, leaping off the stage into the auditorium after a known killer. But what worried me more, a desperate man.

Moira—Saturday evening: at sea

I don't know what possessed me to chase after him. Probably anger. I felt furious he could get away with it. I saw the bright orange suit streak through the top doors of the theatre and barrel past a stunned crowd, a few of them still clapping.

At the entrance to the theatre, I thought I'd lost him, but the orange suit was a beacon, directing me to the main atrium. From my vantage point on the landing, I watched him get into an elevator to the pool deck. What did he plan to do, jump off the ship?

I rushed toward a hidden door next to the theatre that led to a crew hallway, deciding to risk taking the crew elevator up to deck eleven. By now the security guards had exited the theatre, duplicating as they spread out, fanning down the stairs toward the main atrium.

When my elevator arrived, five crew members and an empty laundry cart were already aboard, but they beckoned me inside with smiles. Always the more the merrier. This time I didn't argue and gladly accepted helping hands as they placed me in the laundry cart.

We rode up in silence. After having offered all crew members free Wi-Fi for the duration of their contracts, and a blow-out crew party during the next cruise, they had forgotten most, if not all the issues.

I smiled and thanked them as I ran out into the passenger area and stopped dead. On the other side of the glass, a storm raged. They'd either removed or tied down all deck furniture, and while I knew protocol was to empty all the pools, from here it looked liked they'd filled them up again.

As the ship listed to one side, the pools emptied their contents onto the deck, then in the other direction, the water sloshed back in, all the while replenishing itself from waves dumping water over the side of the glass walls separating deck twelve from the ocean below.

It took me a moment to spot Bandini at the other entrance, trying to open the locked doors to the pool area. When he spotted me, he stopped and bolted in the opposite direction. Despite my better judgement, I rushed toward the doors and, using my keycard—which now had cruise director clearance—overrode the emergency lock, and the doors slid open. The strength of the wind slapped me in the face, pushing me back into the corridor.

The rain soaked me in an instant as I pushed myself out, head bent toward the next entrance. At least two feet of water pulled at my feet, racing across the deck, slamming into the glass, then racing back as the ship, more noticeable on this deck, rocked back and forth.

I got to the door in time to see Chuck enter one of the side elevators. I punched for another, dripping water on the carpet as I waited. These elevators only had two floors, deck eleven and deck four, so I knew he'd get off there. What could he possibly be thinking? Or was he running scared?

I entered the elevator, seconds behind Chuck, and hit the button for deck four. As the doors closed, I fell back against the wall, and for one terrifying second, I thought the ship had capsized. I slammed my head into the glass and fell to the floor. If the ship listed too much, the elevators would stop functioning, which would trap me, and I'd have one hell of a view for the rest of the storm.

I pulled myself up as the elevator descended to deck four, the charcoal grey of sea and sky melding in an angry dance of waves and wind. The elevator coughed me out on deck four, opening to the fury of the wind, and I finally realized what Chuck had done.

The side elevators ran off the same system as the main ones. With all outside doors barred from opening onto outside decks because of the storm, no one could access deck four from the atrium. But Chuck had found a way around by using the outside elevators to bring us to deck four, where he could access the lifeboats.

The *Summit* had three different kinds of lifeboats. There were the large main ones that we also used as tenders in certain ports, which didn't work well in storms because the seating area couldn't be closed off from the elements. Another similar but smaller kind lowered into the sea with hydraulics, and a third was in capsules lined around deck four. Unlike the boats, they inflated as they shot into the ocean and would act as a flotation device with room for twenty-five people to crawl into and wait for rescue.

My guess was that Chuck would try to launch one of these into the ocean and ride it away from the ship. It was a stupid plan, but then, here was a man facing a lifetime in prison, possibly a death sentence. I suppose the alternative didn't seem as bad.

I slipped as I exited the elevator, slamming in to the rail of the ship. My heart pounded in my chest, and I realized I could die out here. Let Chuck take a lifeboat. Chances were he'd die in the attempt.

I held on to the rail as the ship rocked toward the ocean, and my stomach rose up into my throat as I watched the grey water get closer and closer. "What the hell am I doing?" I closed my eyes and took a deep breath. After a moment, the ship righted itself, and I stumbled toward the elevator, only to get tackled from the side.

For one terrifying moment, I went airborne before slamming back down on the Tartan Track running along deck four and bouncing and rolling to the edge again.

"What are you doing?" I yelled. A mix of salt and rainwater slapped my face.

He didn't say anything, but I watched as he pulled himself up, readying to slam into me again. I crawled up the railing into a standing position and began running toward the bow of the ship. The only thing going through my head at that moment was what an absolute idiot I was to get myself into this situation. There's a reason they lock those doors. No one should be out here. One wrong move, and I'd go over the side and no one would know. I'd drown in an instant and drop to the bottom of the sea, where my body would become fish food.

"Stop it!" I yelled at myself. It didn't help to panic. When I reached the bow, where the track curved, I dived for a box hugging the side of the ship and flipped open the hatch. Inside, stacked neatly, lay rows of bright orange life preservers. I grabbed one and threw it on as I pushed myself up toward the other side of the ship. If I could make it to one of the port side elevators, I could ride it back up to deck twelve. Just as hellish, but not as deadly.

But I didn't make it. Something yanked me back by my life jacket, and I fell back against the deck. Chuck stood over me with a shuffleboard stick ready to slam it into my head. I kicked at his legs as hard as I could, just as the ship listed and he lost his balance.

I took the opportunity to push myself up to a crawling position. I felt something strike my leg but didn't look back, only kept crawling toward the elevators still half a ship's length away.

Before I could get even ten metres, Chuck grabbed my leg and pulled me back. I turned and kicked with my other leg, this one connecting with his face, and I kicked again. Blood burst from his lip and he let go.

I rolled away, pulling myself up and running. I felt a sickening dip as the deck under my feet fell away. I grabbed for the nearest thing I could find, a tie-off holding deck chairs to the side of the ship, and wrapped my wrist around it just as a wave crashed into me, and for a terrifying moment I thought the sea had swept me up with it. All my senses filled with salt water.

But it receded. When I opened my eyes, Chuck was gone. I spotted the orange of his suit on the crest of a wave before it dropped and he went under.

I took a moment to calm my racing heart before pushing off and slowly moving toward the side elevators. I bashed my fist against the call button and almost cried when the door whooshed open. I fell in and sank to the floor in relief. As the elevator rose, I turned to see if I could spot Chuck among the waves, but he'd disappeared forever.

CHAPTER TWENTY-EIGHT

Moira—Saturday morning: private island, Maldives

I stepped out of the private car, tipping the driver as he pulled my luggage from the trunk, and breathed in the salt of the ocean air. I'd spent over a decade at sea, yet from land it hit me differently. Palm fronds littered the ground, decaying along the sand dunes lining the path to a group of thatched huts at the bottom of the hill.

I stood for a moment admiring the view of the azure bay spread before me. Excitement welled in my stomach in anticipation of the next few days.

I rolled my luggage down the sand path to villa number six, the last one on the left, nestled in lush green vegetation, and knocked on the door.

My breath caught when it opened, and Claire stood there in a bikini and flimsy cover. From the number of freckles and glow of her skin, she'd arrived far earlier. Perhaps even a couple of days. The woman who'd refused to go on vacation for over a decade was now on her second in a year.

The last time I'd seen her, two months ago, standing in the cavernous port authority in Florida, she'd promised me we'd see each other again, but I don't think I believed it until now.

Sunlight streamed in from behind, making it hard to focus on anything but her. And now, even though we'd kept in touch through email and phone calls, I felt shy seeing her for the first time since our adventure. I don't know why because I felt I knew her better than anyone in the world.

"You made it." She smiled and pulled me into the villa, closing the door behind me. Without another word, she pushed me into the door and captured my lips in an urgent kiss. I dropped the handle of my suitcase and pulled her closer.

She shoved her hands into my hair, and for one captivating moment, I didn't care about anything, the past, our future, or even breathing. All that mattered was the taste of her and the unrestricted freedom we had for the next four days.

She pulled back and I gulped in air. "I almost didn't make it," I answered. "My replacement missed their flight, and they weren't going to let me off."

She guided me to sunken seating running a semicircle with a view of the ocean beyond and pushed me down onto the luxurious cushions. "How'd you manage?"

"I put Austen in charge until the new guy could catch up to the ship in the next port."

"And they were okay with that?"

"They had to be. I'm currently their number one rated cruise director."

Claire's eyes brightened, and she curled her lips into a delicious smile. "Congrats. Let me make you a drink." She sauntered over to an alcove that held a fully stocked bar. "A kiss on the lips, wasn't it?"

I laughed. She'd remembered the signature cocktail on that first sea day. The day we'd met in Colin's room.

"Fancy."

"Only the best for you."

She wasn't wrong. Colin's mother had been so happy that we'd vindicated her son. The thought that her son would commit suicide never sat right with her, and she rewarded us by giving us a percentage of Colin's wealth. Even one percent of five hundred million equals a fortune.

"I see you're putting your new-found fortune to good use." She capped the cocktail shaker and began shaking one-handed. "I could watch this all day."

"I have more interesting plans for us today. This is just the beginning."

I settled in, flipping off my sandals and getting comfortable.

I had an idea of what she planned. I had lots of thoughts of my own. I'd spent almost every night since she'd left thinking of all the things I'd like to do with Claire if we ever got the chance to meet up on land.

"I'm not surprised you didn't quit your job," she said as she handed me a martini glass with a frothy orange cocktail.

"My dad and sister sure as hell are. They think I'm crazy." She plunked down beside me on the couch. "Aren't you making yourself one?"

"I thought we could share." She leaned in, took a sip from my drink, and then immediately scrunched her face up. "Nope. That's disgusting."

"Malibu Rum is an acquired taste."

I hadn't shared the information that I was now a multimillionaire, mostly because I'd get the same reaction my family had given me. Why work when you could do anything you wanted?

I loved that Claire understood. In fact, I think she understood before even I did. I may have griped about my job, but there wasn't anywhere else in the world I'd rather be than on ships. And now, having gotten promoted again, I held the top position in my department. I'd made Austen my assistant cruise director, and once Noah signed off, most of the drama and toxicity of the department left with him.

We ran the newest, biggest ship in the fleet, and it felt good to be at the top of the world. I wouldn't get that if I stopped working and became a tourist. That's the last thing I wanted.

"I read your article, the one about Emil Fuchs. It was amazing, Claire."

"Did you see they arrested him in London? One of his business associates turned on him, and now he's looking at a long and unfruitful life in prison."

"They also caught Jack trying to leave Belize with a stolen passport."

"Serves him right. He may not have killed Colin, but he did kill Amy, and thanks to the emails you forwarded and what they found in his room, they have enough to try him for attempted murder. I don't know if they'll ever have enough to prove he also killed Amy when the cruise line ruled it an accidental drowning. But at least he wasn't able to steal Colin's millions, and the majority of it went to his mom." Claire took my drink and set it on the coffee table. "Enough about that. I want to hear about you."

"Me?"

Claire ran her fingers through my hair, and I closed my eyes to her touch. "You. What have you been up to?" She leaned down and kissed the sensitive spot on my neck, and I found it hard to concentrate on what she'd asked.

"Up to?" I leaned back as her fingers found the top button of my shirt and slowly undid each one until she pushed it open, revealing my white lace bra.

"Yes. Have you done anything interesting since we talked last?"

I focused instead on the lightness of her fingertips running down the length of my stomach. My breath stopped when she got to my belt and pulled it out of its clasp. I don't think I could've answered her if my life depended on it. I'd melted into her touch.

"I like these." She dipped a finger into the waistband of my matching white lace thong and let it snap back. "I think I'd like them better on the floor." She slipped off the couch and pulled at my capri pants, tossing them behind her.

Claire sat back, admiring me from her seated position on the floor in front of me. She tilted her head. "This view is good too." She spread my legs, settling herself in between and running her fingertips up my inner thighs.

I wanted to shut my eyes, but I didn't want to miss the fire in hers. I watched as she hooked her hands into the waistband of my thong and pulled it halfway down my thighs. She leaned in and kissed my stomach, inching lower. I felt my hips pulse toward her, anticipating her touch.

Claire slipped my thong past my knees and pushed them farther apart. My whole body trembled as she ever so lightly dipped her tongue in, tasting me. My hands clenched when she pulled back, a smirk on those lips.

"Would you be mad if I suggested we change the venue?"

"Venue?" My thoughts barely focused enough to make conversation.

She smiled indulgently, and, pulling my thong the rest of the way off, helped me off the couch. She led me into a side room off to the side with a glass bottom floor and a giant bed with another gorgeous view of the ocean.

She slid my shirt off and let it drop to the floor. Next, she unhooked my bra and stopped, enjoying the sight of my naked body.

I finally felt the fog clear enough to stop her before she pushed me on to the bed. "Your turn." I pointed to her bathing suit cover and bikini.

"It was getting rather hot in here."

She pushed her cover off her shoulders and untied the knot at the back of her neck. Her bikini top fell forward, spilling her ample breasts. I settled back on the bed to watch as she stepped out of her bikini bottoms and crawled onto the bed next to me.

"We have the whole weekend to explore the island. Did you have anything you wanted to do in particular?"

I tilted my head up and kissed her lips. "This was pretty high on my list of activities."

She sank into me, running her hands up my legs and sides and capturing one of my breasts. She squeezed my nipple, and I let out a soft cry. "They have diving pools."

"Unless you're naked when we go, I think I'll pass."

She bent and took my nipple in her mouth, running circles around it with her tongue. Again, my hips began to pulse; my legs shook from the effort of taking it slow. I wanted her mouth on me, her fingers in me. I wanted to feel her wetness, to taste it, but the first time only happened once, and I wanted to savour it. I'd fantasized for so long about how it would happen, I didn't want to spoil it by rushing.

I moaned when her fingers found my other nipple, and she squeezed at the same time as her teeth bit down lightly.

"Oh, God." I felt a new surge of wetness, and all thoughts of taking it slow vanished.

She settled herself between my legs as her mouth and fingers brought me close. And then she pulled back. "Are you sure you don't want to do some sightseeing first?" The sparkle in her eyes told me she was teasing, and I didn't think I could take any more.

I took her face in my hands. "My God, woman. I'm dying here."

"So what you're saying is, you'd like me to finish?"

I nodded.

She slipped her hand down between my thighs and ran it through my wetness. "You like that?"

I nodded again, my eyes half shut.

And then she slipped inside and my heart nearly burst open from the ecstasy. My hips set the pace for her, which didn't last long. I came fast and hard, my head thrown back on the pillow, my scream caught in my throat, and my breathing erratic.

When I opened my eyes she was smiling down on me, and I knew I could disappear forever into those eyes, so much like the azure ocean lapping at our villa.

Claire—Saturday evening: private island, Maldives

I sat with my feet dangling in the water at the edge of our dock. They'd turned on the lights under the water, and I watched multicoloured fish swim in and around the dock's beams. Above, the sky glittered with a million pinpricks of light like a blanket of dark velvet and crystals thrown over the sky.

"Reminds me of ships. Out in the middle of the ocean, you can see every star that ever existed." Moira set a vodka tonic with a lime wedge on the dock next to me and took a seat beside me. "So, what's next, Claire?"

I tipped my eyes to her bare shoulder, ready for more of what we'd done all afternoon. But she held a finger to my lips. "Later."

"What's next for tomorrow? Or what's next for us?"

She shrugged her shoulder and took a sip of her drink. Resting it next to mine, she leaned back and gazed up at the stars.

After getting back from my so-called vacation, I had renovated my life. I had finished the article about Emil Fuchs, sent my book edits off without the massive revisions I'd wanted, and then took a step back.

I didn't want to work myself to death. Not when I had so many other fun things to accomplish. I also didn't want to plan. I wanted to enjoy life and now—not that I ever cared about the money—I could choose never to work again. I couldn't see that happening realistically.

I lay back on the dock, mirroring Moira's position, and turned my face to the heavens. "Why don't we take this one vacation at a time?"

"I like that idea."

And there we stayed, gazing up at our future until the moon rose on the horizon.

About the Author

CJ Birch is a Canadian-based video editor and digital artist. When not lost in a good book or working, she can be found writing or drinking serious coffee, or doing both at the same time.

An award-winning poet, CJ holds a certificate in journalism but prefers the world of make-believe. She lives with two barky dogs whose life goals include ridding their world of the evil bunnies.

CJ is the author of the New Horizons series. *Death in the Water* is her eighth book. You can visit CJ on social media @cjbirchwrites or www.cjbirchwrites.com.

About the Author

CJ Brott is a Canadian author, bestseller and director, writer. When he is not in a good book or writing, he can be found with his daughters, son's children, ... or ... or Reader time.

As a award-winning [...] CJ holds thousands... to put out better ... quotes ... and found people with ... lives vow with ... brings best ... on his life, stories, art, projects and inspires with... images on ... time.

Read his work on Charleston Intelligencer, Domain, or Brott's ... on the book, website at "You won't be stone caught... sold on www.amplifier.com.